BAD NEWS

He unfolds the paper with a cold rustle. Letters jump at him. Letters cut out of newspapers and magazines in assorted colors and sizes and all pasted together in two short sentences. The letters say "The Defender killed your father. The Defender can kill you."

The person who killed my father is crazy, he thinks, as he turns and sweeps his eyes across the back seat. Empty. He searches the parking lot to see if a crazy person hides in the tan Cougar on the left or the dented Ford just ahead.

But hold on. If someone intended to kill Howard right now, they wouldn't start with a warning. The note is from some very sane killer who wants him to think the murderer is a nut. His heart is still thudding but he holds on to that.

───────────── ★ ─────────────

KILL THE MESSENGER

ELIZABETH DANIELS SQUIRE

W🌐RLDWIDE.

TORONTO • NEW YORK • LONDON
AMSTERDAM • PARIS • SYDNEY • HAMBURG
STOCKHOLM • ATHENS • TOKYO • MILAN
MADRID • WARSAW • BUDAPEST • AUCKLAND

KILL THE MESSENGER

A Worldwide Mystery/November 1993

First published by St. Martin's Press, Incorporated.

ISBN 0-373-28010-6

Printed in U.S.A.

To the interesting variety of newspapers I've had the pleasure of knowing, I'd like to dedicate this book: as daughter and granddaughter of colorful controversial editors; as reporter who covered the meeting or murder trial; wife of the editor who worked late; stockholder grateful for the dividend, or as member of the board of a newspaper. And, of course, as a reader.

Part of the ambiance of *The Defender* comes from each of these papers, though it is certainly not exactly like any one. So, thanks to:

• *The News and Observer* of Raleigh, North Carolina, where my name was first set in hot type.
• Acorn Press newspapers in Connecticut, and especially *The Wilton Bulletin*, where my husband was editor when we were married, and *The Redding Pilot*, where I covered my first murder and learned the basics.
• *The News Record* in Madison County, North Carolina, which still occasionally sends me off to cover murder trials.
• *The Mountaineer*, in Waynesville, North Carolina, where, late in life, I learned how to make up a page.
• *The Smithfield Herald, Mount Olive Tribune, Gold Leaf Farmer, Zebulon Record, Cary News, Canton Enterprise* (all in North Carolina), and the other papers I've felt a special relationship with as a member of their parent company's board.

Also I'd like to thank all those who helped with editing and suggestions including my husband, Chick the editor, and my son, Worth the poet.

And, for encouragement, I'd like to thank Sarah Litsey Nye, Jeff Rackham, Peggy Parris, Rick Boyer, Margaret-Love Denman, Geraldine Powell, Sharon Grant, Pat Gladding, Sam Warner, and more others than space allows me to mention.

ONE

"YOUR FATHER IS DEAD, Howard." Leonora says it again. She sits erect as a watchman at her steel desk outside his father's office. That is normal. But now she is crying, hand over her mouth to hold in the sobs, tears shining.

Howard is out of breath from running up the stairs inside the Defender Building. He was too impatient to wait for the elevator. Now, stopped in front of Leonora's desk, he stands clutching a brown manila envelope.

But, of course, the Old Man is alive. He's so busy publishing the news of life and death and scams and shocks, he hardly allows time to sleep, much less die. And he'll be so pleased at what Howard brings in his manila envelope: more info on the racetrack, from Doc, the country sanitarian. It shows just how many gallons of urine and tons of manure the racetrack will produce if that Florida company gets away with building it. The soil is too porous and the proposed site is right next to the Harley River. Environmentalists will raise hell. The Old Man will love that.

The very idea of the racetrack throws the Old Man into a rage. He believes the Mafia is bankrolling it. This report will make a first-class delaying tactic until Howard finds proof.

But Leonora is crying. Something is wrong. For twenty-two years, since Howard was six years old, she's been quiet, helpful, efficient, presiding outside his father's office. Familiar pictures of successive cats sit on her desk next to the copy of her father's book: *History of the South in the Revolution*. She wears thick glasses like portholes magnifying her eyes above her receding chin until she looks like a gold-fish.

The Goldfish: always calm. Now her dark hair, pulled loose from its tight doughnut, straggles around her wet face. Magnified tears shrink to life-size as they run down below her glasses onto her round cheeks. The round clock on the wall behind her says 4:15.

A Kleenex box in a hardwood holder always sits on her desk in case anybody wants a tissue. She's too over-whelmed now to pick one up and blow her own nose.

Howard kneels by her steel chair. He puts his arm around her—tentatively, because the Goldfish is a don't-touch-me person, and about as wet as a real goldfish right now.

She pulls back and her glistening glasses turn straight on him like headlights. "The police just called Lance. Your father is dead. That's all I know."

My God, she really said that.

He turns toward his father's office, a square cocoon of maps—maps of the whole Southeast, maps of this south-ern state, this piedmont county, this growing city. The Old Man's mahogany desk sits as always, facing the globe of the world and the window. He wants to be able to see the world and Ashe Street at a single glance. He wants to know where and when, at every minute. The Old Man wears a water-proof watch so he can tell time even in the shower. Howard's own watch is exactly like it.

Howard walks across the thick rug to his father's desk. He is in shock. His body seems to move while his mind lags be-hind. At the desk, the Old Man's office chair still has the imprint of his bottom in the red leather. Four cigarette stubs mashed flat in the ashtray show the strength of his hands. A clothespin on a stand holds the latest crop of clippings that the Old Man gleans from other papers. "The New South is where you'll find a BMW pickup truck with a gun rack driven by a Good Ole' Boy eating a quiche stuffed with chitlins.'' Today's amusing tidbit. Howard feels like crying.

Where the Old Man's right hand would rest as he talks on the phone there's a yellow legal pad, a copy pencil, and, near the point of the pencil, one of the Old Man's doodles: small circle in the center, arrows radiating all around, a mandala of nervous energy. To the right of the pad, a large agate paperweight holds down a pile of papers with the Old Man's bold handwriting on them.

Howard makes himself reach across the desk, pick up the phone and call Bullethead Jones. Sergeant Jones is his best contact for police work.

The phone rings three times, dry and metallic like a snake's rattle. Howard sits down on the edge of the desk. His heart is beating so fast that he's shaking, and Bullethead's voice when he answers sounds unreal: politer, more formal than usual. He sounds as if he's standing at police headquarters as straight as a Greek column with one hand over his heart.

"Yes, Howard, your father is dead. I'm very sorry." And Howard hears the undertone in that sanctimonious voice: Now that the watchdog is gone, Buddy-boy, I don't have to take you so seriously, and I like the change!

All of this seems to be happening whether it's possible or not. A stack of paper crinkles under Howard, and as he shifts on the edge of the desk, the paperweight falls to the floor with a thump. The rock embedded with tiny crystals lies near Howard's feet in the soft pile of the rug. Howard notices with amazement that his socks don't match. This morning he was thinking so hard about the racetrack story that he'd put on one blue sock and one green sock and hadn't even noticed. Honey might have if she hadn't been asleep. Distantly, Howard hears the Goldfish still sobbing and the traffic on Ashe Street.

"Your father was poisoned," Bullethead says. Howard says nothing. He's not sure he can hold his voice steady, and this new hostile Bullethead must not hear it waver.

Now Bullethead is crisp and businesslike.

"Suzanne Mancini called an ambulance to take your father to Memorial Hospital from an apartment at 615 Wildmere Road at 3:35. He was Dead On Arrival. Dr. Hissock suspected poison and called us. That's all we know so far. The medical examiner will be doing tests. Someone will need to talk to you."

Howard is numb. So it's true. Poison. There had been threatening letters—Leonora has a whole file of them—but the Old Man never took them seriously. Too late now. And why, goddamn it, does Suzanne have to be mixed up in all this? That damned Suzanne with her swirling black hair. He can imagine it sweeping out over the pillow when she slept with his father, strands like tentacles. Howard mustn't think about that, or about those damn mocking black eyes, or her Je Reviens perfume that lingered in the air long after she'd left the Old Man's office.

The Old Man ought to belong to his family, damn it; to my mother, to me, Howard tells himself—at least in death, at least in memory.

"I have to see my father."

"They've taken him to the morgue, Howard."

"I'll see you there." Howard hangs up hard and pulls himself to his feet. They still hold him up, perfectly, like two weights in the bottom of a buoy, even if his socks don't match. He's going to need those feet to hold firm. Even with belief and disbelief swirling together in his stomach, he understands from Bullethead's voice how much his father had been shielding him from the wind. The Old Man was a tall tree in the middle of the plain to draw the lightning. "My God, I loved him," he says under his breath. But he won't stop to cry.

He sprints down the corridor past the big newsroom just as several reporters rush out. "I'll talk to you later," he calls without stopping.

He tries to calm his panic, steady his whirling brain. How can the Old Man be dead when his body is alive? An old fantasy holds Howard—his father's human body extends to become *The Defender:* his hair the telephone wires, his arms the network of reporters and their machines, his heart the press itself.

When Howard was small, his father's newspaper body was always the most loving part of him. The Old Man would take him to the office and then forget him, letting him explore and make friends: the Lassiter twins in Circulation, reporters who gave him pencils, Lumberton in the composing room.

Howard rushes past the room where computers set type, but in his mind he sees old Lumberton smiling behind the last clanking, hissing, steaming Linotype. Lumberton pressed the keys that made parts move on tracks. Then out came a name in shining mirror image capital letters: DRAWOH. Lumberton no longer speaks to the Old Man, the Linotype is outmoded by electronics—but one of Lumberton's cast lead names sits on the edge of a bookcase at Howard's house right now.

The pressroom is quiet as Howard passes. Tonight the web of paper will be flashing in and out on the big rollers again. The press will be the Old Man's heart still throbbing in the pressroom: the sound of life!

Howard sees Lance coming toward him. Lancelot Jones. Editor. Leonora said the police had called Lance first. Lance is shaggy, stoop-shouldered, but he moves as if he's jet-propelled. His superthick eyebrows pull together in a frown. Lance swoops on Howard, mouth open, ready to speak. He looks stupid, but Howard knows better. Just when Lance looks stupidest, he's ready to jump to the jugular of whatever subject is on his mind.

Lance throws his arms around Howard, practically knocking out his breath but warm with affection. "Boy," Lance says, "I've known you since you were two years old. Boy, I love you. I loved the Old Man, damn him, even when I wanted to kill him. He was one of a kind. My God, he was only in his fifties. The Old Man. My God, what a boss!"

Howard wants to run; otherwise he'll cry. Not now! Lance pulls him into a small room with a Coke machine, metal table and chairs, and shuts the door. Here comes the worst. Lance's eyes hold him like nails. "There's one thing the Old Man would want you to think about, Howard—especially now. He cared about this newspaper. You care too, don't you?"

"Yes, of course, you know I do."

"Exactly." Lance nods his hairy head emphatically. "And so do I. Now, Howard, you know the Old Man had an offer last week from Gemtrex to buy the paper—a very generous offer. He told them he wouldn't sell *The Defender* at any price."

"Yes, I know." This is no time to talk business.

"But their lawyer said their offer to buy would stand. And the Old Man called a family stockholders meeting for Monday."

"To rubber-stamp his 'No.' So?"

"Except now he's gone."

"I know that." Howard wants to run.

Lance grabs Howard by the arm and stares at him intensely from under those shaggy brows.

"Howard, this is hard for you, but stand still. The paper will belong to seven people now. You four kids and Miss Bounce—and he gave a share of stock to Leeroy and one to Suzanne."

"To Suzanne!" Well, of course. Damn Suzanne, damned bitch.

"The Old Man knew, and I know and I'm sure you know, that the first person who recognizes a power struggle has the best chance to come out on top. Fifty-one percent of the stock gives control of the paper. Some members of the family will want to sell."

Howard shuts his eyes. He is not ready to face his father's death—to deal with the idea of poison, much less a power struggle in his own family. The Old Man's ghost glares at him. He opens his eyes quickly. "I can't believe any of us would want to sell. Why, *The Defender* was my father's life. He'd die if..."

"He did die," Lance cuts in gruffly. "Now it's up to us to find out exactly how it happened. I've put Leeroy on the story. He's as thorough as a dose of salts. Leeroy will find out everything we want to know—and everything we don't want to know on top of that.

"But listen, Boy, you need to think ahead, to keep your eyes wide open and watch out for yourself. See things first-hand. Of course. But also give yourself a little time between finding facts, to see whether things look right."

What a time to be giving me stupid obvious advice, Howard rages inside. He has to go where his father is, to see him. And he's held back by a shaggy bear trying to be a wise man. And what does Lance mean, "watch out"?

Poisoning can never be right. But as Howard starts toward the county morgue, he knows that Lance doesn't mean right as in good versus evil. He means right like two socks that match. Only he means something more subtle, something Howard could miss entirely unless he keeps his wits sharp every minute. There is no great tree to deflect the lightning. The tree was hit. The Old Man is dead.

TWO

AT THIS of all times, Howard would sure like to avoid Freddy Norris. But as Howard runs down the wet marble steps of the Defender Building into the February drizzle, he sees the bum coming toward him, rumpled clothes, sideways limp, galling self-importance and all.

It's enough that the Old Man let this bum park himself on the bench across from the Defender Building.

And hasn't Leeroy, who is supposed to be such a hotshot reporter, already given the man delusions of grandeur by listening to him?

Now here comes Freddy like a flu bug, right when you want it least. The traffic slows for him. Sometimes Howard has wondered what secret hold Freddy might have on his father. Why else is the man allowed to sit on that bench whenever he pleases, and drink white wine or whatever from his 7 Up bottle? He makes a great paper look silly.

"I want to extend you my sympathy." Freddy's lips move slowly: superformality greased by alcohol. How does he know the Old Man is gone? Howard just found out.

"Be polite to Freddy," the Old Man had said. "He hears things."

Howard says "Thank you. I have to rush." He jumps in his car and is glad the window is up. Before he sees his father dead he wants to remember what he loved about his father. Please God, not Freddy, not Suzanne, not poison.

So Howard heads for the morgue by Johnson Street past Courthouse Square. There is a shorter way but the courthouse draws him, the courthouse where he fed the pigeons with his father when he was a child.

The courthouse bulks round-topped in the twilight drizzle. Blue-gray pigeons coo on the cornices and meander down the walks as they have done for over 150 years, undaunted by the Civil War, gory murder trials, the impeachment of a judge, or the rape last year of a thirteen-year-old girl not three feet from the old public water fountain. Now the grounds close at dusk. But the courthouse stands solid.

I began here, Howard thinks, as his Volkswagen approaches the square. Under one of the magnolia trees near the water fountain, the Old Man asked Miss Bounce to marry him. That was thirty-three-years ago. Her wedding picture shows her slim and smiling.

Even then she was full of energy. That's how she got her nickname back when she worked in the Society Department at the paper. Even in the wedding picture she gives the impression of jumping up and down when she's standing perfectly still. Miss Bounce.

Does his mother remember how it was under the magnolias? Now she is all pride and bristle and as puffed up as the courthouse pigeons. The Old Man finds his closeness other places.

Howard grips the steering wheel so hard that his palms hurt. Why did somebody poison his father? Suddenly he has the odd idea that Freddy Norris, the bum, had some glimmer about who did. And he cut Freddy off. No. The bum would have said what he knew right off, to gain importance. Forget Freddy.

In the Old Man's face there could be a glimmer of what happened—some expression frozen at the moment of death. Howard shivers. Or will the poison have distorted the Old Man? Will he be lying on one of those sloping tables with a drain in the bottom? Stop trying to imagine, Howard tells himself.

He turns to reality: Courthouse Square. He is about to pass the statue the pigeons like best—the statue honoring mothers of men who died in the Spanish-American war: a large bronze woman, with a bird sitting on her right shoulder in spite of the drizzle. That formidable statue is the same shape Howard's mother is now. And with anguish, he suddenly knows his mother will wear exactly that statue's noble bronze expression at his father's funeral.

He passes the Civil War general. That statue always makes him feel better, always has since he was a small child. He can smile even now at the general on his prancing horse. The horse is as charged up with courage as the war mother. He likes the noble expression better on the horse.

He passes the corner of his own street. Honey, who says he neglects her, will have left home to join the family at his mother's. Family gatherings fill her with joy, even when she's mad at other members of the family.

He drives between the lovely old houses, between the gas stations and motels and funeral homes that are overtaking the heart of the city. There's the Governor James Gordon McAllister House, preserved by such an earnest committee, including Miss Bounce, of course. He passes the high school whose principal resented the paper's drug-bust story so much. Howard knows he is driving too fast—through new housing developments, past a huge new mall, still under construction. There are so many new malls that they compete and advertise like crazy in *The Defender*. Thank God, the Old Man used to say. The Old Man.

Just beyond the county hospital is the morgue, a modern innocuous building. Bullethead waits for Howard by the glass front door, sanctimonious and contemptuous all at once, like an underpaid funeral director. He intends to see

Howard's face when Howard sees his father. Obviously. So
ignore him.

They go down in the elevator to a cold room smelling of
disinfectant. A uniformed man at a desk writes Howard's
name in a book, then leads Howard to a refrigerated drawer
and pulls it out. There lies the Old Man, the wrong color to
be asleep.

"I hardly ever saw my father asleep." Howard hears his
own hollow voice, fighting off tears. "He was always up
before me and down after."

Shut up. No point in telling Bullethead how it was, how
at night the Old Man used to rush in the door breathless and
immediately ask Howard and Madison and Josh and Alice
and Miss Bounce to tell him the high point of the day. How
he laughed. And when Howard was small, before his father
stopped coming home every night, the Old Man used to listen like a dynamo, too, even to the stories of Alice's imaginary friends. Except that you had to talk fast before the
phone rang, before he had to rush out to a meeting. And
sometimes, late at night, when Howard was half asleep and
feeling his way down the dark hall to the bathroom, he'd
hear the short-wave radio through the Old Man's half-open
door, strange squeaks and jabbers, and sometimes foreign
languages. Mysterious and fascinating.

Now the Old Man's wide mouth is closed and quiet.
Those once mobile hands lie at his sides, long smooth fingers together. His hair is not even out of place, except that
as always, its own energy seems to keep it standing like an
electric shock. And the searchlight eyes are shut.

If those eyes could open they'd watch to see if Howard is
noting every detail that could matter. If the Old Man could
speak, he'd say "Get out there and get busy!" O.K.

Howard goes off with Bullethead to downtown police
headquarters prepared to tell everything he knows that can

help the police. That is step one. He stares at the dirty marble floor and listens to Bullethead's new cynical voice imply that every member of the Justice family, including Howard, has a motive for murder.

Howard would like to stalk out, but he has to answer. "Yes, damn it. I know my father liked women, but do you really think my mother is a poisoner? She is too out-front to be a poisoner. She is not sneaky."

Bullethead suspects everybody in every way. His ears stick out from his head at right angles to hear the worst. He seems pleased that nobody saw Howard for four hours before his father died. That Howard says he was out inspecting the site for the proposed racetrack in deserted fields by the river.

Howard works to keep his voice calm. "But the whiskey could have been poisoned at any time, so nobody has an alibi. Well, at least you don't think my father killed himself."

"Would you like me to think your father killed himself?"

"No." Howard could choke his old news source, and that must show. Bullethead's eyes twinkle.

"We might have thought he killed himself, Howard, except of course, he'd been threatened. Over and over.

"Besides, poison was in the whiskey bottle. I could even smell it," Bullethead says.

"He couldn't smell. He had a cold." Howard groans inside to think his father might have lived if he hadn't had a common cold.

"A man just needs one glass of poison to kill himself." Bullethead leans forward. "I never knew a suicide to poison the *bottle*, and your father wasn't the type to waste good whiskey, was he, Howard?" He almost leers.

"And he didn't die instantly. He managed to write one word on his typewriter." Pleased with himself, Bullethead pauses, teeters back in his chair.

Howard is on the edge of his. "What?"

"Murder."

"Then he didn't know who poisoned the whiskey. He would have written the name instead."

"Perhaps."

"You were jealous of my father."

"Wasn't everybody? He could practically blackmail everybody in town by printing or not printing the news about them. He had power. He had women."

"He published the news fairly!"

No answer.

Howard stalks out past the downbeat signs like "Pay fines here," hurries out to the half-lit parking lot tasting anger. The tall aluminum streetlights give the few cars an eerie glow. By the time he gets into his familiar Volkswagen the dashboard clock says 7:30. On the seat beside him, a reporter's notebook looms out of the shadow, small, oblong, and businesslike. The kind of notebook he always uses. He didn't put that notebook there. No? Stop imagining things, he tells himself. He turns on the dome light and flips open the cover of the notebook, hoping to see his own familiar scrawl.

He finds a folded sheet of typewriter paper. He unfolds the paper with a cold rustle. Letters jump at him. Letters cut out of newspapers and magazines in assorted colors and sizes and all pasted together into two short sentences. In the third grade, Nancy Oliver sent Howard a comic valentine made like that. This is not a comic valentine. The letters say "*The Defender* killed your father. *The Defender* can kill you." He stares at the large glossy magazine K, the small newspaper i, the two pink funny-paper L's, and the entire word "you" in a formal but cheerful script as if it was cut from an ad inviting "you" on a special vacation.

The person who killed my father is crazy, he thinks, as he turns and sweeps his eyes across the back seat. Empty. He searches the parking lot to see if a crazy person hides in the tan Cougar on the left or the dented Ford just ahead.

But hold on. If someone intended to kill Howard right now, they wouldn't start with a warning. The note is from some very sane killer who wants him to think the murderer is a nut. His heart is still thudding but he holds on to that.

Or else those crazy words are from a crank. Yes! A big story about someone like the Old Man brings out cranks, twisted but harmless. And word gets around fast. Look how Freddy Norris knew the Old Man was dead, practically before Howard did. Howard needs to believe in a crank. He sees Lance leer at him from under his shaggy eyebrows and say "power struggle." The vote to sell or not to sell *The Defender* may be hairbreadth close.

Howard knows this crazy glued-up letter is a threat to him. But the threat implies the whole family may be in danger. They all own the paper. Alice is just childish enough that this note might persuade her to sell. Josh can be a nut. Why stir up trouble?

Howard carefully closes the notebook and puts it in the glove compartment. He will say he put it there without opening it. Then he will "find" it again in a few days, after the meeting. Howard slams the glove compartment shut. "I know your priorities," he says to the Old Man. "First we save the paper." He feels so noble that all the aching parts of him ache less. If he could see himself he might be warned. His mother may not be the only person at his father's funeral with a look on her face that is not right, not in tune with hard reality. As he slams the glove compartment, Howard's own expression is a dead ringer for the Confederate general's noble horse.

THREE

4:50 P.M. LEEROY LOPES down the hall toward Suzanne's office with a spring in his step. It's just possible that after she left the Old Man dead, she came back to her office. He investigates small chances, and any chance of talking to Suzanne sends quivers through Leeroy's long body. He knows he looks like a scarecrow, so loose-jointed he could scatter like a broken string of beads. That's what Cynthia, the ex-Mrs. Leeroy, used to say, before she moved out.

Never mind, at least he can listen. Sometimes he listens so hard he feels like he ought to hear not only human words, not only the traffic on Ashe Street, not only the phones ringing all over the building and the small clicks of information punched into the computer terminals, but also the beating of every heart in the building and maybe even the hurtling of planets and stars through space.

A woman in trouble wants a good listener. But don't think, you fool, that just because the Old Man is dead Suzanne is going to notice you beyond that. So be glad he's gone. Even if you once loved him. But don't give yourself airs. It was you, Leeroy, who let the old bastard treat you like a wimp for six months as he gave to Howard all those stories that should have had your byline on the front page. Howard, who is twenty-eight and forgets he has a pencil behind his ear. So why would Suzanne think you mattered at all? Suzanne is whipped cream. So be professional, damn it. Because now the Old Man has gone to the only place he could have gone to do you a favor. He has handed you, Leeroy, the most ticklish, most demanding, maybe the most dramatic story in the history of *The Defender*. The story of how the publisher was poisoned.

Leeroy hesitates outside Suzanne's door. She's so alive she flusters him. She's worked hard as the Old Man's executive assistant and been damned casual about sleeping with him. In his mind Leeroy sees her walking down the hall, breasts high and lively, eyes sparkling as if she takes your rise in blood pressure for granted. She never walks as if she wants you to look at her. She walks as if she knows where she is going. Her family run a small Italian restaurant: Giovanni's. They sweat and scuttle. They christened her Suzanna Antonietta Mancini and wanted her to be a beautician, he happens to know. But Suzanne is a Stradivarius, a Rolls-Royce, a signed Picasso among women. The Old Man did not deserve her.

Leeroy smooths down the cowlick at the back of his sandy hair and opens her door without knocking. If she's there, he wants to surprise her as she is.

She's there. Sitting perfectly still at her metal desk. Framed against the window with its swath of rainy sky. Sitting like death. Death beautiful. He swallows. Suzanne has not turned on the light. She has not bothered to take off the new raincoat with the hood that must have disguised her return to the building. The hood that frames her face in shadow like a New Year's cartoon of the Grim Reaper.

By a slight change of focus, her shining eyes register his presence. Otherwise her face is without expression.

"Can I get you anything, Suzanne?" he asks. He feels her need like a blast of cold air. Need is what Leeroy understands. "Can I get you anything, a cup of coffee or a drink, or anything else?"

"No."

Leeroy arranges his lanky form on the edge of her desk. At least he knows how to sit, waiting as if he's hardly there, all six feet six of him; listening so intensely and courteously to silent pain that he's a magnet to draw it out. That's his talent. On bad days Leeroy asks himself if he is a walking invasion of privacy. But then on bad days he wonders if he is breathing more than his share of the air. Today is a good day. Maybe.

Suzanne stays silent, shrouded in her hood. He leans forward gently like a mother about to comfort a small child with a skinned knee. "What happened?"

"I was late." Her usually musical voice is flat, even harsh, and so faint he has to strain to listen. "The Old Man expected me at 3. At 3:15 I was sitting in my own apartment brushing my hair." Abruptly she runs her fingers through her dark curls, notices the hood and pushes it off, rocks back and forward, back and forward in her chair.

Leeroy is perfectly quiet. He is sorry for Suzanne. He is also excited. He knows the signs. She's cried herself out of tears, and now she's trying to make sense of what happened.

"I stood outside his door, Leeroy. Someone down the hall was frying pork chops, pork chops and onions, and I stood there for three minutes smelling onions and getting angry. He'd been so strange for two weeks, so up and down, so cruel and generous." Her voice swells with need. "I couldn't stand it."

"How was he strange?"

She shuts her eyes, compresses her lips, then opens her eyes wide and slowly answers, reaching for the right words. Good.

"It all started the day after that offer from Gemtrex to buy the paper. He was fine that day. He said every other independent paper in the country could join a chain if it wanted to, but he wouldn't sell until hell froze over. He called a family meeting, the one scheduled for next Monday, to rubber-stamp what he did. Nobody had enough stock to outvote him, but he wanted the family members in on the decision."

She sits straighter, then jumps up, turns on the light, and starts to pull off the raincoat. Leeroy helps her out of the sleeves. She smells of new coat, rain, and a subtle perfume. She walks away from him, around and around the desk, agitated. "The next day the Old Man changed. Didn't you notice it, Leeroy?"

"No. Except that he was damned nice all of a sudden. He gave me a raise I didn't ask for. He sent the Goldfish a big bunch of roses for twenty years of excellence."

"Nice in public." Suzanne stops her pacing, sits down hard in her chair and challenges him with her eyes. "You intend to use everything I say, don't you, Leeroy? You look so human, Leeroy. But you're going to write this story true even if you do it in my blood, aren't you?"

"What worries you?" His voice says "Where does it hurt?" His eyes say "I need your help."

"I don't need my sex life on page one. My grandmother Mancini would have a heart attack. She still goes to mass every morning with a black lace scarf around her head."

"O.K. You get to censor everything about sex I can't also get from another source."

She hesitates. He waits. Finally, she plunges. "See this watch, Leeroy?" She stands up, sticks her wrist almost in his face, pulling back her suit sleeve to show emeralds and diamonds around a digital face, all winking in the fluorescent light. A cash register in his mind rings up $5,000.

"This watch said 3:25 when I stood outside his door and 3:28 when I opened the door. Looking at this watch made me hesitate to go in. You see, Leeroy, he gave this watch to me for a reason. The day after he said he'd never sell the paper he called me to that apartment in the onion building, which he kept secret from everybody else. He was working on his autobiography there. I had the key. But, Leeroy, he didn't want to work that day, just go right to bed. And after we began to make love, after we were hardly more than undressed and in that damned uncomfortable fold-out bed, he suddenly turned his back on me and said, 'Suzanne, go away. Leave me alone.' So I asked why. And he began to yell that it was because I was the kind of girl who would ask why. Then he was totally irrational. His back was cold and sweaty wet, and he smelled funny. I can't explain how. But not like he always did. And I was scared and angry and I left.''

The lucky ungrateful bastard, Leeroy thinks. But he ran out of luck.

''The only reason I came to work the next day, Leeroy, was because he hadn't fired me. I worked for him before I loved him, damn it. He had to come right out and fire me if that's what he wanted.''

She stands staring at the watch the whole time. Now she looks up at Leeroy, puzzled. ''The next day he gave me this watch.''

She sits down slowly. ''And then in a few days he did it all over again. Only that time he gave me a share of stock in *The Defender* to prove he trusted me, he said, and a bunch of orchids. So I came to the workhole today to tell him he had to explain what was wrong. He was strange out of bed too. Moody, or extra nice to make up for it. Not normal.

''I thought it had to do with me at first. And then I began to wonder if it was some sort of breakdown, Leeroy. Now I think he was afraid of something.''

Leeroy imagines kissing the skin under her eyes. Her skin where it shines because earlier tears have made it tender.

''Anyway, today when my watch said 3:28 I opened the door. And before the door was all the way open I heard the quiet. He wasn't banging on the typewriter or pacing the floor in a fury the way he did when he stopped work. I started opening the door, angry at him, and when I opened the door all the way, there he was, dead.''

She stares at Leeroy in wonder. "Dead. Hanging forward over his favorite old typewriter, his arms dangling down beside him.

"The phone was off the hook on the table by his side. Maybe he tried to call somebody. Oh God, maybe it was me! When I ran to touch him I almost fell over a glass lying on the floor. His favorite hand-blown glass that he liked his whiskey in. By the glass, on the rug, were two ice cubes. Not even melted yet. There was a strange smell to the spilled whiskey. He had no pulse. I called the ambulance. And then I guess I began to scream, because the neighbors came.

"I hope my three minutes weren't the minutes that could have saved him. But how could I know?"

Suzanne rocks back and forth, back forth in her chair, and Leeroy sees her grandmother in the black scarf and her great-grandmother rocking, too. As a primitive motion of despair. "I've tried, tried so hard, Leeroy, not to count on him for anything. Just to enjoy him and my job. That's what he needed. That's all he could give. I knew that. That's why I held on to him longer than any of the others did." Suzanne stops in mid-rock, leaning forward. "But I did count on him for one thing, damn it." She gets up, coming over to stand near Leeroy, arms folded, tears wet in her eyes, so beautiful he can hardly stand it.

"I counted on him not to die! He was too tough, too selfish, and too alive."

"But not," says Leeroy with some satisfaction, "too careful."

She tosses her head, challenged. "No. Never. Never dull, never careful of himself. But he wouldn't have killed himself. No matter what."

"But," says Leeroy, "if he'd known he was going to die I'd accuse him of a practical joke on his family."

"Why?"

Leeroy listens to the music of the spheres, half smiling. "I think there's bound to be a big family fight at the stockholders meeting Monday, and the Old Man has arranged for us to be there: you, the other woman; me, the investigative reporter."

FOUR

SUZANNE HAS LEARNED that life is naturally both grief and happiness. That it is given to shriek and wail with misery, the way her grandmother did when her Uncle Chico electrocuted himself trying to wire his chicken house. It is given to cry with joy the way her mother did when Suzanne's brother Nello brought back a bride from Italy, from Luciano, the very town where Suzanne's mother met her father. But it is not given to let go of the rungs of the ladder.

So it is with a firm step late that evening that she goes down to grab one of the first papers off the press. She doesn't think from his questions that Leeroy has found out about what happened in Arizona. Thank God he doesn't know that she has been married and divorced. He doesn't know that her husband, the Shakespeare scholar with his gold cufflinks, milked a computer of $100,000. Who would believe she really didn't know what was going on?

Now she has to see just how bad her discovery of the Old Man's body is going to look in print.

So she hurries past the powerful presses with flowing rolls of newsprint whirring in creamy webs through the rollers; hurries past newly printed papers jackknifing into the folders. She does not know the blond man with a decided squint in his right eye who hands her a copy of the paper. He must be new.

But even as he holds out the paper between ink-grayed finger and thumb, she is startled that *The Defender* with this story is so much the usual. Same vertical columns of crisp black type and horizontal headlines with enough white space around them so that, as the Old Man said, the eye can breathe. THE DEFENDER, marching smartly in blocky modern letters across the top. Date, February 23, and price, twenty-five cents, in their neat little boxes. She remembers the Old Man's pride as he flourished an edition that pleased him and said that, damn it, there was no reason his paper shouldn't look as modern as *The Minneapolis Tribune or USA Today,* and still have nice old-fashioned thunderbolt headlines to goose the reader to get mad or laugh or tremble with prurient interest. Then he winked and said "Prurient. Try it. It's a nice word. Makes you pucker. Lets the reader have fun."

And now the Old Man is the headline, top right:

DEFENDER'S PUBLISHER FOUND DEAD; POLICE CALL IT CYANIDE POISONING

Not, thank God, as prurient as it might be. Next to the headline is one of those photographs with snap that he demanded. The Old Man jumps right off the page, eyes hypnotic, mouth smiling as if he's running for governor. She swallows and takes the paper, annoyed that tears wet her eyes because she is so eager to read Leeroy's story, now a square block of blurred print. A square block wedged above a longer, thinner headline: one of Howard's pieces about the proposed racetrack.

Business almost as usual. That braces her. She reads:

Isaiah Justice, owner and publisher of *The Defender,* was found dead at 3:28 P.M. yesterday in a hideaway at 615 Wildmere Road where he was writing his autobiography. Ice cubes from a glass that may have contained poison had not yet melted when Justice's executive assistant, Suzanne Mancini, arrived at the apartment and called neighbors and the ambulance.

Thank God the doorman remembered seeing her come in. Suzanne shudders involuntarily. She is relieved to see how little there is about her in Leeroy's first story. Undoubtedly there'll be more later. She skims down: Police investigating threats... Tests show cyanide... Then details of the Old Man's life.

Justice, a controversial newspaperman, came to *The Defender* in late 1945 after serving in the U.S. Army in World War II. He was on the staff of *Stars and Stripes* in Europe. He joined *The Defender* when it was in financial difficulties under the ownership of Byron Dougdale, a poet and philosopher known for his nature editorials.

Justice persuaded Dougdale to give him a free hand in exposing environmental polluters such as the Vrestoll Company, responsible for frequent fish-kills in the Sluice River.... He took over the news direction.... Dougdale, who was childless, died in 1950 and left the newspaper to Justice.

The Old Man always seemed to have good luck. Howard, who thinks he's such a hotshot reporter, and his brother Madison, who thinks he's such a business whiz, don't seem the good-luck type. Sister Alice is a featherbrain, and Josh lives on a communal farm in the mountains of Georgia, and wears sandals.

The paper will continue to be published just as it is now, said Justice's widow, Wilhelmena Saxon Justice, "carrying on my late husband's tradition." (Turn to page 3).

Suzanne opens the door of the pressroom and steps into the quieter hall where she can stand against the wall and finish reading. She skims through the list of prizes the paper has won for outstanding reporting. Some winners she's almost forgotten, like Leeroy's series that resulted in the discovery that the wrong man had been convicted of murdering that librarian. That was before Suzanne came to the paper. But, boy, she sure was in the middle of the investigation of that religious cult that turned out to be a drug ring. Took some of the hate calls herself, because she was the Old Man's assistant. But with the Old Man to back her up, she felt more important than threatened.

Her throat tightens again. Her eyes plow on:

In recent weeks, members of the newspaper staff in close contact with Justice, such as Miss Mancini...

(O.K., Leeroy, that's putting it as subtly as you can),

...report that he seemed to have been preoccupied with some private worry that he would not discuss.

Justice was a man who frequently spent 14 hours a day at his office. Friends described him as a man who worked hard and played hard. He took out time to belong to such organizations as the Rotary Club...

She skims through the list of organizations until she comes to the one that always surprised her the most:

He was a member of the Park Heights Bird-Watching Society and would go out with a group at 5:30 in the morning, binoculars in hand, especially in the nesting season.

Then funeral services.

Suzanne lets out a long breath of relief at what Leeroy hasn't said. She glances over a sidebar with comments on the Old Man's death by U.S. Senator McNalley and others. Damn hypocrites, she thinks. She folds over the paper and clutches it tight with one hand, while with the other she smooths back her long dark hair, smooths it as she might pet a nervous cat.

It's like Leeroy to start low-key. There's no telling what he'll find out and print before he's through. But Suzanne relaxes. At least so far she is safe. Nobody knows.

FIVE

HOWARD HAS NO WAY to know what his mother feels. All he sees is rigid bronze bravery. The head held high. Why can't she cry? Why is she so careful not to talk to him alone? Every time he thinks he has her to himself she gets a headache or visitors arrive.

So many visitors: Miss Bounce's club members who gawk, snobbish relatives like Great Uncle Charles who does genealogies, nice relatives like Aunt Earnestine who teaches third grade, even two of the ex-convicts Miss Bounce taught to read in the prison release program. Also, the *Defender* staff from Lance to newspaper delivery boys.

Howard came over at eight o'clock this morning to ask Miss Bounce "Will you vote to keep the paper?" And even at that hour, a pressman's wife showed up with a chocolate cake with the pearly gates in gold icing on top. Miss Bounce has insisted on accepting in person each cake, even each of the thirty-five pecan pies (the Old Man's favorite), each casserole and every arrangement of flowers.

"Life must go on," she keeps saying, even while she and Howard and Madison work out the details of the funeral with Father Martin of Trinity Church, asking him to include the hymn the Old Man's mother sang.

Howard doesn't think the hymn fits the Old Man in any way, but with his will he'd left written instructions to include it at his funeral:

Weary of Earth and laden with my sin,
I look to heaven and long to enter in.

But there no evil thing may find a home
And yet I hear a voice that bids me 'come.'

Minor as a dog howling. Wrong for the well-washed hypocrites who came to the funeral to be glad. Wrong for the Old Man's admirers such as tearful Sarah Johnson, whose garbage was rarely collected on her dead-end street until she called the Old Man and the paper did an investigation.

At the funeral, Howard's vocal cords ache to sing something upbeat like "How Firm a Foundation," as he dutifully howls about sin. He is so distracted he can't even grieve. Even outside, a storm is brewing.

On top of that, Miss Bounce has insisted that the stockholders meeting to hear that buy-out offer must go on at exactly the time the Old Man planned.

So the meeting is the afternoon of the funeral. Howard is appalled. He feels as if he is shot from a cannon almost straight from the graveyard to the meeting room. The new-smelling suit he bought for the funeral seems to be surer where it's going than he is.

In fact, he arrives early for the meeting and stands disoriented in the cavernous room, too large for the occasion, complete with rows of folding chairs. The fluorescent light blinks around him.

He holds onto a folder that contains the Old Man's words, prepared for this meeting and miraculously found in a drawer of the Old Man's desk. He believes that, if anything can, those words will make a difference at this meeting to decide the fate of the paper.

"Why worry about the paper?" his brother Josh asked him shortly after the funeral. "The whole world will probably be blown up in the next few years, anyway." Josh is not an optimist.

The round clock on the cement block wall says 3:45. In exactly fifteen minutes, Prompt Herbert, the old Man's—and the company's—lawyer, will be here to explain how the company can be exchanged for sixty million dollars. Prompt Herbert is never early or late. So nobody in the family except Howard is early, even to hear about money.

Howard's eyes avoid the one other person in the room: Suzanne. She sits near one end of a back row of folding chairs. Already waiting, damned bitch, unwilling to miss one second of whatever is going to take place. Suzanne in her blouse covered with four-leaf clovers. Broadcasting good luck, when she was the one who found the Old Man dead. Undoubtedly also the last one to sleep with him. She could at least have the decency to be a little tearful.

Howard would love to think she killed the Old Man, maybe in a fit of wild Italian jealousy. He mustn't show how he feels. In a tight vote, her one share of stock could actually hold the balance of power.

The round clock over Suzanne's shoulder shows thirteen minutes to go. Howard squirms. He's used to the Old Man being after him every minute, to look into Mayor Wilder's expense account, the safeguards at the Warren nuclear plant. Always something to act on.

But now, he stands and listens to the clock tick, thoughts loose, undisciplined, zigzagging in and out of dark alleys. Suppose.

Suppose someone of his own blood, Miss Bounce or Madison or Josh or Alice, killed the Old Man. My God, why am I thinking that! Am I Bullethead? But most people who are killed know their killers, are joined to them by blood or passion. Howard saw this when he was a police reporter. Also, killers can be mild mannered and ordinary, or even charming outside of the situation that drove them to kill. Like that typist who stabbed her lover with a carving knife. And then went to evening Bible study at the Methodist church.

The heavy fire door begins to wheeze and he stares at it hypnotized, wondering which prospective killer will come through next. A head covered with gold ringlets peers around, a hand jingling with charm bracelets waves at him. He almost laughs with relief. It's Alice. Twenty-five, but what a baby face.

Alice hasn't got enough direction to kill anybody. Not even for ten million dollars. Of course not. If she shot, she'd miss. If she mixed poison, she'd forget and lick her fingers. He could hug her for being so inept. She nods formally to Suzanne and jangles to a front seat. Her string of scalps, Howard used to call those bracelets, because she's got a charm for every man who's ever gone with her; a football for Elon, a tennis racket for Teddy, a beer mug for Elbert. Howard can't remember or count them all. And why, when she could collect all those scalps, she finally married Arthur (who follows just behind her), Howard has never known.

Arthur is good-looking in a 1920s-shirt-ad kind of way, except his ears and feet are too big. In his alcoholic haze he would never be able to get away with murder. Of course not. And yet, Howard remembers, when he does approach sobriety he becomes smarter and sadder. He likes money. He's undoubtedly got his good luck coins in his jacket pocket: a Maria Theresa silver thaler and two Susan B. Anthony dollars. All during the meeting, he'll be fingering and clanking those coins and dropping them at all the worst times.

"Arthur gambles," the Old Man once said. Howard could kick himself because he never asked "Where?" or "How much?" Alice will vote two hundred shares of stock in *The Defender*. If the paper is sold she'll have plenty of cash for Arthur to play with.

Alice leads Arthur to seats at the far left of the front row, leaving diagonally the maximum possible space between themselves and Suzanne. There are more folding chairs than the stockholders will need to sit on, chairs left from some other meeting. The chairs, Howard sees, are going to be part of the tension. Lines will be drawn by where each person sits, and how much space he puts between himself and somebody else.

The fire door squeaks on a nerve-piercing note and here comes a moth-eaten Mexican sombrero. Obviously, it's on top of Josh with his head leaning forward like a bull—Josh, who insisted on wearing his Mexican cotton shirt and un-ironed pants to the funeral. Josh waiting for the world to be blown up.

Is that why he took to drugs in high school? Howard pictures the shoe box with teaspoon, syringe and matches, the heroin kit that Miss Bounce found on Josh's closet shelf after the screaming I-wish-you-were-dead fight with the Old Man forced Josh to leave home four years ago.

A familiar skinny hand removes the sombrero and Josh bows to Howard with a sweeping gesture of the hat. Always a ham. That's why Howard and Josh laughed together a lot when they were kids. Josh bows low to Alice and Arthur, who are plainly bored by the performance, and to Suzanne, who smiles.

Strange that Josh, with his door-squeaks and hat-sweeps, walks without sound. Like a cat stalking a mouse. Always has. And now he has a trapped angry look in his brown eyes. Howard could almost imagine him as a mad bomber, maybe with a homemade bomb in the paper bag he carries under his arm. But I don't believe he'd kill, thinks Howard—even if he's a junkie with needle marks under that shirt, he's not a killer.

Look how he holds the door open for Virginia, who wears enough unironed cotton to match him and carries their red-haired son on one hip. The baby has Josh's wide-set eyes and triumphant nose. Virginia is rather a wow, with that long red hair and intelligent blue eyes. Josh did well.

They sit down in the back, one chair from Suzanne. A statement? "We outsiders stick together."

Howard hurries up to say "Hi!" to Virginia and Josh. He sits down one row in front of them and turns around, saying he's glad the baby is better. The paper bag Josh carries isn't a bomb. He hands it to Virginia and she pulls a diaper out.

"Do you miss the commune?"

Josh's pupils are large and humorless. "I miss the nonviolence. I miss the peace."

Was he practicing nonviolence this morning when he almost drove Miss Bounce to a heart attack by demanding to bring Virginia and the baby into the family pew for the funeral? Of course Miss Bounce didn't help much by explaining that she considers the baby a bastard and Virginia a loose woman, since there is no marriage certificate. Luckily the baby got diarrhea and Virginia had to stay at the motel and look after him, preventing a confrontation in the church. Now either the diarrhea is better or Josh figures the family deserves it. Is he cockier now that he votes two hundred shares of stock? He's sure cocky.

But Josh wouldn't kill. Madison might. Madison manages to open the door without a squeak. He knows its natural rhythm. And he manages to look perfectly at home in his dark suit and tie. He could be an undertaker. An expensive undertaker. But that doesn't explain why Howard doesn't trust him.

Madison says hello politely to Josh and Virginia and Howard. "Cleo won't be here. She has the flu."

"There's a lot around. Honey has the flu too." But, Howard thinks, that's all his wife and mine have in common.

Madison smiles and nods at Suzanne. He may want her vote. Which way is he voting? He doesn't say. He walks down solemnly and says hello to Alice, who is combing her gold ringlets, and Arthur, just nodding off. Madison. Always the diplomat.

And what Madison ought to be doing if he is a normal human being is blowing his stack. Madison is no swinger. He's so conservative that instead of Kleenex he uses monogrammed cotton handkerchiefs. There's one in his pocket now.

And all the time his blond, orchid wife, Cleo, is probably saying she has the flu so she can cheat on him. He must know how much she sleeps around. She even fluttered those long slow I-need-you-in-bed glances at the Old Man. Madison never seemed to see a thing.

Howard and Madison walk back to the table at the front of the rows of chairs. The clock says one minute to four. Just about time.

Miss Bounce will be almost late. That is her style. And where is Leeroy?

Prompt Herbert plunges energetically through the door carrying his briefcase of legal papers. He says hello briskly all around, joins Madison and Howard at the table, snaps open the case, and takes the papers out with a businesslike rustle. He's a small man, wearing those glasses that always reflect the light, overshined shoes and an oversized wrist watch that also reflects. His skin gleams as if he's printed on that extra-thick glazed paper used for art magazines. He's the only person in the room besides Suzanne who is relaxed. Even the baby is fretful. Changed now, he begins to whimper. Virginia unbuttons her blouse and pops a pink nipple in his mouth. He sucks greedily and strokes her breast with one small hand. Miss Bounce will be shocked.

Then Miss Bounce explodes through the door. "I am here," say her feet. "Now everything is under control." She stands quite still, looking around. Like a general when taps is played. She's dressed in simple black that manages to look wickedly expensive without hiding her stubby figure, stiff and round as an old-fashioned clothespin. Or that statue. "Well, I see we are all here," she says cheerfully, managing, however, not to look at Virginia, or at Suzanne.

She walks purposefully to the front and joins Madison and Prompt Herbert and Howard behind the table. This is awkward because there are only three chairs. Madison sits firmly in his, showing Herbert a column of figures, and so holding the lawyer in his place too. Howard is half inclined to be polite and give Miss Bounce his chair, but he stops himself. Sitting at the table would give her an advantage. He's not sure exactly what advantage she wants, but if she didn't feel she needed an advantage, she would not be trying to take it. He puts his folder on the table.

"Mother," he says, "Madison and I will run this meeting. Madison will get Herbert to explain all the ins and outs and tax ramifications of the offer to buy, and I will read the statement that Father had prepared." (Big flash of self-importance.) And, he adds, "Mother, I want you to sit in the front row." He leans forward and somehow knocks the folder of the Old Man's words on the floor. Miss Bounce smiles wryly as he hurries to pick up his papers, then she shrugs and sits down next to Alice with a thunk of bottom against chair. Her mouth curves up in a hard smile as if she's overjoyed to see Howard about to play his ace because she's going to trump it. "All right, son—" her eyes are both angry and triumphant "—go ahead and read your father's words."

Shining in his mother's eyes, he reads this message: "I hated your father." Like a headline at the top of page one. Howard reads it with shock of recognition. He's always known this. Seen it and told his eyes they must be wrong. Heard it and not listened.

My mother hates my father, even now, he thinks. Hates him in the only form in which she still can. As *The Defender*.

Now, for whatever is about to happen, the cast is assembled. All except Leeroy with his one share of stock. Howard remembers what Lance said about Leeroy. "He'll find out everything we want to know—and everything we don't want to know on top of that."

SIX

LEEROY SPRINTS ALONG the wet brick walk across the park, wind at his back blowing his hair up the wrong way, sculpting his body into bones and raincoat flaps. The wind is cold and sharp all the way down into his lungs. He feels light-headed.

He's frantic to get to the meeting on time, and yet he started with no time to spare because he was nervous. If the family members vote at the meeting to sell the paper, his job may be gone. The wind jabs him in the ribs like a practical joker as he sees himself being interviewed by some strange hostile editor, a man half his age with a carpeted office: "What have you written in the last six months?" Nothing impressive. "Howard took all my best ideas."

"Good," says the man. "I'll hire Howard."

Leeroy's raincoat flaps whip with laughter at him. "You," they say, "you're like the wrong pole of a magnet. You repel money. And things. And therefore beautiful women. Why is the bottom button missing from your raincoat? And what do you own of any value? Records and books. Eat those! Your furniture should have been sent back to the Salvation Army. Your car has a dented fender. Your bank balance is $108.75."

Still, thinks Leeroy, by sheer chance and the grace of God and the Old Man's final insanity, I own one of the 1,200 shares of stock in *The Defender*. Cash value probably about $50,000. Better to have a good job than to sell.

That stock entitles Leeroy to go to the meeting about the proposed sale, to be on the inside instead of the outside of what's happening. To speak up if he can think of anything to say against the sale. But what? A great derisive gust hits him right in the middle of the back and knocks out his breath. Then there's a lull.

The Defender Building across the park grows larger as he hurries forward. A squarish glass-brick building, wonderfully modern in the 1930s, passé in the 1940s, now Art Deco and "in." Name across the front: THE DEFENDER in huge aluminum letters shining like pewter in the drizzly afternoon. At the back stands the new red-brick wing with the modern press and composing rooms.

A wave of possessiveness comes over Leeroy. I own part of that! I'm a stockholder. He feels as he does when he fingers his first edition of *The Sun Also Rises,* his autographed Hemingway.

He peers at his watch. Four minutes to four. Prompt Herbert will start the meeting exactly at four. Just time.

And then Freddy Norris rises up before him with that Glory Hallelujah look in his red-rimmed eyes. Good grief. I should have thought of Freddy! Freddy in his seedy raincoat, with a 7 Up bottle in his stubby right hand.

Freddy never rises up with that Hallelujah look unless he knows something that Leeroy needs to know; because Freddy's other high, besides white wine out of the 7 Up bottle, is sparking news. His greatest triumph so far was alerting Leeroy to look into a leaking chemical dump in an old warehouse near the Harvey Street Elementary School. He's been wrong, too—the police chief was not bringing prostitutes to his office.

But Freddy knows his power as he sways and gently flaps in the lulled wind. "You came at the right time, Leeroy." His voice is as gravelly as a loud bellow, but so soft Leeroy has to listen carefully. His right eye with the scar always makes him appear on the point of winking. He lists toward a gimpy leg. Freddy the pipeline.

Secretive types squeal to Freddy. Because they hold grudges. Because they are bored and might otherwise turn in a false fire alarm.

So who has blabbed this time? Leeroy rarely finds out. Maybe a nobody feels powerful by knowing a somebody's secret, and letting hints drop to Freddy. Even the jokers test Freddy. Or are they testing Leeroy? The bit about the garbage truck drivers selling drugs was couched in a pun.

Freddy grins like a sphinx, whatever his source. And it could be somebody scared stiff, hiding his tracks, because he knows of danger or abuse and doesn't dare be discovered as the source of the story. That's how Leeroy discovered the dump near the school.

But, damn it, Lecroy thinks, why does this man always have to be coy with me? I made him what he is, even if I did it by accident, by listening. If I didn't listen, these people wouldn't tell him things. I give Freddy Norris power. Even the police allow him to claim his bench outside *The Defender*. They make other winos move along. Frantically, Leeroy wishes they'd made Freddy beat it today.

"Freddy, I'm late for a meeting," says Leeroy briskly. The Glory Hallelujah in Freddy's eyes merely increases. "There is no meeting worth what I know." He's so full of self-congratulation, he's about to rise and fly. And whatever he knows, he'll take half an hour to tell it, with a seventy five percent chance that it'll be true when checked out. Freddy's tips have to be handled with care, could even be hidden traps. Curiosity and impatience wrestle inside Leeroy, whacking him this way and that like the wind.

Freddy puts out his hand and takes hold of Leeroy's arm. Leeroy knows without looking that the man's stubby fingers have nails bitten to the quick. The "7 Up" is not enough. Freddy pulls Leeroy toward the bench and a gust of wind pushes Leeroy down hard beside him. Their raincoats whip in unison. And involuntarily Leeroy shrinks back. Not because Freddy smells. He looks as if he smells, but he never does, except of wine. Leeroy shrinks from that terrible need to hold that quivers in the man's fingertips.

Now Freddy turns his wind-tangled head in every direction. No one else in sight. He smiles, showing his teeth with the broad space, center top. Leeroy remembers reading once that Egyptians believe people with teeth like that can cast the evil eye. Two minutes to four.

This is Freddy's moment of importance, and plainly he wants to make it last as long as possible.

Leeroy could kick himself and Freddy, too. Because the fastest way to find out what Freddy knows is to be patient and sympathetic. He tries to squeeze out some sympathy. Freddy is a lost soul, he reminds himself savagely. And in a way, damn it, I'm a lost soul, too. Nothing helps. Freddy takes a long slow swig from his bottle and offers it to Leeroy.

"No, thanks." One minute to four. Leeroy jumps up to leave.

Freddy's face goes slack and startled like a whipped child's. Leeroy almost expects to see the red imprint of his own hand on the weathered cheek. His sympathy is at last about to flow when Freddy's eyes go sly.

"Got any leads on who killed the Old Man?" The wind can't mask the smugness of that voice. The vibrating tangled hair can't hide that superior tilt of the head. The eyes glisten. The hand with the bottle is still raised as if Freddy is toasting himself.

And why should I have to care more about finding who killed the Old Man than looking out for my own business? Leeroy seethes. If Freddy really knows anything, he won't be able to keep it to himself in the long run. Only long enough now to drive me crazy. But then, what he knows will eat away and make holes in him like acid in a tin can.

"I'll be back in an hour and a half and we'll go over to Sluder's for a few drinks," Leeroy offers. He does not look at Freddy's face, but down at his dirty tennis shoes, one untied, the other with a hole worn over his toenail. An unnecessary hole because plainly Freddy's wife, a nurse at Memorial Hospital who pays the rent, who mows their small lawn on Saturday and furnishes Freddy's telephone—plainly the wife would buy him new shoes.

Freddy gets up as Leeroy does, laughs gaily and throws one arm around Leeroy as if they are old affectionate drinking partners. "Oh, I know about you," he chortles. He rocks them back and forth, back and forth in the gray rain as if they were swaying to music. Leeroy sways, still torn two ways. "Oh, I know what's got into you," chortles Freddy. "You're a stockholder now. A stockholder in that paper the gang wants to buy. You want to make your loot and get out. That's what makes the world run. Greed. And now you're a part of it like all the rest."

So Freddy is jealous. It's after four o'clock. Prompt Herbert has started the meeting. "Listen," Leeroy hisses in Freddy's cauliflower ear, "unless you can give me one good reason why they shouldn't, the members of that family are going to vote to sell the paper at that meeting and that will kibosh my job, your power, and your place on this bench into the bargain." He pulls back and looks Freddy straight in his bloodshot eyes.

Freddy stops swaying and sits down again hard. He empties the 7 Up bottle, takes another out of a six-pack in a plastic bag by his feet, removes clear plastic and an elastic band that cork the top, and takes a long swig. The Glory Hallelujah has been knocked out of him. "Yes," he says, so softly that Leeroy has to lean forward to hear. "Yes. I believe it. I believe in greed."

He stares up thoughtfully at Leeroy, frowning, now old and wise as Methuselah. How old can Freddy be in reality? He says he was born rich and lost all of it. He says every scar has a history: the livid line at the base of his thumb comes from a knife fight in Alaska; the limp from being tossed by a bull at a rodeo in Texas; the mutilated ear because he was once a prizefighter. If his stories all were true he'd have to be 100. Leeroy doubts they're true. Freddy probably fell down the stairs.

"Listen," Freddy whispers, "what I have to tell you is about the people who want to buy the paper and how they killed the Old Man." Leeroy shudders. He'd almost walked off.

Freddy takes a long slug of wine, head tipped back. Behind him, *The Defender* lights make the whole glass-brick building glow in the gathering gloom.

Leeroy breathes deeply, feels suddenly at home and safe outside the building that belongs partly to him. "What happened?" he asks quietly. Even the wind has lulled.

Now Freddy looks embarrassed. That's his way. Even if he has only a small clue, he has to get the maximum drama out of it to begin with. Then he can only offer what he has, and he twists himself into "Aw, shucks."

"Anything will help."

"I don't know exactly what happened," Freddy says. "But I do know that a man with one eye was mixed up in it. A man with one eye who is a card shark. You talk to him. He knows the people who want to buy the paper. Something smelly there. And those people have some kind of link to the racetrack, too. The one you folks keep yelling about. And all that has something to do with how the Old Man died. I couldn't quite get the details. In fact that's all I know. You ask the one-eyed man."

"What's his name?"

"I don't know."

"What does he look like?"

"I haven't met him."

"Who told you about him?"

"I protect my sources."

Great. But Leeroy knows Freddy well enough to know that's all he's going to tell.

"But I know this is a good lead," Freddy says.

And that has always been Freddy's talent. He usually knows the strength of what he's got. But what good will this vague trail do at the meeting? "The bum in front of the building says a one-eyed card shark is a link to finding out how the people who want to buy the paper killed the Old Man. No proof." That, versus millions. Leeroy restrains himself from groaning.

He is now cold, damp, depressed, and late. And all he has to show for being late is a handful of smoke, a leaf from the grapevine of drunks. Freddy puts his arm around Leeroy again and Leeroy does not recoil. Yes, they really are sad sacks together. Brothers under the skin.

"Listen," says Freddy. "Listen: what I've told you has solid feet. And you're smart, Leeroy. A lot smarter than me. You can find out what happened. Now hurry up, you're late to the meeting."

SEVEN

HOWARD STIRS, impatient, as prompt Herbert repeats "sixty million dollars." He says it in fifty-seven varieties and twenty-eight flavors in a voice like he's reading aloud from a mail-order catalog. Well, nobody ever called him Brief Herbert. The members of the family who might get that money for *The Defender* listen as raptly as if they were hypnotized by his reflecting eyeglasses. They breathe slowly, their pupils enlarge. The baby falls asleep at Virginia's breast and she forgets to button up. Howard feels as if the air is being pumped out of the room. Money is all around them flapping in the air, a green whirlpool of lust. He imagines that the hungry line of each mouth says "I deserve mine."

Even Prompt Herbert is not on my side, Howard thinks. Prompt Herbert is never on anybody's side. But now he enjoys arousing lust: his mouth twitches and seems to water.

"Madison and I have done some checking," says Herbert. "This is a generous offer to buy." He grows larger as the focal point of total attention.

He explains what can happen. This is a closely held company. The executor will vote the stock in the Old Man's estate as each stockholder wishes. Each share of stock gets one vote. It's necessary that a majority of the shares be voted in favor of selling before a sale to an outsider can be made. If the majority of shares vote to sell, the paper will be sold.

Suzanne is the only stockholder besides Howard who is not leaning forward eagerly. Howard notices that Suzanne's eyes stay critical, digesting everyone at the meeting as well as Prompt Herbert's words. A fixed spot in the rushing tide. Howard is almost grateful to Suzanne for being there in her four-leaf-clover blouse. But then, the stakes are lower for that bitch Suzanne with her one share.

"Of course, if you decide not to sell," Herbert says, "there are certain tax laws designed for the protection of small businesses." Immediately, Herbert loses his hypnotic grip. Josh scratches his heel under the strap of his sandal. Alice pats her curls. Only Suzanne and Virginia hold the tension of their listening. The two outsiders. Suzanne, who wouldn't have a share of stock if she hadn't slept with the Old Man. Virginia, who is only the mother of a stockholder's son. Josh's woman.

And where is Leeroy, the other holder of just one share?

Finally, Prompt Herbert begins to pick up his papers and Madison says, "We'll take a five-minute coffee break and then Howard will read Father's statement before we vote." Is Madison as carried away by lust as the rest? He hides behind his formality. If Madison committed a murder, he would do it with such formal politeness that the corpse would be sure it couldn't really be dead; would try to get up and walk away.

They all get up and stretch briefly. Alice comes back from the ladies' room in three minutes and sits down again beside Arthur, who is impatiently flipping one of his Susan B. Anthony dollars. He drops the coin on the floor, leans over and picks it up, and spins it even higher. The baby laughs. Family members take their coffee back to their seats with them. They fidget.

Howard feels dizzy. Isn't what he is about to read, in effect, a letter from the grave? He straightens the typed sheets, lines them up at right angles to the boards of the table in front of him with reverent fingers. To him it was a miracle that he found this draft of the words the Old Man had expected to say at the meeting. If the Old Man had lived, he would have spoken as if these words were inspired on the spur of the moment by his concern for each person. He would have carried this meeting by the force of his emotion and personality. Can all of the Old Man's magic die with him?

Hurry up, say all the eyes. But Howard pauses. "Something wrong" suddenly flashes in this windowless room. Flashes, and vanishes before his mind can grasp it. Something he's half known, so that his heart recognizes it and starts to beat hard with panic.

Not just the obvious whirlpool of money. No. He remembers a flicker of movement that saved him when he almost stepped on a copperhead at camp, a flicker in dry leaves. Now he feels or sees or smells a flicker of warning— so subliminal that it is gone before he knows which sense was warned. Why? What? Is it something one of the people here is doing?

At the back of the island of chairs, Josh's shining eyes peer out of his jungle of hair like impatient tigers. In the front row, Miss Bounce stares Howard down, a dark column of impatience.

Howard goes hot with a wave of anger and frustration, and opens his mouth to begin reading.

The fire door opens. Howard almost expects the Old Man, come to save the day. But it's only Leeroy. Leeroy wrapped in a wet raincoat, hair blown awry, sliding into the chair next to Suzanne, out of breath. Heads turn briefly as he asks Suzanne what's happened. She boils down Prompt Herbert's legal ramblings into just two sentences. "We can vote to sell the paper for sixty million dollars, or not. If we vote to sell, you and I will be the only ones in this room who aren't multimillionaires."

The potential millionaires all glare at Howard, and Miss Bounce taps her foot. Howard begins reading the Old Man's words:

Family and my dear friends. You all know that what we have to consider today is an offer to buy our newspaper. I gave you stock because I believe you care about The Defender *the way I do.*

At the back of the room, the tigers in Josh's eyes snarl. His top crossed leg begins to move up and down, up and down like the tail of a cat watching a rat. Howard knows what his rebel brother is thinking: To hell with that fancy talk. The Old Man started giving us stock before he died for tax purposes.

Howard's mouth is as dry as if it were full of feathers. He stops, takes a sip of water and reads on:

It is a privilege for us to be able to do something first-rate; to have power to make the world a better place.

And at that, Josh shifts so violently in his metal chair that Howard expects him to get up and walk out. Howard sees him equally mad five years ago. "You get the praise, Howard, and you know what I get? My father was so busy helping Leeroy chase a lead in that story that won the Lamont prize that he forgot to come to my high school graduation. Just forgot. Did that make the world a better place?"

Two hundred sure votes for selling. Howard's head begins to ache. He continues reading:

Some of you have been hurt because The Defender *makes enemies. Alice wasn't invited to a big Christ-*

mas party one year because the paper exposed a political payoff to her girl friend's parents. When you're sixteen that's hard to take. You've all had to be good soldiers.

Alice pouts and looks sorry for herself. Minus two hundred shares more?

But our job is to be a watchdog for all public officials or large powerful institutions and to print the truth no matter who gets hurt. Why? Because it's human nature to cheat when no one is watching. I have done it myself. So have all of you. I remember when Howard was six he filched the change I left in an ashtray on my bureau and never counted. After I found out, I counted each day, and he never filched change again. In the same way, our newspaper holds the community to accountability. We can all be proud of that.

Miss Bounce is smirking. Howard filched change from her marmalade jar in the kitchen into his teens. She knew and didn't care. Howard reads on:

I believe we use our power—the power of information—wisely. When racial tensions were high in our schools, the community was at least spared the wild rumors which made such trouble over in Greenburg where that kid was shot as a result. People knew if an incident really happened here, the paper would print it. When the white teacher slapped the black first grader who bit her arm in three places, we published the details and were criticized for making trouble. I know that made life hard for Madison, who was a third grader at that school. But our reputation for fair reporting helped the leaders of the black community refute wild stories about the teacher locking three black kids in a closet.

Alice yawns luxuriously and flutters a twinkling hand in front of her mouth. Howard imagines throwing his glass of water in her face.

And yet he knows that as he reads his father's words they sound wrong. Inflated. Almost pompous. Not at all warm and spontaneous, not like those same words would have sounded from the Old Man himself.

Leeroy and our other reporters have helped tell the community about needs that were being ignored. You know, Wilhelmina....

Miss Bounce raises her head, startled as if it has really occurred to her that she is being addressed from beyond the grave. Nobody but the Old Man uses her full given name.

"... You know, Wilhelmina, that many of your good ideas, such as starting the center for battered women, have turned into realities as our reporters dug out the facts.

She bows her head and Howard believes his mother could be on his side: 398 shares to the good. "Please vote no," Howard prays. Once he was her favorite. She still keeps pencils in the pickle jar covered with bright bits of paper that he made for her in kindergarten.

Now I want you to think about the Gemtrex Group, which is offering to buy The Defender. *They run shoddy newspapers. When* The Atlantic *did an exposé of inadequate sewage systems around the country and mentioned Bright City, the editor of the* Bright City Sentinel—*a Gemtrex paper—did a whitewash job, quoting local officials and saying no national magazine had a right to bad-mouth their city.*

Two of the Gemtrex papers are in known centers of organized crime and largely ignore it. Do you want to see our city served by a newspaper like that? Do you want to sell it to a group that will change the character for which we have all worked and even you children had to make sacrifices? I don't believe there is one of you who really wants that.

Sure, we'd make a lot of money in the short run. But in the long run we enjoy good income from our paper already. You young ones don't get much yet because you don't have much stock yet. You need to learn how it feels to earn your own living. But your future is assured.

As of now, Howard knows that even after high inheritance taxes he and Madison and Josh and Alice *will* get mor dividends, because of the stock they have inherited. Wh can't that be enough?

He reads on:

I hope you enjoy knowing that we contribute to something worthwhile. I hope you will always care enough about yourselves and the community to keep it that way.

Howard puts the typed sheets down. That's all. The fina words. Eyes are still hostile. Miss Bounce leans forwar studying the Xeroxed copy of the offer to buy which Promp Herbert gave her earlier. Howard can't see her face. The abruptly she looks up and straight at him. Her mouth sucks in. There's triumph or the expectation of it in her blue eyes. Howard feels sick.

Miss Bounce stands up. "I'd like to make a motion that we vote as Herbert has suggested."

Arthur opens his eyes wide, leans over and whispers something in Alice's ear, and she says "I second the motion."

"Is there any discussion?" asks Madison. How can he be so calm?

Leeroy shifts in his chair at the back, but says nothing.

"Smart people are not selling newspapers, they're buying papers." Howard has to make his family listen. "Buyers are making money, even foreigners. Like that Australian Rupert Murdoch who bought the *Boston Herald* and all those other papers."

Miss Bounce's arched eyebrows raise high. "Hogwash. People watch television now, Howard. This paper will be obsolete in five years. We're damn lucky somebody will still buy *The Defender* at a good price."

"I move we vote right now!" Josh picks now to agree with his mother, for the first time in twenty years.

"And I second." Alice nods her curls.

Leeroy jumps up, his hair still blown askew. His words are askew too. He stutters, pauses in the wrong places. "Look, would you just give me forty-eight hours to prove or disprove something before you vote?" He peers around at their startled faces, swallows, plunges on. "I mean I can't tell you for certain now that the Gemtrex Group somehow had something to do with the Old Man being poisoned, but it's possible. I can't even tell you enough to convince you how I can find out. I mean, some of my sources are pretty strange. But I know when a tip is worth something. You know that's been true before."

Howard's heart begins to pound.

Arthur sits up very straight, wide awake, turns around in his chair and stares at Leeroy as if he were covered with running sores. Josh says "Oh, my God!"

"Tell us exactly what you know." Miss Bounce glowers.

Leeroy presses his cowlick down with the flat of his palm. It pops back up. "Just a tip from a bum," he mumbles. "The description of a man who may know something. No name. No address. But give me two days."

"So we wait two days. In two days, Leeroy, won't you find a slightly better clue? How long can that keep up?" Miss Bounce's eyebrows wander up so deftly that there's a ripple of laughter.

"We should vote now!" Josh demands.

"Please stop!" Virginia hugs the baby as if for comfort and stands up. Heads turn to see that there are tears in her eyes. "I don't have any right to say anything about this." Her clear soprano becomes hoarse. "But how can two days matter to you so much?" She turns to Josh. "He was your father!" Josh puts his arm around her. This morning just before the funeral, Josh told the family how a white Cadillac ran over Virginia's father and killed him while she watched when she was just thirteen years old. Does Virginia's grief make them all feel a little second-rate? Howard hopes so.

"Gemtrex hasn't set a deadline for selling the paper," he says quickly. "Forty-eight hours won't matter."

Miss Bounce doesn't give up. "If the sale of *The Defender* is mixed up with murder by the buyers, certainly it will be declared illegal. So we can go on and vote whether to sell, and Leeroy can investigate, too."

Prompt Herbert opens his mouth below his tinted eyeglasses and at first nothing comes out, maybe because Miss Bounce is staring at him so hard. His words escape: "Can of worms! If you sell and then try to say the sale was illegal, that would be a legal can of worms!" Imagine Prompt Herbert using slang. He adds, more formally, "I believe the top people at Gemtrex are off in South America trying to put together another deal. They have a variety of interests. I gather they'll be almost impossible to reach for a few days. They won't know if you delay."

Madison gets up slowly, impressive, like three or four presidents rolled into one, laying out his stake as head of the family. "I believe we would be wise to grant Leeroy's request to wait two days. But our motion should say that after exactly forty-eight hours there must be substantial proof that Gemtrex is mixed up in our father's murder or we will definitely vote right then whether to sell."

Miss Bounce says "Amen." And finally they all vote to give Leeroy forty-eight hours. Howard realizes he's been sweating. He's wringing wet.

EIGHT

5:40 P.M. I'M EXECUTIVE assistant to a ghost, Suzanne tells herself wryly, noticing she can smell the Old Man's cigarette smoke. The Old Man's office is still full of his presence, a force like air before a storm. That is why nobody sits in his chair. Her grandmother Mancini would be able to see him, but Suzanne can only feel her skin prickle.

Howard and Leeroy sit facing each other on the edge of the Old Man's desk. Howard holds a large envelope marked "Threatening Letters." Lance stands facing them, hunched a little, hands in pockets, elbows out.

"I can help," Suzanne announces. That is a demand.

They look up, surprised. Leeroy pleased. He beams. Howard annoyed. He squirms. Lance polite. Leeroy brings her the chair that usually sits by the globe of the world. She turns the chair and rests her elbows on the sharp ladder back, facing Howard and Leeroy. She does not intend to be looked down on.

Leeroy repeats Freddy Norris: Gemtrex, the company that wants to buy the paper, is in some way linked to the Old Man's death, and in some way linked to Howard's racetrack exposés, and a one-eyed card shark can tell them more if they can find him. Sounds like a B-movie plot.

Lance rubs his jaw as if he's stupid. Howard leans forward in his funeral suit as if he's trying to hear Leeroy's words before they come out of his mouth, and frowns like he thinks Leeroy is maybe crazy.

"That's all I can tell you," Leeroy says firmly. Why was Leeroy all feet and Adam's apple at the meeting? Now he's more convincing. "Freddy is onto something, I'm sure," Leeroy adds. "He's given us good stuff before, beginning with a few odd facts like this."

Lance still rubs his jaw. "The police seem to think one of us put the poison in the bourbon. They even asked me if the Old Man made passes at my wife."

Good question. Lance's Alexandra is twenty years younger than he is, red-haired and yeasty. Out loud, Suzanne says "That's how they treated me: like a number-one suspect. And with their eyebrows raised."

"And even me!" Howard is plainly surprised. He thinks he's special. "But we don't have time to worry about that." His voice rises, "We've got to get started." A clock face is all but printed in the worry lines on his forehead. Forty-eight hours minus fifteen minutes. He may self-destruct from trying so hard. That won't help.

Lance takes his stubby hand out of his pocket and points. First at Leeroy. "You look for the one-eyed man." Next he points at his own old blue plaid necktie. "I'll take the past. If something happens to a man that I don't understand I look back into the time before I knew him, before the people I know knew him." Then he points at Howard. "What do you know about your father before he came here, Howard? What should I look for, Boy?"

"He said the time before he came here was too boring. He never would talk about it. I just know he came from Mason County. Even his autobiography starts after he left home." Howard is defensive. Relax, Howard.

"If we don't know exactly where he came from after all these years, then exactly where he came from must be important. Why, Boy, that could be the key to the whole thing." Lance likes to sound like a good old boy. Sometimes he acts like a good old boy. He winks at Suzanne. He says he'll take on Mason County. He says he'll assign one of the boys from the newsroom to find out everything there is to know about the Gemtrex Company, even if the brass is out of the country. Howard has already looked for dirt about the racetrack people. Cagey types.

Lance points the stubby finger at Suzanne. "You took some of those threatening phone calls, Girl. You track down the threatening letters. The Goldfish, God bless her, copied them all before the police took 'em."

So Lance is taking charge. And was Mrs. Lance too sassy with the Old Man? Sassy enough. Suzanne does not trust Lance. Is he giving her the threatening letters job to keep her a safe distance from the office family and the Justice family?

Howard thrusts the folder of letters at Suzanne. "Don't tell anyone you have those. Leonora sold her soul to get them." Is he trying to pique my interest? she wonders. To divert me from what?

"You know how the Goldfish is," Howard says. "How you can always tell by her tongue if she thinks she's breaking a rule. How her tongue wiggles."

Everybody laughs, almost breaking the tension. Because of course they all know how it is. The Goldfish loves rules. The Old Man used to say that was one reason she got straight A's at State College. Pre-med, yet. Until she had to look at blood and then she gave the whole thing up and took a secretarial course. No guts.

"When the Goldfish gave me these," says Howard, "her tongue began to rub the corner of her mouth, tip in and out, the way it does when she worries about a rule." Howard over-explains. But the gist is that Leonora let the police think they took the only copies of those letters. Of course, Leonora would cheat for the Old Man.

That is not what Howard is getting at. What he obviously means is that he is giving Suzanne something super-important.

Suzanne takes the folder, but not the soft soap. "If one of these letters is from the poisoner," she says, "one of these letters is from somebody close to the Old Man, maybe one of us."

Lance rubs that stubby jaw. Leeroy freezes at attention. Howard stares back at Suzanne hard, as if preparing for a duel.

"The poisoner had to know the Old Man had a cold and couldn't taste or smell, right? He had to know where the Old Man's secret apartment was. He had to know the Old Man drank bourbon when he had a cold and scotch when he felt well. I never heard of anybody else doing that. Only the bourbon was poisoned."

Howard clutches the edge of the desk. Does he think it's going to run away? "Yes," he says as if the word gives him heartburn. "Yes, somebody had to know my father had a cold, and that wasn't easy. After two sneezes he always took Contac. He said he might not be able to help being sick but he sure could manage not to act sick."

Lance begins to pace up and down, up and down behind Suzanne. He says he thinks better on his feet, but he acts like an animal in a cage. "I never knew he had a cold."

"I knew." Howard's lips are stiff as if they'd love to stay shut. "I knew because the whole family went out to supper together for Madison's thirty-first birthday, and my father was upset because he couldn't taste the pecan pie. But who could have known besides the family?" Howard's crossed leg pumps up and down, up and down. He'd like to kick somebody, Suzanne thinks, maybe me. Now that's more human. If he kicked somebody I'd like him better. He did kick before, but he was the Old Man's foot on a jerk string.

He smiled when he did it. Now he frowns. That's an improvement.

"O.K." Howard blurts, "You do the damned letters, Suzanne, and I'll talk to all the people who were closest to my father, even my mother."

Suzanne sucks in her breath. For a moment she actually admires Howard. Nobody in her family would be capable of suspecting his own mother, even with good reason. Why, her grandmother Mancini would like Howard. Not because he can suspect his mother, but just because he tries so hard. Because his intentions are so good. But then, Grandmother liked Mussolini. For a while.

Howard and Leeroy jump up. Jack and the beanstalk. "Be careful, Howard," Leeroy warns. "If organized crime is mixed up in this, and you are the family member trying to stop them, you could be a target." Dutch uncle. But also some spite in that: better you than me.

Amen. And why does Howard look at me like that? Goddamn, Suzanne thinks, he's wondering if I'm related to the Mafia! The sanctimonious son-of-a-bitch! I may be Italian, I may have married a con man by mistake, but I, myself, am squeaky clean, and he should know it.

The phone rings. Howard reaches across the polished desk, picks it up, answers it, then holds it a little away from his ear. Even Suzanne can hear that it's Honey and she's screaming.

"You're never coming home! I thought that at least when he was gone you'd come home. You don't even come when I'm sick. What do you care about anybody but yourself? What do you care about me?" What lung power!

"I'm coming right now, and I do care." Howard hangs up, very collected. Maybe he thinks they haven't heard Honey yell. "I will start," he says, "by having dinner with my wife. I think her flu is better. And as a matter of fact,

I'm starving. And if I question Honey, she may remember something or other that will help.'' He grins at Leeroy. "Even the killer would not be alarmed to see me eat dinner with my own wife."

Just surprised, thinks Suzanne. If I were Honey I'd have killed the Old Man for making Howard forget me so often. But I would have killed Howard first for being the kind of man the Old Man could do that to. Oh, he was a persuader. But each of us had damned well better look out for himself.

And look at Honey. She may put on those arty airs, but she's naive. If she ran a restaurant, she'd take bad checks. If Honey knows anything related to the Old Man's death, she won't know she knows it. Will Howard be smart enough to pull it out of her? The odds, Suzanne decides, are fifty-fifty. There is a part of Howard that desperately wants to know what happened, and another part that is afraid to find out.

NINE

HOWARD STARES AT the crazy cutout letters: "The Defender killed your father. The Defender can kill you." Now that the family meeting is over, the vote at least delayed, he can admit finding this thing. He slips the glued-together note into an envelope marked "Sergeant Jones." The envelope also contains his white lie: he just found the threat this minute. Thank goodness the police are a zigzag away from the *The Defender*. He's hardly delayed leaving the envelope. Then home to Honey.

At 7:45 he parks in front of his apartment in the old clapboard mansion on Chestnut Street. The February dark is already thick, moon obscured by clouds, drizzle turning the night clammy. Occasional gusts of wind. And Howard is tired.

Why else would the man walking slowly past his house across the street make his heart begin to pound? So it's not a good night for walking. That doesn't prove anything. The man walks too slowly. Oh, come on, Howard. Out of the gloom, the man's round face and plump hands seem unearthly white. The dark clothed part of him vanishes.

Howard turns quickly toward his own porch. No outside light. Only what glimmers faintly through the windows. Honey forgot. Howard slips inside fast and locks the door behind him.

Inside, lights are low. Just for a second, he allows himself to stand and smell the blooming narcissus in the blue bowl on the ledge of the small window by the front door. He married Honey because she created this kind of haven around herself, right? The inside of one of those globes that you shake and snowflakes fall. Her screaming is entirely out of character. Honey pouts. And arranges goldenrod. And plays parts.

He saw her first at that wild art show. God knows why he'd gone with Miss Bounce except that the twin gallery owners are distant cousins. There, Honey was a Persian princess in flowing soft blouse, purple harem pants and gold filigree earrings. He stood with her in front of that unbelievable wooden sculpture of an angel that flapped its wings and stuck out a pointed red tongue if you pushed a button. She smelled not like narcissus but like honey, and she moved, slow, sweet and smooth, like honey pouring on a cool day.

He remembers her hand was small and cold, asking to be warmed. But I haven't warmed her, he thinks bitterly. In a strange way, he's not even sure he knows her very well in spite of all the signals she sends. We live together, he thinks, but we are alone. I have no reason to trust her. She has no reason to trust me.

Today's signal is a vase of peacock feathers. There it stands on the low Japanese table in the middle of the old blue and green Oriental rug with her careful mend in one corner. Whatever sits on the table is the key to her mood.

Last spring, right after the wedding, two branches of dogwood in a Steuben glass vase (wedding present) meant happiness. She explained that.

The prettiest arrangement combined goldenrod with asters, and Honey put it on her signal table to greet Madison when he dropped off extra work from the Old Man, the last Sunday in September. The goldenrod was plainly designed to give Madison hay fever, and it worked.

So why is it that today the glass pitcher holds seven peacock feathers with faded golden eyes? They shimmer with age, smell like somebody's attic. Obviously they are one of Honey's finds at the flea market where she manages to buy cheap, sell expensive, and meet strange characters. The Old Man said she should work for the paper, not be a junk dealer. The Old Man.

Then it happens again. The sudden jolt of something almost perceived. The copperhead almost stepped on. But Howard can't tie his alarm to anything in this room. The built-in couches with big cushions are no danger. The many-paned windows on the far side of the room show only a ghostly white bit of paper blowing across a small lawn and then the next old retrofitted mansion. Art gallery there. Nobody at night.

Copperhead inside, strange man outside. Yes, I'm tired, Howard thinks. He does not call out to Honey. Ground rules. Part of her peace. He walks down the hall past the kitchen, office, and bathroom doors to the bedroom.

Honey is sitting in the middle of their double waterbed wearing a green kimono and balancing a large watercolor pad on her spread knees. And she's painting—what else? A peacock. A peacock amazed at itself like an illustration in a child's book. She concentrates absolutely on the painting as if nothing had happened. No murder. No family meeting. No flu. No screaming. Her Chinese jade earrings suspended from gold ear wires do not even sway, still as silence. The Old Man gave her those for her birthday. Her black hair is tucked Chinese style into a smooth bun with huge tortoiseshell hairpins.

She places one last dab of paint, then lifts the picture, gets up from the bed and attaches the peacock with a quick jab of a pushpin to the wall.

He goes over and kisses her and feels his own loneliness and her slight withdrawal, like a conch going deeper into the safe fastness of its shell. She smells sweet and fresh like the narcissus in the window.

"Honey," he says. "I've been off a lot. I understand why you were mad."

She smiles, green almond eyes inscrutable. Of course. The smile goes with the costume. Her coolness hurts. He feels guilty. He remembers she is an orphan.

His stomach rumbles loudly. "Honey, I'm starving to death."

"Well, I'm feeling better. I already called out for Chinese food, Howard. It should be here soon. Bring us some wine."

He brings two glasses and a bottle of chilled Chablis from the refrigerator and they sit facing each other on the edge of the bed.

The silk kimono that matches her eyes is old and shimmering like the peacock feathers. Maybe from the same attic, the same flea market stall. He tries to savor his cold crisp wine, but the clock in his head ticks louder and louder.

"Let me tell you what happened at the meeting, Honey. Then you'll understand why I'm so uptight."

"Maybe."

"My family is going to vote to sell *The Defender* unless we can prove that the people who want to buy it have something to do with killing my father."

Honey sips her wine with no change of expression.

"At least Leeroy has a lead, although it sounds weird: a one-eyed gambler knows who did it. But we've only got two days to find out. Only two days!"

And then Honey laughs, a princess tinkle, but her words come out too loud. "A deadline. That's what you like. A deadline!"

"I like a deadline, but not this kind, God knows. Help me. Then our lives will be back to normal."

"Normal? What's normal? I hope they sell the damn paper. I hate it." She is the woman on the phone again. Shouting.

"Please, Honey, help me get this over with."

"Oh, I could help you." Her eyes are green slits. She's a green snake. "I can feel out the ones who hated him," she hisses. "I read they've found a way to detect cancer by the heat in the place where the cancer is. I can feel the hate in people even if they smile. I can feel it because of the heat in me. Even in you I could feel it sometimes, but so mixed in with hero worship that you couldn't feel it yourself."

My God, Howard thinks, does she mean to be so cruel? He forces himself to stay calm. "Name your list. Who hated him?"

"Miss Bounce," she hisses, "and the women he took and deserted. And the women he didn't sleep with. Because he took so many that if he didn't even try to take you, you knew there was something personal in it."

"He didn't try to make you, Honey?" he asks, and realizes he means that as a return jab. That won't help.

"Oh, he got it across that he'd sleep with me in a minute if I wasn't your wife. He took me with his eyes. That was one way he tried to get me to shut up and enjoy my empty waterbed. The old goat."

Howard's face convulses with anger and grief. "My God," he says. "The funeral was this morning. You are talking about my father."

But Honey is a vial of green acid, come uncorked, spilling, out of control, on this of all days. "Your father! Oh, yes, you told me all the great things he did," she continues, "told me how he was too busy to notice you much until you were five years old and he found you spelling out words on his typewriter. And how wonderful it was that instead of getting mad, he was so pleased and excited he took you out to buy a typewriter of your own, that big legendary shining typewriter with chrome levers and bars. Oh, yes, you told me that. And how after that, instead of having to see your father in little glimpses and on television talk shows, you were his sidekick. How he took you to the office with him and showed you off."

She takes a deep breath and starts again: "You told me all that until I thought I'd vomit. And you became his good and faithful dog. Bow wow."

"Honey! I still have on the suit I wore to the funeral."

"So why don't you take it off?" She's imperious, angry, flirtatious, and sexy all at once. Somehow in her tirade she'd knocked out the tortoiseshell hairpins and her hair falls down around her shoulders, dark and vibrant.

Suddenly he finds her sexually desirable, feels it clear and straight, unmixed with love. The doorbell rings and he goes and gets the food, delivered by a very un-Chinese kid in a raincoat, a wan kid with pimples. The whiff of rain in Howard's face cools him off.

He comes back to find Honey naked to the waist, hair falling around her plump snub-nose breasts. She's wearing the purple harem pants she wore when they met. Must have been under the kimono all along. She has shut the curtains.

She laughs Chinese chimes. "You need one hour for yourself, Howard-San. One hour to rest your brains and make them number-one brains again. To eat supper and make love." She pronounces it "rove," flutters her eyelashes, and stretches languorously, each breast pulling toward its own arm, each rounded breast with a life of its own. She is the Honey who intrigued him first, Honey who is a blood transfusion to the parts of himself he's stopped taking time for: Foolishness. Sensuality. Honey's skin is soft. Howard is hungry.

"Honey, you're right!" He pushes away his grief and anger and begins ravenously to eat an egg roll. "Paradise enow. Two egg rolls, a jug of wine and thou." They both laugh.

He sees the clock over her shoulder. The moon-face clock she found at the flea market: 8:15. "I can't," he cries. "I don't have an hour. There isn't time."

"Time! Your father is dead! But he still drives you." Her uncorked anger erupts again. Honey stomps over to the closet, jerks out an old army jacket and hat, throws them on without bothering to button up the jacket and salutes with an angry snap. "Colonel," she drawls, "I am ready to salute your dictator from beyond." She puts her thumb to her nose and wiggles her fingers.

Howard would like to slap her across the mouth. Great. He gets indigestion from the sweet-and-sour spare ribs instead. He gets up and goes over and opens the curtains.

"Damn it, Honey. Stop. Just help me for two days."

"And then another two days and another two days." She's still wriggling her fingers.

"Damn it, listen," he yells. "Somebody knew my father's habits. Knew he had a cold. Cyanide smells. He couldn't smell it. The killer knew his workplace."

With difficulty he tries to be more reasonable. "Please, Honey, tell me, did anybody, anybody at all, ask you questions about my father?"

Honey whips the army cap off as if she's going to hit him with it, and throws it hard on the floor. "I have better things to talk to my friends about than your father!"

Why did she have to pick today to go bonkers?

The phone rings. He grabs the phone on the bedside table to hush its shrillness after the first ring.

"Hello."

There's no hello at the other end, just someone breathng hard. This, by damn, is no time for a crank phone call. "Hello?" No answer. But the breathing is somehow out ′ the ordinary. He imagines that the breathing is frightned, coming in quick short gusts. As if the caller has just .n up a high hill. He waits.

"They want you at the phone to get you in front of the ndow," Honey squeals. "Get away from the window. ang up. The tarot cards say you're going to die."

All Howard can see through his reflection on the dark ndow is the ghostly frame of the white art gallery bend. No signs of human life. The gasps of breath on the one become deeper. They are working up to something. e puts his hand over the mouthpiece and shakes his head Honey to say "be quiet." Her eyes are whirlpools of ter-r. This is not one of her acts.

"Hang up!" She jerks the heavy blue cotton curtains shut ain.

Finally a voice gasps into Howard's ear. "Come to the rner of Lear and Pine streets." A disguised voice, he is re. Could be a man's or a woman's. Very breathy. Then ck. The person hangs up. He repeats the words.

"It's a trap." Honey runs to his side and holds on to his n so hard that her fingers hurt. "Listen, you're in dan-:. I know you don't believe in fortune-telling, but my end Maurice Poole at the flea market, who reads tarot :ds, has the gift, Howard. He knows."

Sons of heroes don't go to fortune-tellers unless they are eek, and unless the fortune-tellers are oracles. But ward is curious. "Who is Maurice Poole?"

'He is the one who sells occult objects, the one with the ny pimple who thinks he's developing a third eye for en-htenment in the middle of his forehead. The one who

hears voices. He's odd, but he has the gift." She is dea
earnest.

"What did the cards say?"

"Maurice said I would be close to three deaths and soo
be alone."

"That is just general gobbledegook. You might kill thr
mice." But Howard is uneasy. "Honey, I do have to go lo
into this. There's nothing else I can do. For God's sake, I'
a reporter." He puts on his trenchcoat and starts down t'
hall. He hurries past the peacock feathers and has reache
the narcissus when Honey calls out again (against grou
rules) "Howard! Don't go!"

She comes running and stands by the feathers as if she h
something important to tell him, but then seems to flick
and tremble in indecision. He waits impatiently.

"Howard, you mustn't go." She starts to reach out
him, then drops her hands on her sides. "O.K., Howar
Maurice did ask about the Old Man. Nothing importa
Just where he came from."

"That could be important."

She shrugs. "I doubt it. And all I knew was Mas
County. You know that's all I've ever known. But liste
please don't go, Howard. Please. Maurice is coming he
You can ask him yourself. He's coming to deliver a mu
box I bought with astrological signs on it. One sign need
to be touched up and now it's ready. Please stay here."

So how much more is Honey keeping to herself? "I ha
to go." He tries to stay reasonable. "Make Maurice some
your good coffee. Keep him here until I get back or find c
where I can reach him. And keep the door locked for an
body you don't know. I'll hurry."

Honey glares at him with 2000 watts of contempt, a
tears in her eyes. "All right, you skunk, go get yours
killed. I thought things would be better if the Old Man w

gone, but they aren't. And don't hurry. I'm used to waiting."

Nothing he says is going to help, so he shuts the door between them, remembering that he once loved Honey a lot before... He's not sure before what. He is upset, leaving her upset. The clock drives him.

TEN

9:05 P.M. HOWARD SLOWS near the corner of Lear and Pine where the houses seem tired and underlit. Lights shine dimly in a room here, a room there. The overgrown shrubs around them seem to move in his headlights.

He parks near the intersection, slips out of his Volkswagen and takes a deep breath of chilly air, trying to puff up the part of himself that feels like Son of Hero.

"Easy and Quick Extermination" says an unlit sign on a bungalow next to a house with the whole downstairs alight. Howard shivers and turns up his coat collar. The exterminator is just another symptom that this old neighborhood is beginning to go commercial, he tells himself. Nothing personal.

He makes himself explore the porch of each house near the corner, being careful not to trip over the child's trucks scattered around the first, and not to be seen through the living room windows of the house where three forms flicker around a glowing TV.

On the third porch, a note is taped to the door. He slips out a penlight and tries to read it without attracting attention. "Don't bother knocking, you dolt," says a scrawly hand. "I'll never be here for you again. Not tonight. Not ever. Go soak your head." The way part of him feels it could be for him, and signed "God." That is the wrong attitude. He squares his shoulders.

He comes last to the house next to the exterminator, stops and stands in the yard feeling the roots of an old tree under his feet. The roots remind him of something. Something ugly. The peaky shape of the house tries to connect itself to a memory. He's been here before! He begins to think of balloons, a clown holding a bunch of bright balloons. But that was inside the house. Outside was snow, just a dusting, though he came out with a bunch of kids and ran around the yard. He came to a birthday party. When he was five years old. Now he remembers. A birthday party for Lumberton's daughter, Cindy. Lumberton of the steaming Linotype machine. Cindy lost her mind sixteen years later on her twenty-first birthday. A terrible celebration.

But Lumberton was always his friend, almost an uncle when Howard was small. Lumberton looked to him like a picture in the book of fairy stories Aunt Earnestine gave him for his sixth birthday, like the shoemaker who was helped by leprechauns. He was thin and pointy and craggy all over. His hair stuck out in wisps around his face, like wisps of steam mingling with the hiss of the Linotype machine. His cheeks rose in knobs around his grin, his eyes popped with laughter. He always joked. "Well, I see the President has come to town just to see you and the Old Man." Actually it was the candidate, but the Old Man had advised him and he did go on to win.

Howard starts at footfalls on the sidewalk. Someone is walking out of the shadows near the "Easy and Quick Extermination." Pale face, dark clothes. Could this be the same man who was in front of Howard's house on Chestnut Street? Too dark to tell. Whoever it is walks on with slow measured step.

Then before Howard can decide what to do about the man, the door of Lumberton's house begins to open. A wedge of light widens on the porch floor. Howard stands rock-still, heart pounding. That's silly. He could explain to his old friend why he's here. A white cat comes out, then vanishes into the shadows and the door shuts. So why am I

afraid of this house? he asks himself. Lumberton is my
friend, no matter what happened between him and my
father.

Why, after Lumberton left the paper he still beamed at
Howard from half a block away every time they met on the
street. Beamed as if it was the old days and he was about to
give Howard a lemon lollipop. He was still joking when
Howard was ready to graduate. "I hear you've taken over
the university, and now that they can't do without you
you're going to leave."

Someone turns on a television across the street. Maybe
someone deaf, for even with windows shut Howard can hear
wave after wave of canned laughter, out of place, almost
sinister in this cold darkness.

Laughter out of place. Howard plays his memory backwards: begins with Lumberton's laughter sounding thin
without the clank of the Linotype to back it up. Before that
came the handclasp, tight. As if Howard was valuable. Before that, Lumberton's craggy face breaking into a smile.
Before that—and this is the point—Lumberton before he
saw Howard, or at least before he knew Howard saw him.

Howard slows the picture. Zooms in closer. The hands by
Lumberton's sides are clenched. Lumberton has long tapered hands with knots at the finger joints like the Dürer
print of praying hands that Mrs. Jamison keeps by her desk
in the Classified department. Those hands clenched into
angry fists. Howard shivers.

He slips up onto the porch. A screen left from summer is
still on the window to the left of the door. The room shines
through, blurred. There's someone in a large reclining arm
chair. Lumberton. In the frame of a door beyond stands a
woman. Maybe Mrs. Lumberton. He remembers her from
office Christmas parties. Plump with a wildly contagious

laugh. Comfortable, like a favorite chair. Behind Lumberton is a fireplace, no fire. A television, off. Faintly, Howard hears music. An opera. There is a large framed picture on the table by the lamp. Maybe the daughter. She was so beautiful you wanted to eat her like peach ice cream. With faraway violet eyes. She worked in Classified for a while. But she tripped out on drugs. Now she sits in the state mental hospital and smiles like an angel and won't wear clothes. That's what Mrs. Jamison told him.

And Lumberton blames the Old Man. Because it happened after the Old Man slept with her. But that's not fair! Howard clenches his own fists.

He walks over firmly and knocks on the door. Mrs. Lumberton answers and, good Lord, she must have gained 100 pounds. She wears a pantsuit designed for an elephant. She jiggles. She opens the door, sees Howard, and draws in a great gasp of breath, dropped jaw pushing down double chins. Then she steps outside fast and shuts the door behind her.

"You mustn't come here!" That's an order. Yet in the dark her voice is still throaty and warm as he remembers it. Why didn't she turn on the porch light?

"You mustn't come here! He has a weak heart. You know that. The doctor says he must not have any shock. You mustn't come in."

"Am I a shock?"

"Don't you know, Howard? He's been saying he wished our father was dead. And now he is dead. And my poor husband feels like it's his fault for wishing so hard. Hurry. Go away."

"I got a call to come to this corner. Why?" He can't let her push him off without an answer.

"I don't know, but for God's sake go away." Even in the dark he can see the whites of her eyes go round as if she's seen a ghost.

Behind her, the door opens inward and there is wispy Lumberton who lets out a cry of surprise so exactly as predicted that Howard wonders if he is imagining Lumberton's face contracting in pain. Mrs. Lumberton turns, cries out, and tries to catch him as he sags to the floor, so light and boney he hardly makes a thump. In the background an Italian opera is throbbing and wailing. Lumberton in his faded plaid shirt and brown pants, both too big, could be a tragic clown in an opera. This is surreal, Howard thinks, like a bad joke played on no one . . . or everyone.

Howard leans down and feels for a pulse in the slight wrist. There is none. No pulse. No joke. He kneels quickly. "I can do C.P.R. Call the emergency medical service." Mrs. Lumberton moves like lightning.

Howard leans close to Lumberton and makes sure there is no breath. "He was my friend, wasn't he?" He begins to alternate breaths into the old dry mouth with rhythmic pressure from his interlocked hands on the boney rib cage. Lumberton is so frail that Howard expects the ribs to crack, but the pressure is necessary to replace his heartbeat. The ambulance seems to be taking forever.

Now Mrs. Lumberton is kneeling on the floor next to her husband, praying. The grand opera from the stereo is reaching a crescendo. How horribly appropriate. Still Howard breathes into Lumberton's lungs, finally hearing the gentle return of breath.

Once he was my friend, Howard thinks, but he's done more than wish for my father to die, or else the very sight of me wouldn't give him a heart attack, even if his heart was sick. And whatever he did, his wife doesn't know, but only guesses. That is part of why she's praying.

"Let him live," Howard prays. "Live because he was once my friend, and live to tell what he knows." Now the up and down of a siren swells from faint to earsplitting and stops. Thank God. Two men in dark blue uniforms take over.

ELEVEN

MIDNIGHT. SUZANNE FEELS the revolver in the bottom of her shoulder bag, the gun her father usually keeps under the cash register, the gun her brother Tony once borrowed to kill rabbits in his garden. Tony overreacts. Suzanne stands in the half-dark Defender lobby thinking: Nobody is going to take care of me but me. Not the Old Man. Not my family—we don't think the same way. Not the police. At least her marriage to Gordon, brief as it was, taught her that. She raises her chin a quarter inch.

Now Gordon is out of prison. She called this morning to check. How amazing that he got out two days after the Old Man was poisoned. Otherwise, considering how violent Gordon turned, she'd wonder if he did it.

He is probably not dangerous to anybody but Suzanne. She is his obsession. He said so in those letters she didn't answer.

He used to recite Shakespeare and polish his guns. And she'd been so naive she thought he was just a little eccentric because he was rich. I was a fool, she tells herself bitterly. But nobody needs to know it.

Strange that when Gordon stole money he used a computer, not a gun. In a jealous rage he used his fists.

Her tongue tip touches the false front tooth where he hit her in the mouth. The bruises on her body passed.

She feels safer with a gun. She touches rough stippling on the gun's handle, touches the smooth, almost sexy metal barrel. Six bullets are in the cylinder. Six if needed.

Why on earth did she park her car around the corner? Why did she have to stay so late looking through back issues in the newspaper morgue?

She opens the door and steps out into the damp cold. Ashe Street appears deserted, streetlights glimmering on the pavement.

Exception: one car up the next block either illegally parked or waiting for the stoplight to change. The visible edge of the park across the street is empty except for the trees and their shadows. She adjusts the briefcase of threatening letters under her arm, raises her chin a half inch more defiantly, and starts down the marble steps that gleam pale in the half-light.

Her steps echo. Another pair of footsteps echoes. She freezes. Out of the dark park into the brightness of the streetlights comes a tall lanky figure, a marionette on loose strings. It's only Leeroy. What a relief. She waves and hurries into the street toward him.

The car, a darkish blue that fades into the night, starts up with a zoom, hurtling down the street right at her. Good Lord, is she the target? Suzanne zooms too. As a kid she learned to outrun her teasing brothers. Thank God for the practice. She's on the sidewalk fast, jerked behind a tree by Leeroy so fast that the car is still three lengths away.

The car races straight on as if the driver is merely trying to create a new speed record on Ashe Street. So fast she's not even sure what make it is. Something powerful.

"Damn drunk," she gasps. She wants Leeroy to think it's a drunk.

The arm Leeroy puts around her shakes. Even his voice shakes. "I'll take you by the police, Suzanne."

"No. It was only a drunk, and too fast to get the license number." If it was Gordon, she thinks, perhaps he just wanted to scare her.

"Maybe it was a drunk, maybe not. I'll take you by the police just in case."

"No. Not again. The police are getting to be like my family. One nosey family is enough."

He tightens his arm. "After the police I'll take you home."

"No! I don't want to go home. I want to talk about these to somebody." She holds up the briefcase of threatening letters, amazed to see that she's still got it clenched tight. The park is still here. The Defender Building across the street glows with a few lights deep inside. All as if nothing had happened. Except Leeroy is upset. Even smells upset.

"If you'd rather, after the police we can go to my place and I'll give you a drink, Suzanne."

She laces her fingers through the fingers of his large firm hand. "That would be great. I wish I knew who was in that car."

"Naturally," says Leeroy.

Naturally? Nothing seems natural to Suzanne. It's too much to bear that Gordon should show up just after the shock of the Old Man's murder. If that was Gordon. A man obsessed with one woman, one poet, and violence. Suzanne's grandmother says troubles come in threes. But please, Suzanne prays, not now.

LEEROY RELAXES IN his dingy kitchen, warm with Suzanne. He admires the casual way she kicks off her high-heeled black shoes under his old kitchen table. She wriggles her toes.

He tells her he can't find a sign of the one-eyed card shark who is supposed to know who killed the Old Man. She listens so well.

"What a day," she sighs, and leans back in the straight kitchen chair and stretches. Arms up, back, almost popping the buttons off her four-leaf-clover blouse. Then she rests both elbows on the table near the file folder with the threatening letters.

Two hundred percent alive. Leeroy thinks, I wish I enjoyed my body that much. She'd stop to eat strawberries while the world was coming to an end.

He crosses the linoleum on a worn path to the clanky refrigerator, takes out a dented metal ice tray and a bottle of California Chablis, and from the cupboard one thin-stemmed wine glass, which he shines with the dishtowel and fills with Chablis for Suzanne. A mouse skitters across the floor. He hopes she doesn't see it. He puts ice cubes in an old peanut butter glass with a roller-skating duck on one side, and sloshes on bourbon for himself. Then he brings these and a chunk of cheddar cheese and some Ritz crackers back: the best offering he has. He sits down next to Suzanne, almost cozy except for the dead windows of the office building across the way. Someone could be watching from those windows unseen, could be armed. His many-paned window, as wide as the kitchen table, as tall as Suzanne and jutting outward a foot almost like a greenhouse, gives maximum exposure. That big window, sunshiny in the day, sold him on this small apartment, eighty-year-old landlady, unreliable front door lock and all. He wishes there was a curtain to draw just in case. He wants to protect Suzanne, who seems already to have forgotten danger.

A few city lights still show outside. The Defender Building is faintly luminescent in its glass-brick casing off to the right, marking the spot where somebody may have tried to run Suzanne down. The police were no help.

In the near distance a bar name blinks. On. Off. On. Off. Like a crazy stop signal.

"Some of these threats are signed," muses Suzanne, holding up a piece of Xerox paper containing a copy of a small letter.

"From Marvella T. Johnson, whose son Dan found out that his motorcycle buddies were also a dope ring. And, as you know, Dan told Howard.'

"I saw the original letter," says Leeroy. "It was lying on the Old Man's desk next to the report on sewer extensions he wanted me to look into. That letter came right after the gang shot Dan Johnson in the head. Howard wrote that story. I won't ever forget it. Dan's mother found him dead in a pool of motorcycle oil and blood on the garage floor." He shudders and glances again at the dark windows across the way. No sign of life.

Suzanne reads the note aloud in her clear musical voice. Alto sax. "Your drug story killed my son. Someday I'll kill you."

Suzanne shakes her head. "It makes no sense, Leeroy. Howard wrote about Dan, and maybe that's why Dan got shot in the head. So why did Marvella Johnson threaten the Old Man?" Her eyes are wet, though her voice stays firm.

God, he thinks, what I wouldn't give for her to care that much about me. The duck on the peanut butter glass seems to be laughing at Leeroy as he swirls his drink. He stares out the window at the bar sign. On. Off. On. Off. "It's sexier to kill someone powerful." He spits out the words because they taste bad. O.K., so he was jealous.

With one outstretched little finger, Suzanne makes an X on her misted wine glass, then sighs and adds two more lines to make a star. "Yes, he had sex appeal. Also death appeal. Related. Both power."

She sighs again, then presses her lips together, determined. "Let's put the letters in three piles, Leeroy: most likely to be a killer, least likely to be a killer, and maybe. I've only brought the most alarming letters with me, but even so, I think Marvella goes in 'Maybe.'

The next letter is ugly, even in Xerox. Words and letters cut from magazines and newspapers were glued into uneven sentences. Leeroy picks it up, not wanting to see Suzanne touch it. The date at the top is January 24. The type is familiar, cut from the top of *The Defender*. Then crazily assorted letters say: "You remember what today is and I haven't forgotten. I won't let you forget this anniversary till you're six feet under." At the end, two words of spidery handwriting: "The Father."

"That letter got to the Old Man." Suzanne's voice lowers, wavers. The low timbre gets Leeroy in the gut. "The Old Man said threats were a natural professional hazard, Leeroy, like policemen knowing they might get shot. He said the ancient Greeks would kill the messenger who brought bad news. Now people just write poison."

Leeroy admires the way she swallows hard but then goes on. "That letter from 'The Father' disturbed him more than any other I knew about. He got mad at the Goldfish for not filing it faster." She takes a sip of wine, leaving her lips moist. Why does she have to be so damn beautiful?

"I've checked the paper for this January 24, Leeroy. All editions. Nothing rings a bell."

Leeroy touches the word "remember"—big R, tiny e, "member" all in one slanty calligraphy. Yes, ugly. "Whatever happened on this date that the Old Man was supposed to remember may have been years ago."

"Yes. I looked in the back file in the morgue, but of course I don't know what I'm looking for." She reaches for the letter and he tries not to show electric shock when their fingers touch.

"Most likely pile," they say in unison and then laugh at the unplanned harmony of their voices.

Next one is less likely, they decide. From Gustav May, whose doctor father was put in prison for Medicaid fraud after he tried to collect from the government for an appendectomy on a two-day-old baby and an abortion on a great-grandmother. Gustav May is a professional mime and has his picture on his letterhead. "I'll see you in Hell," says the letter, but the man doesn't look up to it.

Finally they come to a letter with handwriting so black, even in the copy, that Leeroy imagines the paper almost tearing as the writer banged the typewriter. Signed Roosevelt Lincoln Worthington. Leeroy winces. "Here's our old friend." He imagines the man angrily whacking out the letter with his single hand. For Worthington has made it clear in his constant letters to the editor that he lost two legs and one arm in a bomb explosion in Vietnam—that he's black, that he's a Ph.D., that he is unemployed.

"His mother gave equal time to the Republicans and the Democrats when she named him. I'll say that." Worthington's constant tortured letters and the fact that the paper can only print a few of them upset Leeroy. He has to joke.

Suzanne reads the letter out loud: "'You print a damn letter from the garden club about bird feeders, but not my letters about real discrimination. You only printed three this month. I may be a damn cripple you wouldn't hire, you racist pig, but I know something about you. You're a coward. I am not. I was a Marine. I know how to kill.'"

"He wrote the Old Man asking for a job as an editorial writer, but that was six months ago." Suzanne picks up the letter and holds it over the "Most Likely" pile. "I don't know what he could do from a wheelchair. And yet..."

"I agree," says Leeroy. "He was angry enough. And he has brains."

She drops it into "Most Likely" and sighs. "That's all Worthington and The Father in our most likely of the most-threatening letters pile. I'm tired. It's two o'clock."

Leeroy pours her another glass of wine and himself another bourbon. "Here's to us." He keeps his voice light. "To us, the survivors. Toilers in the night."

Suzanne raises her glass, savors a sip, and then puts the glass down, excited. "Hey, you remember you told me that old Linotype operator who left used to do handwriting analysis? His hobby. You said that, before they replaced him with a computer, he'd done it for just about every member of the staff."

"Sure."

"Well, that letter signed 'The Father' couldn't be from any member of the staff now. The cops checked all their handwriting. But Lumberton might recognize the handwriting of somebody who used to be on the staff. Hey, I'll go see him."

"And why don't I go see Worthington, Suzanne. I'm not getting anywhere with the one-eyed card shark business. Something's wrong with it."

"Good." Suzanne sits straight, revived, ready to start.

"You can't go anywhere at 2 in the morning!" Leeroy laughs. "And look, Suzanne, I don't know how much Lumberton will want to help. His daughter had a fling with the Old Man and a nervous breakdown in that order."

"Still, he's always been fond of Howard since Howard was a little kid. Maybe Lumberton will help."

"Howard." She yawns, relaxed as a cat. "If we solve all this, the one we'll be helping most is Howard. And we don't even like Howard. You don't and I don't. That's crazy."

"I used to like Howard." Leeroy yawns and stretches his neck. "Before he was teacher's pet I liked him." Leeroy takes a comforting swallow of bourbon. "Howard has been a horse's ass for a year. Today at that meeting I was damned well tempted to shut up and let him lose the paper. But then I thought about his eyes."

"His eyes! Why?"

"Howard has good eyes. Always has, since he was a little kid wandering around the office asking questions. Howard has got the kind of eyes that make people act uncomfortable when they try to bullshit him. Did you ever notice that? Because he looks like he might suddenly wake up in the middle of the night and comprehend how the things they said didn't quite fit together. Howard has eyes that might someday be wise."

"Eyes that could someday be wise?" Suzanne tosses her head and laughs, a laugh with a sharp cutting edge but a nice warm center. "Bullshit you, Leeroy. You want to be father of the world. You're more interested in what might happen some day than in paying your rent. You don't even poison mice."

Damn. She'd noticed.

"But as for me, Leeroy, what I care about is now. Fold out your couch for me and we'll both get a couple of hours of sleep and then go to work and find out who poisoned the Old Man. Then I'll sell my stock to the highest bidder." She lifts her wine glass. "To the good life," and finishes the last few swallows. She gives him a quick kiss goodnight, touch of butterfly wings, breath of perfume, not an invitation. Suzanne still belongs to the Old Man.

TWELVE

"I HAVE TO GET my back to a wall." Howard is running, wet with panic. There is no wall. Only endless ground and sky. The ground is shaking more and more violently. Alice's little-girl voice comes out of the shaking.

"Howard, wake up. Why are you sleeping in your clothes? Where is Honey? And why was your front door open at 7:30 in the morning in February?"

"Damn," he says, barely awake, "I overslept."

He opens his eyes to baby doll Alice, sitting on his bed as if she had a right, patting her poodle curls in place and smiling around her small even teeth. Her baby-blue dress swears at the peacock-blue bedspread. She thrusts a cup of coffee at him, bracelets jangling. "I locked the door. You look terrible."

The coffee is the murky instant decaf that Honey kept to serve Madison. Otherwise, Honey makes real coffee.

But Honey who makes real coffee has left him. No hurt comes. Only sadness. Love can wear out. He has no time to think about that.

And what's with Alice who waits like a baby time bomb? He needs more coffee, even such as it is, before he asks.

A big pearl hatpin that Honey found at the flea market still lies on the bedside table next to the swan lamp. Last night that hatpin fastened Honey's scrawled note to his pillow: "I have gone with Maurice. I am tired of being alone. Don't look for me. I won't be back. Honey." Now the note is gone. That is damned odd.

"Last night I locked the door, Alice." His voice is still rusty with sleep. "I checked the windows." He doesn't tell her that nevertheless somebody came into this apartment while he slept, and stole a note from Honey. That's too crazy.

He sits up straight and puts his coffee cup on the bedside table. "O.K., what's wrong?"

"Howard, why did you ask Arthur if he gambles? Why did you accuse him? Tell me, Howard, and don't pretend you don't remember!"

But he doesn't remember. The Old Man once said "Arthur gambles." And Howard's mind was so much on that election story that he didn't realize the significance or ask more. He certainly didn't ask Arthur.

"Listen, Howard, when Arthur dropped his good luck coins on the way into the funeral, you asked him how often he lost money, Howard. You pretended it was a joke, Howard. He says so." She picks up the pearl hatpin in her small hands with the long sharp tapered nails and points it at him. "You want to prove the Mafia killed the Old Man. You'll say Arthur was mixed up in it because he gambles. Well, if you do, you'll be sorry!"

Howard stands up. "Does Arthur owe a lot of money, Alice?" He can't keep his mind steady. Why was the front door open? As a little kid, Alice used to make up fantastic lies for no known reason. Always with the same totally innocent look she has now.

Could Alice have made up the open front door? Did she take Honey's note to confuse him?

"You think I'm dumb, don't you, Howard? Because our father thought I was dumb and you were smart. You think I'm so dumb I'd let Arthur go right down the drain and not help him!"

Howard staggers into the small kitchen to get some real coffee. Alice follows close. She's left the water boiling in the brown enamel kettle. One point for Alice.

So, O.K., the Old Man did think she was dumb. He'd smile that big country humble smile around determined city eyes and then with great charm he'd drawl "Alice, you're too pretty to need brains. You'll knock 'em dead like you are." And Alice used to grin like she was pleased and work on being pretty.

Why, look, even now Alice has on just the sort of dress the Old Man liked, sassy and expensive. The kind that makes people on the street wonder if she's a model. She also looks so mad she'd like to bite. She doesn't give him time to answer her question.

"Howard, Arthur is a good person, whatever you think. And we're going to have a baby if I die trying. I'm going to all the best doctors. You leave Arthur alone!" Her little-girl voice cracks. Her eyes fill with tears.

The kitchen clock says quarter of eight already. Thank goodness he has a filter to brew one cup of the strong jolting coffee he likes. The first gulp helps.

"You don't care whether I have a baby, do you?" She looks like she's going to grab the frying pan and throw it at him.

"Howard, do you know what the Old Man said when I told him about Arthur having to do it in a jar, and the doctor putting it in? He said that cows and pigs found that extra titillating! He said that to me!

"The only person on my side is Arthur, Howard. You hurt him and I'll kill you."

Howard has heard that women who can't have babies can become deranged. But Alice has only been married three years.

"Alice, I'd like to prove Arthur had nothing to do with the Old Man's death. Help me find out what really happened. I need help." The word "help" hurts. It's like Howard is admitting he is stupid, too. What he feels is totally alone.

At least Alice knows what it's like to be lonely, to need an imaginary friend. He hesitates, wondering what to ask her first. Never hesitate with Alice.

"Howard, where is Honey? She never gets up this early. Where are her coats? Why is the coat closet open and empty?"

So he has to tell her about the goodbye note. Of course she is totally thrilled. She vibrates like a hummingbird. Alice loves drama. "Maybe the note was a forgery, Howard. Maybe Honey was kidnaped or something. Maybe Honey is in danger!

"Howard," she says, "did you and Honey fight a lot? Did you hit her?" One hit would be worth half a kidnaping. Howard hears the clock tick.

"Howard, did you know Honey was unhappy? Did you think she might leave? Why didn't you tell me when I got here? Is she having an affair with Maurice Poole? He read the tarot cards for me. Do you think he can really read the future? He said I would have plenty of money to go to the best doctors and that I'd have a baby of my own."

"Alice, tell me what you know about Maurice Poole. Come sit on the couch."

He lets her ramble on about how Honey said Poole has no telephone and how Poole is only at the flea market on weekends and this is Tuesday, and how he has such strange eyes. Finally she pauses.

"Alice, what did Maurice Poole ask you when he read the tarots for you? Did he ask you questions about the Old Man the way he asked Honey?"

She pats her curls in place and looks him over as if to say "Why are you asking that dumb question?" but she answers. "Of course Maurice Poole asked me about the Old Man, Howard, in order to understand the background of the reading. The Old Man was my ancestor. Maurice Poole said that was important. I was glad I could tell him where the Old Man came from."

Howard's heart beats so hard he is afraid Alice can hear it. Can Lance be right, that where the Old Man came from is the key to who killed him and why?

"Oh, Howard, I told Maurice that my father came from Mason County. But everybody knew that. And I told him the town was such a little place it wasn't on the map. I told him we'd never been there and the Old Man almost never talked about it." She reaches and puts a cold hand with bracelets on top of his. "But that's no secret, Howard. Why do you look so uptight?"

"And that's all, Alice?"

"Oh, there was just one other thing. I don't see how it could be important, Howard." She frowns the way she used to do with her math homework. "You know, it's funny, Howard, but while I was talking to Maurice, there by his table at the flea market with all the crystal balls and things, and while he was looking back at me in that strange way, right in the eyes and so quiet he made me sleepy, something came back to me that I had forgotten since I was a little kid."

Howard's breath feels hot in his lungs. He works at not breathing hard. Alice gives him a show-and-tell smile. "Maybe I remember this because the Old Man didn't take me to walk very much, Howard, but one Sunday he took me a walk by Low Creek, and he stopped in that place where the banks on each side are so high. He stopped and just stared at the creek running over the rocks like it does there.

And in this really funny faraway voice, he said 'Heaven high, hell deep and river wide.'

"And I said 'What?' because the way he was talking kind of scared me. I was really a kid. Maybe nine or ten. And still in that funny faraway voice, he said 'That's what they used to call the place where I came from.' And then he said 'I will never go back.'"

"And that is all?"

"And that is all I remember. Except it was in the spring and we found an old glass jar and I caught a crawdad with one claw missing. And he said that meant it was a crawdad who knew all about life and I should let it go."

"When did you tell Maurice Poole that our father came from a place called 'Heaven high, hell deep and river wide'?"

"A few weeks ago. Could that possibly hurt?"

He jumps up and walks up and down, up and down. Outside the blue curtains Honey had made, it's raining again. "I don't know. Something may have happened where he came from that led to his death. We need to find out."

Why did the Old Man tell Alice what may be the only clue to the place he came from? Not Howard or Madison, whom he said he trusted more, or even Josh, but Alice. Because he could relax and pretend she didn't matter? For a moment Howard is actually jealous. Then he sits down and hugs Alice. "You're not so dumb!" She flushes with pleasure. He can see how badly she needs to be told that.

But Alice is about to burst with more questions. Isn't it about time for Alice to go to work? The fancy blue dress is for the gift shop run by that elegant Mrs. Koch.

Alice draws her breath for a question. Howard beats her to the draw.

"Alice, do you remember anything strange about the Old Man or the people around him in the last few weeks? Not the kind of stuff you tell the police, but just anything odd?"

She gets up and stares out the front window. He has the impression she's trying to hide her face.

"Would you count that the Old Man tried extra hard to be nice to me? Is that odd enough?" Her voice is suddenly more grown-up. And bitter.

"How do you mean, 'nice'? What did he say?"

Her blue shoulders quiver. Why, she's trying not to cry! "I'm not good at saying how, Howard, but it wasn't just words. Why, he was humble! And maybe sad at the same time. And he said 'Alice, I haven't given you enough credit for doing the best that you can.'" She turns back toward Howard, swallows, and her eyes glisten like wet blue glass. "And he was nice to Arthur, too. He usually acted as if Arthur was about to bet my wedding ring on a horse. And he said 'Arthur, you make Alice happy. I appreciate that!'

"And it wasn't just us. He gave the Windham sisters in Circulation a box of chocolate-covered cherries just to show how he appreciated all the years they've worked so hard for the paper. And he even took the Goldfish out to lunch three times the week before he died. I learned that when I went into the office to use the john when I was out shopping on my day off."

She frowns and begins to finger a small pistol on her charm bracelet. From Teddy who belonged to the NRA. Her voice rises. "And he gave that damn Suzanne Mancini a share of stock. You know that, Howard. And he also gave that woman a great big expensive vulgar watch." Alice's face goes ugly with rage like a baby struck with a pin. "That gold digger!"

Howard is amazed to hear his own voice rise. "Alice, for God's sake, you're jealous! Alice, daddies don't give their own little girls great big vulgar watches."

Now she's shouting. "I figured all you cared about was yourself and that damned newspaper. Do you care about that bitch, too?"

"I don't know why I said that." He doesn't. He's amazed.

"Well, believe me, whatever happens, I intend to sell all my stock in the damned newspaper." She's shaking hard. Her curls quiver, her lips tremble. "I want all the money I can get, Howard, to pay for the best specialists in the country so I can have a baby. And if I can't have a baby, at least I'll be filthy rich."

Howard has blown it with Alice. Damn, damn, damn. He has a thundering headache and it's only 8:30 in the morning. Stop. Mahatma Gandhi, who was once a newspaperman, considered a setback as a challenge. So did Benjamin Franklin. So did Frederick Douglass, or Henry Morton Stanley, or the Old Man. So must Howard.

He's blown it with Alice, but he knows where the Old Man came from! Lance will turn Alice's clue into a spot on the map. Dear God, let it be so.

THIRTEEN

"HAD ALL HIS HAIRS been lives, my great revenge had stomach for them all." Gordon hurls his words at the picture of Isaiah Justice on the front of the newspaper. He has folded the paper to display Isaiah's arrogant face, and propped it next to the silver-framed photo of Suzanne on the motel table.

Gordon doesn't read anything but newspapers and Shakespeare. Newspapers to keep him informed, and Shakespeare for continuity. He keeps the complete works of Shakespeare by his bed and reads a little every night, wherever he is. There's a quote for every person in his life, even Suzanne who looks so innocent in the photograph. "O thou weed! Who art so lovely fair, and smell'st so sweet, that the sense aches at thee, would thou hadst ne'er been born." And Justice was her lover. He deserves to be dead.

But why did they have to kill Isaiah Justice before Gordon got out of prison, when he would have so enjoyed doing the job himself.

The prison grapevine said that Justice was killed by amazing coincidence just when the big boy wanted him out of the way. Gordon's experience tells him this isn't true. There must have been a connection.

Justice is dead meat. Gordon endures. He looks at himself in the motel mirror—the mirror covers almost the whole wall at the other end of the long room. So smooth and lustrous that he can almost see the suave man he used to be staring out through the pale fat man he hates. He can see Gordon Long, the man that women and headwaiters spotted across a room, almost see the disciplined stomach, the trendy clothes, expensive jewelry, thick blond hair. The fat came in prison: unhealthy flab.

With the rolls of fat showing through his silk shirt, he is a maggot. Maggots destroy what is rotten. "Sweet are the uses of adversity."

His friends and clients do not care what he looks like. They respect his talent and versatility. Gordon, the scholar, never commits the same crime twice, except on purpose to terrorize, to leave someone waiting for the other shoe to drop. He has never committed the same crime twice since he made up his mind to prove to himself that there was no God. God is the excuse parents use when they can't think of a reason. If there were a God, Gordon Long would have been stopped permanently, not allowed to be so clever. Not allowed to discover that the way to fool the law is to have no pattern. Police always look for repetition. He smiles, self-satisfied, then frowns.

He can handle "accidents" or murder. What he can't handle is love. His love is turned to "shuddering fear and green-ey'd jealousy." He can't live without Suzanne and she's a bitch. He looks at her picture and feels that familiar emptiness as if he is floating alone in space, without stars. The bitch wouldn't even answer his letters from prison.

He made good contacts in prison and got word out he'd like a job in this city, danger no object. He's even been paid in advance. That's how well he is respected among those who know. They may call him "the scholar," halfway joking, but he is paid cash in advance.

What they want now is negligible: accidents to keep the family that owns the newspaper upset and off balance. So that the scales are sure to be tipped for selling.

He gathers through his grapevine that the man who had hired him is obsessed with this city. Gordon can under stand that: to want what you want and nothing else. The man wants his racetrack, his drug-dealing center, his power here. Gordon has heard he was born here and treated like nothing and he wants to get back. Gordon has also heard there's a woman who won't move anywhere else. To Gordon, it doesn't matter. He has been hired as insurance that the boss can acquire the paper which gets in his way. No problem. Gordon is going to give his employer even more than he bargained for.

He gets up from his chair, walks over and pats the small trunk of bomb makings that sits on the foot of one of the twin beds. He found that old trunk in a thrift shop in Omaha. Faded stickers tell where it was going twenty, thirty, forty years ago: Istanbul, Athens, Florence, Rio. He would like to add a tag that says "Hell."

Closer to the mirror he sees himself larger, a maggot plotting death, the man who needs Suzanne, dead or alive. He remembers how she gasped with amazement and pleasure when he gave her a diamond bracelet. An old-fashioned girl. He told her his father made the family money finding oil.

But of course, he'd been busy making the family money with computer fraud because he didn't want to put Suzanne in danger from his other work. He'd been a fool. And then, because she called the police after he lost his temper and hit her, his company checked his work. So in effect the damn bitch sent him to prison and divorced him. "Thou stick'st a dagger in me." And still he loves her.

The police were too thickheaded to find out about his other crimes. And Suzanne never knew. She hasn't got that excuse.

Gordon sits down in the plastic motel chair and picks up the newspaper, jostling the white box of pizza from last night with his elbow. He studies the dead face once more:

the late Isaiah Justice. The wide impatient greedy mouth, needing the full width of the square jaw to give it room. Most people would look at that mouth and think eager, think determined.

That Justice mouth is poised to suck in as much of life as possible as fast as possible. It takes one to know one. And you can tell he thought he was good-looking, Gordon thinks. Tilt of head. By God, you can tell he was used to giving orders. Angle of chin. Arrogant. But sneaky arrogant. Look at that smile.

And the eyes. Hot eyes. Because of the please-like-me smile, you might not notice those eyes are skeptical. He was a man who knew about women, knew they could never be trusted. Therefore he was a magnet for them.

The young man who now concerns Gordon, the son, is just a pale imitation who inherited what his father couldn't take with him.

In the bars it's still the Old Man they talk about: who knew more jokes than any other man in the county—dirty jokes, Gordon assumes. Who could drink any other man to the blurting stage before he himself showed any signs of being drunk. Who always carried a motheaten rabbit's foot in the right inside pocket of his jacket and pulled it out sometimes late in the evening and patted it. So, being dead, he has become a glorious bar myth. May he enjoy it. May the son become Glorious Bar-Myth Jr. Gordon throws down the paper, which slaps the floor as if he's slapped a cheek to declare a duel.

With shaking fingers he opens the large square box on the other side of the table from Suzanne's photograph to eat the rest of last night's pizza for breakfast. He has to keep up his strength.

There are so many ways to destroy. His last job before the computer fiasco was drowning an unwanted wife in the bathtub. Her husband believed she'd philandered in the bathtub with another man.

Explosives take more talent than drownings. He has it. He can rig a car with a device that will blow it up when key triggers starter, rig a device so quickly that the target has hardly turned his back before the car is wired for eternity. His father's leather suitcase, which was all he left Gordon after the oil shale fiasco, does fine for portable jobs.

The mushroom-sausage-green-pepper pizza is not bad. Gordon savors the tomato sauce, chewing slowly and swirling the richness around his mouth. The tomato gets on his ringed fingers. "Out, out, damned spot." He licks it off the gold death's-head ring with the ruby eyes like small red lights. A little cold breakfast for a man who needs strength, who didn't get to bed until 2:45. Who knows how to frighten a victim before he kills him. Who can even wander around inside the intended victim's house and leave a few clues that make him wonder if he's lost his mind. That touch particularly pleases Gordon. Who would expect such subtlety from a man who can also put a booby trap so artfully into the ground? Gordon can arrange it so the victim who goes for a brisk walk toward the east will blow sky high when he returns west. Gordon Long, trained by his Uncle Sam in Korea—thank you, Uncle. Gordon can even rig a whole restaurant or bar to self-destruct, even a whole building. Nice. But that takes a little longer.

He looks at his watch: 7:45 A.M.

He throws the pizza box in the trash basket, puts on a shoulder holster, because he never knows what he'll need, and sets off with his suitcase in hand to keep watch.

FOURTEEN

8:15 A.M. SUZANNE STOPS HER robin's-egg-blue Fiat in front of the Lumberton house. That blue Ford she's seen in the mirror several times is out of sight. Good. After last night she's a little paranoid. But I don't intend to be bottled up like a rabbit in a hole! she tells herself. She jumps out of the car and clicks up the front walk. The sky behind the peaked roof almost matches her car. Vibrant.

She hurries up the three steps onto the porch with the wood rail that needs paint and pounds the unpolished brass door knocker, hoping 8:15 is not too early for Mr. Lumberton to identify the spidery handwriting on the letter in her briefcase.

Nobody answers. A rolled paper lies on the porch near her feet. It's today's *Defender*, the daily reminder of the Old Man. She's read it: The police are getting nowhere. A soft white cat rubs against her ankles and meows. Suzanne peers in the window to the right of the door and, through the haze of screen and glass, sees lights burning. That's odd, she thinks, at this hour of the morning. The cat continues to rub and moan loudly.

Suzanne turns the tarnished doorknob and the door opens. The cat runs through her feet and she calls "Mr. Lumberton? Mr. Lumberton?" No answer. A half-full glass sits on a ringed coffee table by a big wing chair. She sniffs Bourbon and water. Warm.

A color picture of a pink-cheeked girl with fluffy blond hair dominates the table. Is this the girl who lost her mind? The eyes are normal, only too eager to please. The Old Man would have grown tired of that. Poor young girl. The picture has been here awhile. The mat is yellowed. Nothing too strange downstairs except an obviously expensive hi-fi set punctuated by one dot of light, left on but silent.

Suzanne runs up the scuffed stairs to see what's above. The first door is locked. She opens a second door and, good Lord, the room behind is so full she half expects the contents to fall out on her, the way they do out of Uncle Mario's hunting-gear closet.

The walls are covered with pictures of the pretty girl with an older man and woman, all smiling. The man is tall and thin, the woman pleasantly plump. At Disneyland. In front of the Capitol. At the Grand Canyon. The girl at all ages as if they went one big place each year. There's her picture in ballet costume, on a horse, in graduation robes, being hugged by a clown.

They spent a lot of love and money on that girl and then she tripped out on drugs and lost her mind. Suzanne feels like crying, but not for long. She's too curious.

Under a mustard spread the double bed is unevenly made, probably not slept in. A huge pair of women's pants are draped over the back of a rocking chair to the right of the bed, pants even larger than Suzanne's mother wears after tasting pasta sauce all day at the restaurant. A huge blouse hugs the chair's other arm. Runover shoes dot the floor. The bureau on the right side of the bed holds two dusty bottles with china flowers on top. There's a pile of change, a clutter of jewelry, a brush with a few gray hairs in it, all reflected in a peeling mirror. The woman has gone to pot since she smiled like Santa Claus in the pictures on the wall.

The bedside table on her side holds a worn Bible and a new library book, open and spine up. Beneath clear plastic casing, a broad-shouldered young man without a shirt embraces a young woman with her hair and scarf blowing behind her. The Bible and *Young Love Against the Storm*. Comfort and escape. Nothing is exactly wrong on this side of the room, so why are Suzanne's eyes wet again?

She moves to the left side of the bed and glances at the bookshelf near the bed. There's one fat book: *Thirty Famous Operas*. One cheerful book: *The Art of Clowning*, well-worn with clown face on spine. Lots of detective novels: *Revenge at Schroon Lake, The Bishop's Revenge, Revenge at the Opera*. Revenge in almost every title. A small badly printed paperback reads *Fifty Ways to Get Revenge*. Upsetting. The girl losing her mind was just the first step to some kind of dry rot, it seems.

The left bedside table is like the other. Small, flimsy, square with a cheap white china lamp, but no Bible. A nearly nude blonde leers up from an uneven stack of magazines. Girlie magazines. Cheap and dirty. Not as well done as *Playboy,* more like the *Hustler*s Suzanne's brother Tony used to hide under his mattress. A little more explicit.

A torn piece of white paper marks a place in each magazine. The top magazine dates from five years back.

Downstairs there's a quick rat-tat-tat of brass knocker on door. Damn. Suzanne quickly opens the top magazine to the marked page. A stark-naked redhead sits akimbo. She appears to have just had her hair done at the beauty parlor—above and below. She smiles with bared teeth. Suzanne's grandmother Mancini would cross herself and turn the young girl's pictures to the wall.

But there's something familiar about the woman in the magazine, familiar if she weren't red-headed, her eyebrows overplucked, her lips overpainted.

Suzanne hears the front door wheeze open and a woman's high-pitched voice calls "Flora?" A man's voice calls "Are you there?" Suzanne hurries to open the second magazine to the marked place. The same girl. This time the face is a shock, less made-up and easier to recognize. Stuffy old Madison's Cleo. The only member of the Justice family except the Old Man who has never treated Suzanne as if she smells. Cleo never put on airs with Suzanne. Lumberton collected lewd pictures of Cleo.

Suzanne feels a little sick. But she grabs the book on *Fifty Ways to Get Revenge* and the magazines that will fit and stuffs them in her briefcase. She clamps the rest under her coat. The voices are getting closer.

Suzanne meets the man and woman at the foot of the stairs. She's a girl reporter looking for help, worried by lights left on. Inwardly, she can't help thinking about the expressions that would be on the faces of this earnest couple if the magazines slipped out and fell to the floor. The man and woman are plain and clean. They both look like horses. They're about seventy. They introduce themselves as the Smiths.

The Smiths take turns explaining how the ambulance came in the night. They know where the extra key is hidden. They offer to see that everything is O.K. and lock up.

Then Suzanne drives too fast to the hospital to see Mrs. Lumberton, to see what she can pick up. If that's the same car following her, it's going to have a hard time keeping up. But she's glad for broad daylight.

In the hospital lobby, Suzanne stops at the phone booth to call the paper. The Goldfish can't reach Leeroy or Howard. Out. And so, although Suzanne does not entirely trust him, she tells Lance about Lumberton, about Cleo.

He whistles long, low and sad. "My God, what next?" And Suzanne wonders.

FIFTEEN

9:06 A.M. SUZANNE HURRIES to the waiting room for the cardiac unit—a small, oblong room where people fidget in chairs around the wall, read magazines fitfully, whisper to each other as if it were a library, and do not smile. Mrs. Lumberton, the only enormous woman in the room, sits in a molded plastic chair too small for her bottom and looks at her tapered hands.

"Mrs. Lumberton?"

She looks up from her hands, smiles vaguely, then frowns. "I don't remember . . ."

"You don't know me, but I know what it's like to wait here near the cardiac unit. My father had a heart attack."

"Did he get well?" The blue eyes beg for "yes."

"Yes."

Immediately Mrs. Lumberton takes Suzanne's hand in her large moist hands. "Pray for me," she whispers. "Pray for my husband." And then, "Why are you here?"

"I went to your house to ask your husband a favor because he's a handwriting expert." What else can Suzanne say? This is no place to mention porno magazines or revenge. Suzanne would like to leave Mrs. Lumberton alone. Not ask her questions in this time of despair. But she feels the pressure of the Old Man's ghost, almost as if he sat beside her instead of the skinny man reading *Popular Science*. The ghost eggs her on.

"Your neighbors told me what happened, Mrs. Lumberton, and since I needed your help so badly I came here."

Mrs. Lumberton is silent, picking a ball of wool off her sweater. Suzanne presses on. "I remember when my father was sick, the only thing that helped was to have my mind on something else."

A woman across from them with her head on one side begins to snore. That's one solution.

"So I wondered, Mrs. Lumberton, if you could help me in spite of what has happened."

A vague smile quivers on Mrs. Lumberton's generous mouth. She squeezes Suzanne's hand. "Yes, yes, I'd like to help."

Go on, says the Old Man's ghost without mercy. Ask her now.

Suzanne pulls the threatening letter out of her briefcase. "I understand your husband used to read the handwriting of the members of *The Defender* staff back when he was on the paper." Suzanne puts the letter in Mrs. Lumberton's hand. "If he's well enough just to look, could you show him this and ask him if he recognizes the handwriting?"

Mrs. Lumberton's face goes vacant and slack as if the letter has electrocuted her. Suzanne feels the shock. Mrs. Lumberton's eyes are scared. Also mad. Why?

"It's my fault my husband's here," the huge woman gulps. She nods in the direction of the intensive care unit, chins shaking. "It's my fault. I let Howard Justice into the house. I did it. Howard Justice sent you here, didn't he? And everything is my fault." The other visitors stare. The woman who nodded off gets up and moves across the room.

Mrs. Lumberton is plainly about to launch into major sobs, but a shadow falls over her. She and Suzanne look up together and there's a doctor in his ominous white coat, ominous face. Mrs. Lumberton freezes. A rabbit runs over Suzanne's grave. "Can you come with me, Mrs. Lumberton?" he asks, very formal.

Mrs. Lumberton's blue eyes flash terror. "He's dead, isn't he?" Her voice rises and squeaks. The doctor takes her arm and she shakes free. Poor woman. She turns to Suzanne, screaming "It's my fault, do you hear? Don't you or Howard Justice ever come near me again."

Suzanne drives back to *The Defender* with hands still firm on the wheel, but she's shivering inside her coat. Her intuition tells her who signed that letter. Lumberton.

There's Howard walking up *The Defender*'s front steps, bent forward as if he's carrying a 150-pound bag of something that smells. And he probably does not even know about Cleo yet. God help him. Howard always jokes with Cleo. Now, he disappears up the stairs by the elevator as Suzanne enters the lobby. He's going up to Lance's office, no doubt. "And I deserve two minutes in my own office alone before I take them these dirty magazines," she tells the ghost defiantly, then realizes the ghost is no longer prodding. She is alone.

She sits down at her desk and cries, for the poor woman in the hospital, for herself, for the Old Man, for Cleo, even for Howard.

When the door flies open and Howard comes skidding to a stop in front of her desk, she's only a little mad at him for acting like he wants to run right out again. Can't she cry if she feels like it? Does he think she'll melt and make a mess on the floor?

All right, she thinks, I can be businesslike too. She sits straight and blows her nose. "Lumberton died, Howard. The doctor just told his wife. I was there at the hospital."

Howard slumps down in the chair by her desk and rubs the back of his neck, as if everything that hurts him is right there. "Died." He holds onto the word. He stares toward her, but not exactly at her. Dazed, he says "Lumberton was my friend. I think."

She tells him exactly what happened at the hospital. He keeps rubbing his neck. He tells her how Lumberton saw him and had a heart attack. His friend? He tells her about a phone call directing him to Lumberton's corner. Very fishy. Then he just sits there, frowning, wrinkling that space between his hazel eyes where there have never been enough frowns to leave a permanent trace. She actually likes him when he's like this, too confused to be arrogant.

"Howard, Mrs. Lumberton thought her husband's death was her fault." Tears run down Suzanne's face. "How awful for that poor woman. Howard, I know. I felt like it was my fault the Old Man died." She sobs out loud and wonders, why did I tell Howard that?

"Your fault?" He's more confused.

"My fault because I was late. Don't you see, if I'd been on time I'd have smelled something wrong with the whiskey before he drank it. I didn't have a cold. I could have saved him but I was late."

Howard jumps out of his chair and comes behind her, putting a firm hand on each of her shoulders, gently squeezing in the valley of each shoulder. Comforting. "You mustn't think that way." He's so intense. "We can't think that way—about what we ought to have done." She almost gets up out of her chair and turns and puts her head on his shoulder. Howard has a solid shoulder.

And then he says "We can't think that way because there isn't time."

"Time!" she screams, jumping up to face him. "What has time got to do with feeling? If I didn't feel the way I do about the Old Man I wouldn't be helping you at all. I wouldn't be stealing dirty pictures and deviling a poor woman whose husband was about to die. I wouldn't do it."

She glares at him, but no anger bounces back. He only sags, which is worse. "Lance told me about the pictures of Cleo, Suzanne. He sent me here."

Howard's brown hair is soft and curly, but under it his mind is a one-track rock. Suzanne's briefcase is still lying next to her on the desk. She takes out the magazines and thrusts them at Howard. He doesn't have time for frills or tact. O.K.

He turns one dog-eared magazine after another to the marked places, bites his lips, swallows. She hands him the small book on how to get revenge. He looks pretty grim. "Blackmail?" he asks. "But then why murder? And what's the connection? Is there a connection?" Obviously, he doesn't have time to waste if there's no connection. He's got his deadline.

Suzanne could kill him. Why did I get mixed up with this damn family? she asks herself. I used to decide what I'd put up with and what I wouldn't, and I did what I pleased. And mostly I told the truth. Now, somehow, I can't.

Howard picks up the magazines, still grim. Does he have to be as rigid as a cardboard mask? His mouth hardly moves: "I'll go talk to Madison and Cleo." He turns and walks doggedly toward the door and then stops. Arrogant S.O.B. "Suzanne?"

"So?"

"Lance says there are rumors that a woman was mixed up in the Old Man's death, a woman he was seeing quite frequently, whose husband found out. Did you know about any such woman?"

Suzanne goes hot and cold and knows she's flushing. She does not like Howard asking her about the Old Man and sex.

But, by damn, he is handing her a dare. Well, if he can question Cleo and Madison, Suzanne can find out about other women.

"I was not aware of any woman recently, Howard. But, don't worry, I'll look into that."

SIXTEEN

"DAMN IT, HOWARD, I'm being threatened because of you!" Madison grabs Howard by the arm in the little room with the coffee machine.

Howard is impressed. Madison has never seemed the kind of colorful combative person a threatener would choose. In fact, the Old Man used to say that Madison sometimes reminded him of the groom on top of a wedding cake. Madison can also be as quietly stubborn as quicksand. But, like all the Old Man's lines, the wedding cake one sticks in the mind. Now Madison grips Howard so tightly that he feels Madison's alarm in his own gut. And on top of that, Howard is going to have to ask him about Cleo posing for those magazines.

Why does Madison—who is, after all, only thirty-one—have to be so damned stuffy that Howard can't feel close to him? Even now when he wants to so much?

At least most of Madison is stuffy. He has the disturbing knack of looking several different ways all at once, and even several different ages. His small pink mouth seems vulnerable and maybe twenty. But then his mouth seems entirely out of place below his thirty-year-old skeptical brown eyes and his fifty-year-old British-ambassador haircut with a white streak in front. Under pressure, those eyes could maybe kill. But his mouth could cry like a sick baby. The rest of him could apply for the diplomatic corps or play poker and win. But there is nothing diplomatic about that right hand with the panic-hold on Howard.

"Who threatened you, Madison? How?"

Madison puts one long rectangular finger to his lips and pulls Howard toward his office. O.K. That's where Howard was about to go anyway. But then what is he going to say to his brother? If Madison needs to look like the British ambassador, how is he going to feel about Cleo's picture in sleazy skin magazines?

Madison's office doesn't help. Madison uses the walls of his office to display some of his collection of old movie posters. He says they are a good investment, they appreciate in value. With the measured tread of an usher at a funeral, Madison passes James Cagney, gun in hand, leering at Lauren Bacall and Humphrey Bogart.

Madison reaches under a copy of *Presstime* on the right side of his overorganized desk and, with an accusing flourish, pulls out a piece of paper. Behind him a glittering devil waves a baton as if he's directing Madison.

The devil dominates a poster right beside the map of the retail trading zone. Satan, complete with horns, leer, pointed mustache and goatee, is directing the passion of Lars Hanson and Greta Garbo. Their eyes are riveted together in lust, their lips are a few inches apart. A huge caption says *Flesh and the Devil*. Vintage 1920s? And why on earth does Madison, whose wife and father have both been loose with the flesh, hang that behind his desk?

Madison thrusts a piece of typing paper at Howard and waits, self-righteous. Howard shivers. He recognizes the note. Yes. Just like the one he found in his car the day the Old Man was poisoned, just as ugly, and made of cut-out many-colored letters. Some pervert threatening a newspaper family with letters cut out of a newspaper. The note says "The Defender killed your father. The Defender can kill you all. Look and ye shall find out things you do not want to know."

"Now, you stop playing detective, Howard, and let the police handle this." Madison is red and pompous all at once. And Howard realizes he would love to pinch him, like when they were kids. That won't help.

"Madison, if someone is going to hurt us we need to know who and why and when, don't we?"

"No." Madison's eyes are as cold as the devil's, but without as much humor.

There's nothing to do but plunge right in. "Madison, listen, a man who sells occult objects at the flea market and tells fortunes, a man named Poole, has been worming information about the Old Man out of Honey and Alice. Has Cleo talked about him?"

"No." The small vulnerable mouth opens the minimum, then snaps tight shut. Why does Howard suddenly remember his father leaning back in a chair, legs up on a coffee table and singing "Oh, I want what I want when I want it!" or "I am a gambling man" or whatever, always from a mouth wide and generous with music. The opposite of Madison.

"Madison, I need your help. Do you know of anybody who might be able to blackmail Cleo into revealing where the Old Man's workhole was, or what his drinking habits were, or anything that might help an outsider to kill Father?"

Madison jumps up so fast he could be on springs. He charges around the desk like a bull in a pinstriped suit and stands next to Howard, eyeball to eyeball.

"You don't take warnings, do you? You stay away from Cleo!" Howard does not back up.

Madison's eyes are on fire. But then his mouth trembles. "Howard, Cleo didn't have any more way than you or me to know where the Old Man's secret workhole was. How could she?"

There's a quiver of doubt in his voice. My God, is it possible that the Old Man seduced the wife of his own son? Howard's stomach flips over with revulsion. But he remembers what the Old Man taught him: First look into the things that you believe are possible—then don't neglect the things that you think are impossible, or you haven't done your job.

"Madison, did the Old Man ever make passes at Cleo, or did Cleo ever . . . ?"

"No, goddamn it. No. What kind of a brother are you?"

Howard wishes he was a brother who could just shut up and walk out. He can't. "Look, Madison, when Cleo was younger she posed for girlie magazines."

Madison flushes so red that the black and white poster devil is pale behind him. Howard can actually feel his brother's heat.

"For God's sake, Madison, we didn't look for dirt about Cleo. Suzanne went to get Lumberton to look at a letter threatening our father. To get him to identify the handwriting. He wasn't there and she found a book on revenge and sex magazines with Cleo in them."

"Damn bitch!" Madison spits out the words so wetly that this time Howard does step back. "Stay out of my business."

Howard has got to stay calm. "Madison, could Lumberton have been blackmailing Cleo?"

"You mean did Cleo help to kill Father? You listen to me, Howard." Madison leans forward like a cobra and words hiss from his small pink mouth like steam. "You listen." He waves the ugly pasted note. "This threat means Cleo. Somebody will expose Cleo. What else could it mean? Nobody needs to know about Cleo but you and me. And Suzanne—well, tell Suzanne to keep her mouth shut!"

Howard almost admires Madison furious. Now he is real. Sweating. God help him.

"Madison, Lance knows. So does Leeroy. Maybe Mrs. Lumberton knows. Maybe the person who's sent you this threat knows."

Madison closes his skeptical eyes, drops his hands. Actually grits his teeth. His red face has gone gray and he rubs it with his hands as if he's trying to wash away a layer of dirt. Then he speaks very slowly. "I've always tried to do the right thing, and what good does it do?"

"Listen, Howard, two weeks ago Cleo said there ought not to be any secrets between us. And she told me she posed for pictures when she ran away from home and was too proud to go back. She was hungry and naive. Does she have to pay for that for the rest of her life?"

Now the devil conducting in back of Madison is an actor in a tragedy. Madison's voice is desperate, choked: "I love my wife, Howard. She needs me. She really needs me. She's fun, a lot of fun. And, damn it all, I need her. I need to protect her." He collapses into the swivel chair behind his desk. "What a stinking mess!"

Nothing Howard knows about his brother prepares him for Madison without armor, like a soft-shell crab. Madison defending weakness.

It was Josh who always tried to bring home stray dogs and cats, fed them secretly out the back door when Miss Bounce said "No." Not Madison. Josh made friends with the retarded kid in the next block. Madison was embarrassed because it wasn't cool. Madison always wanted to be in the "in" group and didn't quite cut it. He got straight A's in high school and won the chess championship. He was Phi Beta Kappa in college, but never quite "in." Just that groom on the wedding cake.

Sweat oils Madison. He rubs his face and this time his hands slide over the sweat. Compared to Madison, Howard is safe. And empty. He tries to put his arm around his brother but Madison retreats.

"Cleo is going to a psychiatrist, Howard. And when everybody knows about those magazines, what will that do to her?" The small mouth is trembling again. "Cleo is just a farm girl from Minnesota. Her people ride tractors and go to prayer meetings. And that's how she judges herself. Maybe I ought not to care so much, myself, if people find out. But, dear God, Howard. How would you feel?"

Howard tries not to look at Madison's vulnerable mouth. He concentrates on his brother's eyes, skeptical as always. I have to finish and find out the rest, he thinks. I can't stop now.

He can't bring himself to tell Madison he is going to see Cleo.

As Howard drives across town he has the uneasy feeling he should have asked Madison to come along. He also knows he couldn't do that. Madison does not want him to question Cleo at all.

SEVENTEEN

HOWARD HAS ALWAYS BEEN disturbed by Cleo. Viscerally disturbed. His heartbeat becomes irregular. He wants to move to the other side of the room. He also wants to touch her. Sometimes he wants to slap her. Cleo sends out equal signals that she wants to run away and hide like a hunted deer, and that she wants to be naked in bed with him. But Cleo is his brother Madison's much valued wife, even if she now stands in her half-opened doorway with wide help-me-please eyes and a you're-the-one-I-want-to-see smile.

Howard finds it hard to believe that Madison even managed to meet Cleo. They're so different. Cleo represents some part of Madison that doesn't fit, perhaps the part that chose to collect old movie posters instead of coins or stamps. What else doesn't fit?

"Hello," she says, in her breathless little-girl soprano. "I'm glad you came, Howard. I don't want to be alone today."

The sheen of her black velvet dressing gown highlights the curves above and below. He knows exactly what's underneath. He wishes he hadn't seen the pictures of Cleo in the buff. With her smooth right hand, Cleo slowly massages the side of her round slender neck.

"Cleo, you look beautiful even at 11:30 in the morning." Damn. He didn't mean to say that. But, in her shadowy living room with the bamboo blind obscuring the window, Cleo is a source of light, skin glowing like one of those translucent candles with the flame down inside glowing brighter because Howard pleases her. He swells, almost floats with power. He thinks: watch out!

Cleo steps slowly backwards, eyes beamed to his. She's framed by a huge armchair with a pair of red high-heeled shoes in a kicked-off position beside it—a discard for comfort last night? This morning she wears gold silk slippers. The armchair is big enough for two people to sit in together. (Forget that.) In the small room there's nothing much else but a small fireplace, a love seat (forget that), and a series of English hunting prints complete with red-jacketed men and leaping hounds. To Cleo's right is a print Howard particularly dislikes, titled "The Death." Dogs killing the fox.

"I'm eating breakfast." Cleo leads Howard to a small dining room with a large sunny window overlooking Cullen Park. This apartment is on the fourth floor, only a few blocks from the building where the Old Man died.

Howard has always liked the dining room. Here he likes Madison's framed movie posters: W.C. Fields with his walking stick, Charlie Chaplin with his Hitler mustache, Mae West with hands on hips, huge hairy King Kong carrying Fay Wray atop the Empire State Building. Madison's secret sense of humor. Is that his only secret?

Howard sits down at the table across from Cleo's place. After she pours him a cup of fresh fragrant coffee, she flows into her own seat with her back to the window, W.C. Fields to the right, King Kong to the left. Sunshine gilds her pale fine hair which has always reminded Howard of milkweed fluff. Alice collected milkweed fluff in a box one year because she said her imaginary friend, Jennifer Ann Glorious, liked to feel how silky it was. Howard would like to feel how silky Cleo's hair is now. Damn.

"Cleo," he says brusquely, "I'm not here for a visit. I want to ask you some questions that may be hard to answer."

Her eyebrows rise slightly: delicate, clearly marked brows with a teasing little extra arch near the outside top of each curve. Cleo can say almost anything she wants with those eyebrows and the fine-boned shoulders that now give him a semihumorous shrug. "Shoot."

She ignores the halved orange and unbuttered toast on her plate and fixes him with those hopeful eyes, half-closed to show the rounded lids above the long lashes.

Damn it, he thinks, I like Cleo—there's something about her that's brave.

Brave? That doesn't make sense. The bones under her soft skin look delicate enough so you could break her arm without even trying. He suspects she might like that.

She puts her hands against the sides of her cheeks, little fingers stretched to rest against her moistly pouted red lips. Waiting.

"Cleo, did you notice anything odd about the Old Man or anybody around him the week before he was poisoned?"

The tapered hands move down to cup her smooth neck, head back. She shakes her head so the pale hair flickers in the sunshine. "No." She laughs a little embarrassed Alice-like tinkle. "Madison never let me be alone with his father. I think he thought..." Her eyebrows and shoulders finish the sentence.

And was Madison right? Even if Cleo had the key to the Old Man's secret apartment, she wasn't there when he was poisoned. She was with her shrink. She told the police that.

"But I did notice Leonora was worried about your father, Howard. I don't mean ordinary worried, but unnatural. Panicked inside."

"How could you tell?" Howard had never noticed that.

Cleo hesitates, biting her plump lower lip, then shrugs. "Feminine intuition. That's all. I knew."

Now the tinkly Alice-laugh jars him. "Hahahahaha. I knew the same way I know about you, Howard. Behind that ugly frown, what you're really thinking is that we'd be great together in the sack. Isn't that right? Oh, Howard, my shrink says I only add to my self-hate when I try to cheer myself up in the sack. But it would be nice, wouldn't it?"

Howard thanks God for Cleo's Alice-voice. That helps him not jump out of his chair and unzip her black velvet dressing gown. The whole day is so unreal. He could almost pretend it didn't matter.

She arches one eyebrow and pulls the zipper down an inch. "Some days I feel so terribly lonesome. I can't suddenly be a new woman. It takes time."

Howard stands up. Cleo stands up too, holding out her slender arms in welcome. "Cleo—" he raises his voice, angry—"I'm not here to jump in your bed. I have a job to do."

She raises both eyebrows and pulls the zipper all the way down. The black velvet slithers to the floor and she stands before him naked, pinky golden from that candle flame inside. The triangle of hair between her legs is silky milkweed pale as the hair which swings forward rakishly to half hide one of her begging eyes. Her smile is so welcoming that he feels only a monster could rain on her parade. He hesitates. She shimmers in happiness, waiting. Nothing has ever made him feel so powerful. "I like you, Howard"—words low as if she's out of breath. She picks up a large red scarf from the sideboard and, with both arms held out, she drapes the scarf over her face with only the eyes showing. Eyes from an Oriental Harem.

The sheer red scarf hides nothing. Turns the nipples on the rounded breasts bright red, the pubic hair redder than it must have been when the photographer took his pictures. Unreal. She laughs and runs ahead of him, scarf fluttering, her firm cheeks softly undulating. He follows her past the picture of the hounds cornering the fox, through the bedroom door. The bed is not yet made and the sheets and quilt are pushed back. There's one chintz chair, a mahogany stand on which Madison's clothes must be set out each night. Stuffy Madison, Howard thinks. Madison, my brother.

Cleo lies down on the bed, leans back, throws one arm up, the tapered hand against her cheek, doe's eyes vulnerable and eager, in equal parts. The red scarf lies, blood red, along one side of her slender body, her bones delicate enough to break. He feels like a drunk gorilla, not a Justice.

He makes himself look up, removes Cleo from his field of vision. And there on the wall are Miss Bounce and the Old Man. Madison has hung his mother and father on the bedroom wall.

Howard runs into the bathroom and vomits. Mostly coffee. The sour smell makes him vomit more. He is saved from the quicksand. He also feels wildly cheated.

He returns to find Cleo in the doorway hugging the pillow as she would a teddy bear. Eyes frightened. Breathless. "Are you all right?"

"Cleo, your shrink is right about you, and about me too. We'd both hate ourselves." He sounds sanctimonious. He goes back through the dining room to the kitchen and makes himself a large glass of ice water and drinks half, splashing the other half on his face. He sees himself reflected in the mirror on the end wall and thinks: I do not like myself.

Shredded Wheat sits on the kitchen counter. Howard and Madison fixed their own breakfasts when they were kids.

They liked Shredded Wheat best. He fixes himself a bowl with milk from the refrigerator and sits down at the dining room table. The Shredded Wheat does not take him back to the safety of the past.

Cleo does not come back to the table. He prays he does not have to go back to the bedroom to get her. He can't.

As he's chewing the last spoonful, she comes in the room—in a green V-necked housecoat this time, hair damp and curly. She's taken a shower.

She sits down across from him, leans forward, two hands together, very solemn. "Thank you, Howard."

Which doesn't make what he has to ask any easier. "Cleo, has anyone been blackmailing you?"

"No, and you don't look like the type either." Pixie grin, turning this into a joke. She's wary, but Madison hasn't warned her. She's not that threatened.

"Cleo, Lumberton, who believed he had reason to hate the Old Man, collected some pretty raunchy magazines with photos of you in the nude."

She has turned pearly white and both arms are crossed on her chest, hands clutching her shoulders. "Perhaps is wasn't me. Maybe it was just someone who looked like me?"

So Cleo is ready to lie when it suits her. "It was you."

She massages her arms as if she's cold in spite of the sunlight around her. Then she straightens and puts those tapered hands flat on the table. "All right, it was me. But no blackmail."

Howard notices his coffee cup is still half full and takes a sip. The coffee is now cold, but Cleo makes first-rate coffee. This makes him sad.

"I didn't tell Madison about the photographer before I married him." She crossed her arms again, gripping each shoulder, then raises her chin belligerently. "I was afraid to tell Madison."

"And I was a new person when I married Madison, Howard. I was the straight man for a comic, and I wasn't even sleeping with him. And by then I was blond."

Blond all over. But it didn't hide her from Lumberton. "Cleo, do you think someone is blackmailing Madison?"

Her mouth makes a red "O" around the white teeth. Her eyes go wide with shock. "Oh, Howard! Do you think so? Listen, Howard, I told Madison about those pictures two weeks ago. When I told him how hard I'm trying to change. When I asked him to help me. And Madison is a rock. Not like that photographer. I love Madison."

Howard sees Cleo unzipping her black gown superimposed on Cleo saying, "I love Madison."

"Cleo, I believe those pictures that Lumberton collected have something to do with how the Old Man died."

"Why?" Eyebrows half-raised, voice suspicious.

"Like you said about the Goldfish. A hunch. And because Lumberton also had a book on revenge. Do you know of anything else that might fit with blackmail or revenge?"

"No!" She rubs her face with both hands. The sunshine has shifted and is no longer behind her, or perhaps she's moved her chair. No light glows from inside. Her hair is too blond, plainly dyed.

"How many people know?"

"Me, Suzanne, Leeroy, Lance, Madison, maybe Mrs. Lumberton."

Cleo shrugs. "And tomorrow the world." Her Alice-tinkle fills the room as she flows into a Mae West pose, hands on hips. "What I know, you know. But come up and see me sometime." She means she hopes he'll leave now.

This is awful. At the door, he leans over and kisses her on the cheek, feeling the brush of a lock of her hair and smelling Tabu perfume. "Cleo, I'm sorry." He has the impression that as soon as he closes the door she is going to burst into tears, and he is quite sure he should not wait to find out.

Yet outside in the neutral hall, which smells like somebody's burned bacon, he stops. Considers.

Sexy Cleo never reached out to touch him. Not once. She was not at all straight-to-the-point like that slightly drunk girl who followed him to his car after a political rally last fall and unzipped his fly. Cleo hadn't even tried to kiss him or brush her fingers along his cheek or take his hand. Is there some connection between that and the fact that she fell for a photographer and not a pimp? If Cleo felt she had to kill somebody, would she use a hands-off method like poison? Suspicion turns everything sour.

EIGHTEEN

OF COURSE, LEONORA KNOWS what Suzanne calls her behind her back—the Goldfish. Half the people at the office use that silly nickname. Not Isaiah Justice. He never did. And now he can't call her anything. He is gone.

She minds Suzanne most. And there Suzanne stands in front of Leonora's desk with that give-it-to-me gleam in her eye. Leonora seethes. She remembers spitting at the teacher's pet once in the first grade and getting her mouth washed out with soap.

Usually, Suzanne has flounced by Leonora's desk, glanced at the picture of Baby on the corner and called out "How is Baby the cross-eyed cat?" Small talk. Because Isaiah wanted them to get along.

Baby died last night at 12:37 in convulsions in Leonora's arms. He was a silky cat, a loving cat.

Suzanne pretends she cares. Plainly she wants something. "I was so sorry to hear about Baby. I know he was like a member of your family." Suzanne speaks in exactly the same tone of voice she used when Leonora's father died last year. Suzanne is a wop bitch.

And now that Isaiah is gone, there is no reason why Leonora has to give Suzanne what she wants, whatever it is.

"Leonora, do you think the Old Man was sleeping with some new woman we didn't know about just before he died?" Of course. She wants the list.

Everyone assumes that Leonora knew more about the Old Man's women than anyone else, and they're right.

Now Leonora wonders why she took such pride in keeping track of his appointments with women. She even selected the flowers for them. He was so delighted with the way he could describe "a small wisp of a girl with a sense of humor," or "an earth mother you can tell your troubles to," or "a little bitch who's worth taming once," and Leonora could order flowers to fit: A pompom chrysanthemum, a pot of mixed herbs, a tiger orchid.

Then Isaiah would sit in his chair glowing with gratitude and appreciation and say "Leonora, you're wonderful, you're unique." Now he's gone.

Suzanne remains. "Leonora, isn't there something about his women you haven't told the police because you weren't sure? I know you like to be watertight sure." How splendid to have Suzanne begging.

Leonora is proud she told the police exactly what they could find out anyway, and no more. Isaiah would have been pleased.

"Leonora, the Old Man's ghost is here with us now, begging for help. Can't you feel it?" Suzanne is trying so hard not to show she is impatient that her voice cracks.

Leonora does not believe in ghosts. Not quite.

"Leonora, I need to know. Who did he go out with secretly during the last months of his life? Anybody? You know, don't you?"

Leonora has promised to keep the names of those women secret for good. Promised Isaiah because some of them would be damaged if anyone knew.

"The last month," she says, "he didn't go out with anybody but you. He seemed depressed."

"And before that?"

Leonora names a few names already familiar to Suzanne. Inside she laughs. All sorts of people would have fun with Isaiah's list. What would his family think if they knew that at least once, Isaiah and Cleo might have slept in the same double bed, but on different days. Cleo was actually flagrant about her fling with Albert Koch, the big ham who teaches chemistry at State. Nobody but Leonora knows that the Old Man had slept with Koch's wife. (She liked yellow roses.)

Suzanne waits. She probably learned that trick from Leeroy. He keeps waiting until people can't stand it and tell what he wants to know. But Leonora knows the counter-trick. Talk.

"Everything began to go wrong here when they got rid of the typewriters." She walks back around to her own type-writer and pats it. "Now there are just a few typewriters left in the building and the sound is wrong."

A flush is stealing onto Suzanne's face although she keeps her features calm.

Keep talking. "Typing is the first sound I remember, Suzanne. My mother used to tell me that she was so busy helping my father write his books that she propped me up with a bottle in their workroom. I think I came here to work because of the familiar sound of the typewriters. And be-cause I could be important to somebody. I always wanted to be important to my father. I got straight A's in pre-med be-fore I quit. But he wanted me to be pretty. And now I've even lost my cat."

Leonora is suddenly on the verge of crying. Her throat aches. Her eyes burn.

Suzanne looks like a fashion model even now when she's so frustrated with Leonora that her lips press together.

At least I have good level eyebrows, Leonora thinks, a good nose. But my eyes pop some. My chin slopes right down from my lower lip into my neck. Why in hell should I help Miss Beautiful? And why should that bitch be so sure she can do things better than I can? Be sure I can't have better ideas first?

Damn it, I can even think of some better way for Suzanne to look for the woman who killed the Old Man—so she thinks.

Leonora jumps up from her desk, and leans toward Suzanne. "You're right! There could have been a new clandestine paramour." (Long words annoy Suzanne. Use lots.) "Several times, when the Old Man wanted to work late, we went to a bar to have a little libation while he worked. And the bartenders gave me a double take, as if they expected somebody else. So talk to the bartenders in all his favorite places, Suzanne. Maybe they can help."

Suzanne stops dead still, plainly surprised. She hasn't really expected Leonora to help, has she? She hasn't expected an idea so smart that it seems completely obvious.

"That's a good idea. Thank you." Suzanne is taken down a peg.

And Leonora has kept her promise to Isaiah Justice not to reveal his secret list of loves.

SUZANNE GOES FROM bar to bar, getting tired of the smell of alcohol and not learning much; tired of giving all the bartenders her most appealing smile and knowing she'd be dumb not to. What a day.

The Iron Bar was one of the Old Man's favorites. The Iron Bar is next to the old brick state penitentiary, now overtaken by the town. The Old Man even liked the supposedly funny cartoons on the walls: cartoons of prisoners grasping iron window bars and yelling "Let me out!"

The place is in a lull when Suzanne arrives. Willie the one-eyed bartender, tells her more or less what the keepers of the Old Man's other favorite haunts have said.

"In the last month I didn't see him here with a single pretty girl except you. He didn't pick up any girls at the bar if he came in alone. He just drank." Willie turns his head a little sideways so that his one eye is on Suzanne. "But he did bring in one woman. Could have been some relative, maybe, but they didn't look alike." Then, in slow wonder, he describes the Goldfish.

When Suzanne tells him who it is, he shakes all over with laughter, strange laughter because he doesn't make a sound. Finally he stops shaking. "I didn't think she fit in the same category as you, kid. I just couldn't believe that one." He laughs again as he picks up a large cloth and begins wiping the bar.

Suzanne should feel glad. At the end, apparently, whatever was getting to the Old Man didn't keep him from sticking to Suzanne as much as he was able to stick to anybody. There was no new woman. If Suzanne cared about him she should feel good about that, right?

She feels a gathering evil. The Iron Bar is so thick with it she wants to run. Not just because of laughing Willie, who lost his left eye in a brawl years ago, so they say, and wears an eyepatch. Not just because the eyepatch is pink and his pink face appears to be unfinished. A half-finished man shaking with silent laughter is eerie.

But not eerie enough to make her want to run out screaming into the February afternoon.

She thanks Willie and leaves fast. Outside, she leans against the cold building and listens to the whir of cars, feeling a dark current—strong as wind or water, strong as electricity—suck around her. The current is as vital, as terrible, as hard to breathe through as blood. She mustn't faint.

She would love to run to St. Ignatius and seek sanctuary, to smell the ghost of incense in the shadowy quiet. But she can't. That's going back to being her father's good Italian girl. And I'm not that anymore, she realizes, even if I wanted to be.

A large hand touches her arm and she jumps and cries out.

"Are you all right?" It's only Leeroy leaning over her. His eyes come into her focus, deep with concern. That's not whom she expected.

Suzanne tosses back her hair and pulls herself together in the cold February sunlight. Leeroy is waiting so earnestly that she tells him the truth. "I felt the power of evil, right in there for no reason."

"Perhaps there was a reason. I'll give you a ride where you're going."

But the wave of evil has gone as fast as it came. The cars that whiz by are not part of a dark force field but just cars. Nothing sucks at Suzanne and tries to pull her down. And she feels the flame inside her burn higher because she can say "I'm O.K. now, and I'm going back to the office."

She can see Leeroy is disappointed. But he's here for a reason and Leeroy likes to follow his reasons through.

"You're going in the Iron Bar, Leeroy?"

"Yes." He shrugs, and she almost expects his long loose frame to clank. "I'm still looking for a one-eyed gambler, Suzanne, and Roosevelt Lincoln Worthington of the poison pen letters won't be home from college for me to see him until 3 o'clock."

NINETEEN

12:30 P.M. HOWARD FEELS he's being followed though his rearview mirrors are empty. He won't worry. He hasn't got time. He turns and parks in the curved driveway in front of the big brick house that once was home. When he was a child the Japanese hollies on each side of the front door used to be small enough to have secret spaces in back. His hidden fortress. He has no hiding place now.

Still, he will have to be absolutely sure to shake any possible tail before 2:30.

At 2:30, Howard has to call Doc from a phone booth and arrange the exact place and time of their next meeting. Doc has promised to tell Howard something important about the racetrack, something that may relate to the Old Man. Why can't Doc just come to the office? Or tell Howard on the phone? Doc, the sanitary inspector with delusions of cloak-and-dagger. Trust Doc, the Old Man said. He may look like Bugs Bunny, but he's a good source. Doc sure has a four-star electric fear of being spotted as such.

It's hard to think about fear here, where Howard used to lie under the maple on the long silky lawn and read when he was six or seven. Here the Old Man knew the name of every wild plant in among the grass. This house is just five blocks from downtown. Just six blocks from the Defender Building. At the far end of Pritchard Park. The houses by the park back up to busy streets with restaurants and shops and offices. But here it's as quiet as if nothing is wrong, as if Howard didn't have to find out what his mother might be keeping to herself about his father's murder.

Howard walks doggedly up the brick front walk, worn almost soft from so many feet over the years. He's about to pound the shining brass door knocker when the door opens and Aunt Earnestine comes out. His favorite relative. Her twinkly eyes and wide mouth are always bemused, even about Miss Bounce. Maybe she gets that way from teaching third grade. She is the only member of Miss Bounce's side of the family who hasn't let on to Howard that his mother married down, married a man who rocked the boat. The Saxons don't rock boats.

"Howard, you're worn out. You get your mother to feed you some good hot lunch."

Howard hugs his plump aunt and feels better. Feels ready to deal with his iron-plated mother, who stands just inside the door, upholstered in black and chairperson of all she surveys.

Miss Bounce ignores lunch, takes Howard firmly by the arm and marches him across the tan rug over to the tan couch. She marches triumphantly as if she's carrying a flag to claim the couch as her territory. But the couch is already her territory. What she intends to claim is Howard. She lets loose of him at his appointed seat on one end of the couch. She sits down on the other end, next to the silver bowl from the Women's Club, given in gratitude for her two terms as president.

Howard moves as far away down the couch as he can get. Miss Bounce is leaning forward like a cavalry general about to charge. "Howard, your brother Josh has lost his mind."

So? From Miss Bounce's point of view, Josh has never had a mind.

"You've got to talk him out of giving—just outright giving—all his stock to that hippie woman. The gold digger."

"To Virginia?" Why, Virginia might even be on Howard's side, might vote not to sell *The Defender*. Besides, he likes her.

"Josh wouldn't give all his stock to Virginia. They can't afford the gift taxes." Howard tries to be as logical and firm as Prompt Herbert.

"Hogwash!" Miss Bounce grabs hold of the patchwork pillow made by the girls at the Shelter for Unwed Mothers as if she's grabbing Josh for a good shaking. "Your brother intends to waive his right under your father's will. The idiot. His stock will go straight to his son, and he'll give that hippie woman the right to vote it." Miss Bounce seems about to explode with anger like a hot burp. Howard discovers with horror that he is on the verge of laughing. None of that, Boy.

"I'll go talk to Josh." He does not say about what. How else do you deal with an unbending chairperson? She was not always that way.

"Mother," he says, "you used to comfort me. Remember when I fell off my bicycle and broke my leg?" He moves down the couch to touch her hand. "Mother, why can't we comfort each other?" That is not what he came to say.

She does not soften. "Do you remember, Howard, when the Old Man bought you the typewriter?"

"I still have that typewriter."

"That typewriter swallowed you!" She leans forward and hisses "swallowed." He's pushed her button. The cords stand out on each side of her neck. Her ringed hands clench so hard they go white at the knuckles.

For a moment Howard can see his mother choking his father. No. His imagination is carrying him away. And his father wasn't choked.

"I know you were angry when the Old Man started getting the school bus to drop me off near the office. I didn't

mean to hurt you by not coming straight home. But can't
you imagine how exciting that was, Mother? I wrote little
stories that actually appeared in the paper, when I was six
years old.''

Miss Bounce jumps up. She throws the patchwork pillow
down. ''The Old Man took everything,'' she blurts, ''even
you.''

Howard wants to yell ''That's not fair!'' But he's sorry
for his mother. She is shaking. Not like a chairperson at all.

''Listen, Mother, don't say 'choose. Choose me or him.'
You wanted me to choose when I was a kid. I can't.''

His head aches. His stomach rumbles. Aunt Earnestine
is right. Miss Bounce is more than he can handle on an
empty stomach. ''Mother, I'm starving to death.''

''You were always hungry in a crisis,'' she replies tartly,
marching right after him into the kitchen, temporarily de-
used. Good. Howard needs to breathe. The house and his
memories press too closely around him.

As usual the refrigerator contains a package of assorted
cold cuts, a bottle of milk and a loaf of bread. Miss Bounce
lives on sandwiches, club luncheons and microwave pies.
Mostly, in recent years, the Old Man has eaten out, rarely
alone.

Miss Bounce's refrigerator: all that emptiness wrapped in
steel. A self-portrait, Josh once said.

Howard eats a ham sandwich and drinks a glass of milk.
Here in the kitchen, sitting next to him on a tall kitchen
stool, Miss Bounce seems to relax a little. She watches him
eat like a mother, a nurturer. Like she did when he was a
small child, devouring peanut butter sandwiches.

''Mother, what happened?''

She starts. ''What do you mean?''

''In the pictures when we were babies, you smiled at the
Old Man as if you loved him. And then what happened?''

Howard swallows his milk the wrong way, self-conscious. He does not feel free to ask about love or war between his mother and his father.

Miss Bounce squirms on her swivel-top kitchen stool, as if she wants to turn her back to him or leave, to rush out to a club meeting. She has trouble forcing out her words, is suddenly hoarse. "Howard, I needed to be close to your father." She gets up and paces around the table. "When you babies were born I had you to hug a lot. And we talked about you. So your father and I were close in a way." She stops, looks at her wedding ring on a small squarish left hand outstretched for inspection. The hand trembles.

Howard sits very still. It's been a long time since his mother let him see the tenderness inside the steel.

"Howard, I needed to know how he felt. Why he had those black moods. When I asked, he joked or changed the subject or shut the door." Howard remembers the door shutting. Door slamming.

"It was as if, because I had to get closer, he had to run away. And then because I was angry, he ran farther away. He needed you kids to adore him. He needed that. I don't know what he needed from me." She's about to cry, but straightens herself abruptly. "I made my own life! He had his women," she spits. And glares.

"Why didn't you leave?"

"Because I am a fool! Or maybe because I wanted to be around to see him get his. To see some woman finally kill him. Is that what you want to hear? Is that it?"

"No, but I knew something was wrong." Abruptly, she's shaking and vulnerable again. He understands he has to ride the roller coaster, keep as steady as he can. He pushes two images away. One Cleo, the other Miss Bounce, both carrying bottles of poison. Dear God, why can't he get a handle on his thoughts?

"Yes, something was wrong." In raw anguish, Miss Bounce's mouth writhes around her words, like paper burning. She gets to Howard's gut again. "When he came home from work one night the week before he died he went right in his room and shut the door and locked it. When I pounded on the door he didn't answer." A puzzled frown contracts her eyebrows. She leans both elbows on the table. Howard puts a hand on her shoulder in what he hopes is a steadying way, and she does not pull away.

"Your father had done that before, gone in his room, slammed the door and locked it. But that was when he was mad. He didn't seem mad, Howard. He walked in stoop-shouldered and shut the door quietly. He seemed depressed.

And then she shrugs her shoulders and pulls away from Howard abruptly. "But how could you tell with him? How? The morning of that last day he came over to me and he said Wilhelmena, we were happy at first, weren't we?' And I didn't say anything because I couldn't figure out what cruel trick he was going to play. What did he want? And then he said 'Maybe that was the happiest time of my life. I thank you for that.' And then he walked out."

Without realizing it, Howard has taken her hand. It's trembling again. She pulls it away as if she's been caught cheating and stiffens hard.

"You just tell me, Howard, why would your father act like that unless he intended something bigger and worse than usual?" She swells with anger until the black dress is too tight. "He was about to ask me for a divorce. He was softening me up. That was it!"

And then her voice drops and trembles with all the air knocked out. "But he threw me a kiss. The Old Man threw me a kiss, Howard. And then he walked out."

The tears roll down her struggling face and Howard understands that there is nothing he can do because she's furious. Furious that she can't control her tears. Finally he can't stand it, and one last time he reaches out to touch his hot damp shaking mother. She jerks away and cries. "I'm all right. What else do you want to ask? Go on and ask."

The kitchen clock behind her says 1:25. He wishes he could just sit and cry with her, but there is no time. He has to ask a question less charged. Clear the air.

"Have you heard of a man named Maurice Poole who reads tarot cards? Do you know him, Mother?"

She jumps up from her stool and paces up and down, up and down in front of the glass wall cabinet full of Grandma Saxon's china with the gold rims, paces jerkily as if tears inside are still struggling to take over. "No, I never heard of him," she snorts, obviously glad of something to snort about. "What a ridiculous name for a man who tells fortunes. He should be Indian or Persian, something exotic. Why do you want to know?"

"He's been asking the women in the family where the Old Man came from."

She stops short. "Where the Old Man came from?" And then very softly, she says "I'll tell you something strange. When the Old Man left I went in his study and looked around. He had a picture of his mother lying on his desk." Miss Bounce sits back down next to Howard, elbows on table, eyes fixed to his. "You know, that picture in a country dress, looking like a bad conscience? He kept that picture in a drawer most of the time. Sometimes he took it out when he had a big decision to make. That morning he had the picture out. Why?"

The picture of the grandmother who died before he was born had always given Howard the willies. She looked so strict and so sad. So hungry.

Before he can say a word, Miss Bounce shouts her own answer. "Because he was about to ask for a divorce. That's why! But it wasn't to marry that Suzanne creature, because she doesn't act like he asked her to marry him, does she?" That calms her and leaves Howard oddly self-conscious.

Miss Bounce is the chairperson again. In control. O.K., he can stand that.

"Your father was up to something and you'd better find out what if you want to know who killed him." She stands up. If he were company, that would mean she thought it was time for him to leave. She means he should get to work. "Please, Howard, before you do anything else, stop Josh from making a fool of himself. Do that first. Don't let anything stop you, Howard. Not anything."

HOWARD IS EXHAUSTED as he hurries out to his car in the driveway, his familiar Volkswagen with his personal dents in it. Maybe the only thing you can trust is a machine, he thinks. Either it goes or it doesn't. Not both at once. Like a human being. A machine is neutral. You don't love it and hate it, both at the same time.

He gets in and slams the door so hard that he jiggles the pencils on the passenger side floor. Slam, bang, kerthunk. Satisfying. The clock on the dashboard says 5 of 2. Twenty minutes to get to a phone booth. A safe margin. Twenty-seven hours and thirty-five minutes until his deadline. Too tight.

He turns the key and steps on the gas. The starter coughs. He tries again. There's a quick metallic pop and an odd smell. He remembers that same smell the time that lightning stripped the bark off the maple next to the house: almost like chlorine. There's a small puff of black smoke and a stronger smell like plastic burning. Normally he might sit and ask himself what's wrong with the car, but today he's too jumpy. He has the door open in a second and is out and running, hearing his own feet slap the drive.

And his ears hurt from a loud boom behind him. A blast of hot air slaps his back. He turns and the car is surrounded by a mist of smoke through which the door hangs at a crazy tilt. The hood is up, too, askew. The car is burning, glass from the windows glistening in a sunburst all around, tracing the force of the blast.

And Howard finds himself laughing. He's alive. Not even cut. He laughs harder. "I can't trust anything or anybody. Except myself. Now I know."

Somebody has tried to kill him. He is so angry he can taste it, dry and bitter in his mouth. "I'll show them, God damn it!" he shouts out loud. He feels better.

Then he sees the front door of the brick house start to open and he dives through the hedge. He hears running feet from both directions and escapes through his secret childhood shortcut, crossing yards. So let Miss Bounce deal with the riot of curious neighbors. She wants him to see Josh no matter what, right? Let the police deal with who bombed the car. Explosives they know about. He hasn't got time to stop. It's 2:05.

TWENTY

3 P.M. LEEROY DRIVES toward Tuttle Street and Roosevelt Lincoln Worthington's house with Suzanne. Actually she's back at *The Defender* by now, but he imagines her head light against his shoulder, smells her dark hair as fragrant as grass in the sunshine. And he sings off tune: "How Fickle Women Are, Just Like the Evening Star." Not appropriate. Suzanne is not especially fickle. But the song is from an Italian opera and is as full of life and death as Suzanne. That startles him. What does he mean, full of life and death? She's so entirely plugged in: that's how he feels. To be that plugged in, you have to be dark and light together. Whole.

Leeroy, you have champagne taste and beer sex appeal, he warns himself. But the singing side of him sings on.

A band marches toward him, drum majorette strutting, brass twinkling. Through the window that won't roll up the last inch, "The Stars and Stripes Forever" toots and booms louder and louder: Toot toot toot. "How Fickle Women Are." Boom boom boom. A musical traffic jam. Also a real traffic jam. He hardly minds.

Behind kids in band uniforms tooting riotously, there are cars full of other kids, screaming and waving out the car windows. Leeroy waves back. A girl with frizzy blond hair is yelling "Win, win, win, win!" She is already hoarse.

The big college basketball game will be tonight. This must have to do with the pep rally.

"Win! win! win!" he yells out his car window, and a leggy drum majorette throws her baton in a high twirl, grinning at him as if it's his throw.

The parade marches past him into Tuttle Street. Of course. The black star of the team lives there. Leeroy turns in after the kids. He sings with the rousing brass band, sings the words to "The Star and Stripes Forever" that he learned at Lakeview Boy Scout Camp fifteen years ago. "Be kind to your web-footed friends, for this duck may be somebody's mother. Be kind to the denizens of the swamp, where it always is cold and damp."

The day is cold but sunshiny. The parade keeps going but Leeroy parks. Pleasant neighborhood. Tuttle Street has for years been lined with the well-kept houses of teachers, bankers, policemen and other solid black citizens of the city. When the town surged out this way, a developer wanted to buy the area for a shopping center just off the university campus, but the citizens banded together and prevented a zoning change. Worthington lives in No. 27, cheerful white clapboard, freshly painted. Not the kind of house for a poison pen murder suspect. An older black woman with a round enigmatic face comes to the door wiping her hands on her flowered apron. Flour dusts her right wrist. Her eyes narrow, suspicious, especially when he says he's Leeroy Hicks from *The Defender*. Or maybe he looks so happy that she thinks he's drunk. Leeroy works at sobriety. "I'll tell my son you're here." She shuts the door hard.

Then the door whips open and a young man in a wheelchair yells "Come in." A challenge. Man and winking silver-framed chair fill the doorway. The man rolls rapidly backwards to make room for Leeroy. Obviously Worthington.

Worthington has a noble angry face like a cornered leopard, triangular, eyes glowing. His angry eyes never leave

Leeroy for a second. His single arm and hand, the right, emerge from a brown T-shirt, with opposite sleeve flapping loose. His pants legs are empty and tucked under him.

He backs up aggressively into a small neat living room with a small fireplace and artificial roses on the mantle. (That's impossible, Leeroy thinks to himself: you can't back up aggressively. But Worthington does.) He stops with a jerk in front of an overstuffed chair by the fireplace. "Sit down, Leeroy Hicks from *The Defender*." Leeroy lowers his body into the chair.

Leeroy is sure that Worthington won't put up with anything but blunt honesty. "Mr. Worthington, our publisher was poisoned. You sent him threatening letters."

Worthington laughs and his motorized chrome wheelchair winks and skitters forward. He leans forward. "Leeroy Hicks. I used to see your byline on the front page a lot. Before all the glory went to Howard Justice. And you have to ask why I wrote your Old Man threatening letters? *You* have to ask?" Score one for Worthington. He knows how to punch where it hurts.

"Your Old Man was a bastard. I went to your newspaper to get a job as a reporter. Would you believe I'm a Ph.D. and unemployed? Your Old Man saw me himself. I think I was supposed to be grateful. He told me that reporters have to have legs."

Leeroy flinches. That was like the Old Man to tell it like he saw it. And this man would have resented a lie even more. But still, Leeroy thinks, if I ran a paper I would probably have hired him, rage and all. He could use the phone. But the Old Man had to have super reporters. He wanted everything right. Why, even typographical errors drove him up the wall, like that small headline last week about the "Untied Methodists." He loved perfection. And that's why he could make you feel so great, or like dirt, or both.

"Listen, Leeroy Hicks, do you know where I lost my legs? In the Vietnam War. That was our war. Fought mostly by blacks because nobody else wanted to go.

"But I could report the black news better than it's done now with no legs and no arms either. What do you put in your paper about us? That we have riots when things get bad enough. That we get arrested. You damn well ought to have more news about black business; about our churches; about young people working their way through college. Oh, sure, you have token stories. You have token employees. But thirty-eight percent of the people in this county are black. Thirty-eight percent of your news ought to be about us!"

Worthington rolls his chair forward fast, and Leeroy thinks, he's going to ram me! Leeroy has to grasp the arms of his chair to keep from flinching, as the wheelchair screeches to a stop just in time.

Oh, how Leeroy would like to get up and move out of ramming range. Or at least defend the paper. Not now. Worthington is working himself into such a fury that he will forget all about caution. What's hidden will come spewing out.

"I could have killed your Old Man, that sanctimonious bastard. What did he think a man with two legs and an arm missing could do if no one would hire him for a desk job? After all those damn courses I took, I couldn't even get a job in the college library. They said their budget was cut."

"Perhaps you're so angry that people are afraid to hire you." Leeroy is using his "where does it hurt?" voice.

"Yes, I'm angry. Damned angry." The single hand clenches into a fist. "So suspect me. I even know where cyanide is. I could have stolen it easy but I didn't."

Leeroy forgets tact. "Good God, where?"

And Worthington smiles, plainly pleased with his effect. "Professor Koch in the chemistry department at State has a bottle somebody gave him twenty-five years ago. He says he keeps it to hold up at lectures and wake the students up. Like I just woke you up good."

"Where does he keep it?"

"In a locked glass cabinet with other dangerous stuff. I could have picked the lock but I didn't. And don't look so eager. The stuff is still there. After your Old Man died, I looked. I'm the curious kind."

Leeroy believes Worthington. Still, Leeroy makes a note to call Professor Koch and double-check, or maybe go by. Was there a grudge between Professor Koch and the Old Man? Who would know?

Leeroy knows he lucked out. He didn't even come to ask about cyanide.

"Listen," Worthington says, "I take courses because I can't get a job, or nothing but make-work. I'm a writer, a damned good writer. I sell stuff free lance, but I want a real job. Not pity, and artificial legs from the government. That's not me. I can get everything from the government except what I want."

"What exactly do you want?" Leeroy senses that Worthington knows more than he's told. Leeroy mustn't crowd him, just keep him talking.

"Maybe I want to see the world stop fucking itself. Maybe I want to see the people who pretend to be in favor of that, like your Old Man, stop being such hypocrites."

Worthington grasps the arm of his chair and bends forward. He tosses his arrogant head. "Listen, I'm not dumb. I learn a lot more around campus than what's in books. You came here because you suspected me because I was angry. Did it occur to you to come here because I'm smart? No. It never did, but it should have."

"I'm listening."

"I could help you if I wanted to. I know something you don't know. But I only talk to the top man. Send me the Old Man's son. Let him learn a thing or two besides how to use us."

"So we're both angry," says Leeroy softly, envious of Worthington's fire: his rage undiluted with self-doubt.

"Yes, I'm angry. Maybe I'm angry enough to have an idea how your damned Old Man was killed. You see, people talk in front of me because they figure I'm so angry I don't count. So maybe you came to see me for the right reason after all. Now get out."

Leeroy the well-digger knows he is about to hit water. But one wrong move and he'll cut the flow. Worthington quivers, the metal on his chair actually rattles, as he fights his own urge to tell something he obviously considers more important than where to find cyanide. He quivers and then erupts: throws back his body and shouts. "They were blackmailing him!" He's no longer a leopard but a lion roaring. "Blackmailing him! He was perfect. So damned perfect he had something to hide. Something from long ago, Man. From the place where he was born."

He stops. Shuts his broad mouth as if it's been a traitor to him. "Why should I help you? Or help his son?" Then he shrugs his shoulders. "But why should I help those other bastards either?"

"We need your help," says Leeroy quietly, sensing that under all Worthington's fury he has one thing in common with Leeroy. He needs to be needed. That's why Worthington wants a job. He eyes Leeroy narrowly, probably suspects he's being psyched out, but keeps talking.

"The one I met was a detective. Looking for dirt. Didn't give his name. Said he knew there was dirt way back on that bastard Justice. Mr. Detective, or the people he worked for, were going to the town where Justice grew up, to find out what.''

Leeroy tries not to show how excited he is. This could be it. Better than cyanide. The keystone of the arch. The fact that will make everything else fall neatly into place. God bless Worthington.

"Where did Justice come from?"

"Don't his family know, Man?"

"No."

Worthington laughs. "He was a secret-keeping bastard, he sure was. And, Man, how should I know where he came from if his own family don't know? But I do know this. They were looking for something to blackmail him good, and shortly after that Mr. Blind Justice was dead. There's a connection there, Man. There must be a connection. Now I've told you all I know. Get out."

Leeroy rushes back to *The Defender* with the blackmail lead. The cyanide lead. Only ten minutes to the paper. It would take him that long to call Lance.

Correction: it's ten minutes to the bench in front of the Defender Building. And there's Freddy Norris reaching out to grab Leeroy with that scarred left hand, while the right hand clutches that brown paper bag with joy-juice hidden inside. Freddy is as disreputable, snaggle-toothed and pleased with himself as usual. Freddy the oracle.

"Did you find the man with one eye?" he asks. When Leeroy shrugs, he bursts into a big grin. "Never mind. I have something better. They're saying that Howard Justice's wife knows the guy. They're saying that if Howard hadn't been careless enough to lose his wife he'd have his answers."

"Who says it?"

"I protect my sources."

"Where is his wife?"

"I have enough trouble keeping track of my own wife. But I know what the woman looks like. If I see her I'll tell her to go home." He bursts out laughing as if that is a big joke, and takes a long swig from his 7 Up bottle.

Leeroy sighs, pushes his cowlick flat with the palm of his right hand, says "Thank you" and heads across the street. He shakes his head. "Oh Lord, how is it that the world is so full of lost souls who need to be mysterious, and I, Leeroy Hicks, know all of them?"

TWENTY-ONE

NOW HOWARD KNOWS. Somebody wants to kill him. Somebody tried. He's flattered. Maybe he is like the Old Man after all. So he has to be brave. Howard is also horrified. Aware of every part of his body, private and public. He doesn't want to lose even one part. He is also incredulous. For more than twenty-seven years he has lived without looking over his shoulder for death. Now, as he walks along the outdoor mall, he looks into every window for the reflection of what's behind him. Nothing suspicious reflected in the Eckerd's Drug window full of pill bottles. Lots of people go in, though. Sale on diet products, says a sign in the window, and lots of fat people go in. They walk more loudly than thin people. Or is it just that his ears pick up every nuance of sound, even two women mumbling about their operations.

The phone booth is in front of Eckerd's. Next door is the dime store, smelling of popcorn just as it did back when the Old Man used to buy Howard toy trucks. Both stores now have fake marble on the mall side. Like so many of the stores on the mall, these two have back doors onto Vance Street. Vance Street leads to *The Defender*.

Howard steps inside the three-sided glass phone booth to dial Doc. Yes. "Trust Doc," the Old Man said. "He tells the truth."

Doc's message came to the office: Call "True Grits." That's the code name Doc has given himself. Doc is originally from Connecticut and thinks anything to do with grits is funny. A cloak-and-dagger ham. Call from a phone booth, he said. Call 653-2894 at 2:30 P.M. exactly. That must mean that Doc will have some kind of tip about the proposed racetrack. And maybe, by the grace of God, it will relate to whoever poisoned the Old Man.

Howard may think Doc is a little bit of a nut, but the Old Man knew sources better than Howard does. He was a magnet for sources. He'd walk across a room full of people, stop to put his hand on shoulders and tell jokes, or ask "How's Emma? Is your mother's arthritis better? How are the twins liking State?" And by the time he was across the room he had a question that needed answering: Where did the star of the State basketball team get his car? Or, why is the state insurance commissioner acting so rich?

Sources even showed up at the house. Like the auto mechanic who knew that the school bus repair bills were padded. That man rang the doorbell after dark. "I can't afford to lose my job," he kept saying, "but that's my money they're stealing. My tax money." And the Old Man made that mechanic feel like a hero. A safe hero. Because the Old Man would find the details and nobody ever had to know where the tip came from. So why do I feel like I know more about sources than my father did, wonders Howard—am I so smart?

Howard reaches in his pocket for change. He hasn't got any change. No. He's not so smart. It is already 2:29 and Doc is fanatical about his arrangements. Howard sure hasn't got time to wait for another message or another time to call from another phone booth. He pulls out his wallet and searches in the crevices. No change. He reaches his index finger and scoops it along the rounded bottom of the change return slot, then breaks into a big smile. God is on his side. He pulls a quarter out of the slot and places his call.

"I'm so glad I caught you!" His voice shakes with relief. "There's so little time."

Doc sounds in a hurry, too. Rattled. "Meet me at the racetrack site. Under the big maple that stands alone. I'll be there in an hour and a half."

"An hour and a half? Why so long?" No answer. Howard speaks more loudly and distinctly. "In an hour and a half under the big maple that stands alone at the racetrack site?"

"That's right." Click. Howard looks at his watch. He will need about half an hour to get to the site. He has an hour to waste. Which he can't waste. He can go talk to Josh. The company has been lending Josh a car. The Old Man's silver BMW. Howard can borrow it and save the time he'd spend renting a car. Good.

He swivels to leave the phone booth. Turns, and a fat man is just disappearing into Eckerd's. He walks funny, familiar funny. Good God. Is that the man who followed Howard last night? He runs after the man, bumps into an old lady in a lavender coat who grabs him by the arm to give him a lecture. Not now! He pulls away leaving her shouting after him and waving a cane. All the diet-pill people stare as Howard runs into the store. Damn the sale. He can't see his own man anywhere. He runs out the back door onto Vance Street. No fat man in sight. The two women waiting for a bus stare at him and one begins to laugh. Does he appear that crazy-frantic? What do they know? Nobody has given them a deadline. And nobody is trying to kill them.

Howard's man has escaped. Perhaps he ran back into one of the stores. And Howard can't even be sure it was the same man who followed him before. Damn. Damn. Damn. Is his life going to depend on knowing which backside is which? All he can do is keep trying. He sets off by taxi for Josh's hotel.

2:45 P.M. JUST AS Howard looks at his watch, Josh stalks
out of Room 23 and shuts the door hard. Howard was about
to go in. The hallway smells of air freshener and is painted
a sick green. Josh wears his sombrero, his wool poncho and
his knapsack, the old canvas one he had when he camped
out as a kid. He walks flat-footed hard the way he does
when he's being mulish. When he sees Howard, which seems
to take him a minute, he says "Hello. Goodbye. I'm leaving." He keeps walking fast, like he can't stop or he won't
have enough speed to get up the hill. Except there isn't any
hill, only the flat motel hallway with an ugly flowered rug.
The ugly rug must be home for a cricket. Mixed with the
clomp of Josh's sandals is a tiny beep-beep.

Howard grabs Josh's unironed cotton arm. "Wait. Where
are you going? Don't leave me."

"I'm going to get out of here before it's too late." Josh
pushes forward, shoulders hunched as if he's striding into a
gale.

The door opens behind him, and there stands Virginia
very pale, rocking the baby against her shoulder. She nods
at Howard, still holding her cheek against the child's soft
fuzzy hair. Howard has the impression she rocks the baby
for her own comfort, not the child's. Her natural wool shawl
is clutched tight around her shoulders as if she needs a hug.

The cricket or whatever chirps again. Josh used to collect bugs. Drop them in a killing jar with carbon tetrachlo-
ride, then mount them on pins. His bureau drawers were bug
display cases and his shirts were stacked on the floor. The
Old Man said he didn't know whether Josh was going to
grow up to be an exterminator or a naturalist.

Now Josh is trying hard to pull loose from Howard, Josh
twisting hard, Howard gripping. Then Josh and Howard are
actually wrestling in the hall, wrestling like they used to as
kids, but now it's serious. Josh is frantic, trying to shake

Howard off, even slapping him against the wall. Josh who believes in nonviolence. Howard catches a glimpse of Virginia crying. The baby's hair must be wet from her tears and she's too upset to care. Somewhere nearby he hears the cricket again. Beep-beep-beep. A gentle sound in the middle of their stupid scuffle. Howard is not going to let Josh leave without finding what he knows.

"Listen," Howard manages to gasp, "somebody will call the police. Come inside, Josh!"

They manage to stand apart as a head in pink hair curlers sticks out a door, stares and proclaims "Drink is the root of all evil," then retreats with a slam. Low-type motel. But Josh was too proud to let Miss Bounce put him up at a good motel, and too unmarried for her to let him stay at the house. Then Josh refused to use sleeping bags on the floor at Howard's.

Inside the dingy motel room with cheap prints of magnolias on the walls, Howard and Josh both catch their breath and Virginia lays the baby in the middle of the bed on a motel towel. There is a dignity and remoteness, a despair about her. Whatever is happening, she has accepted it. She sits down in the plastic chair as if she's taking a seat for a tragedy.

Josh has not quite accepted whatever it is. He is too restless. He goes over and drops his knapsack next to six oranges and two apples that lie on the fake wood bureau top ready to roll off at the least vibration. One orange hits the floor with a thud, the rest roll against each other.

"There is nothing I can tell you that you want to know, Howard! Be careful, or I'll tell you the whole truth." Josh throws off the poncho and scratches one shoulder blade, an odd nervous habit which goes back at least to first grade. With his prominent shoulder blades and sharp nose, Josh used to remind Howard of a tall friendly chicken. Today, Josh is not friendly. Let him talk. He'll get to the truth.

"I suppose you can tell I'm leaving Virginia. Or maybe it's the other way around." Josh glances angrily at Virginia who does not react. "Virginia won't come back to the commune with me unless I marry her. Marry her! Miss Bounce put that in her head, I know it!" He glares at Virginia from under those heavy black eyebrows. "We were perfectly happy the way we were." His voice hits two notes at once the way it always has when he's upset.

"Why?" he screeches at Virginia. "Why? You were happy there with Dick and Thelma and Sharon and Christianson. Raising our food. Living simply. You were happy!"

"I was almost happy because I love you. I don't want you to go. I love you." Her voice is so choked that listening hurts Howard's throat. Howard is embarrassed because he knows Virginia wishes he wasn't there. But if he wasn't there, Josh would be gone.

"Josh, I don't just want money. I want you, too. I want us to get married. I want us to have a commitment to each other. But if that can't be, at least I want the baby to have his share. I love you both."

"Love!" Josh spits it out like rotten meat. He turns his back on Virginia, turns toward Howard who is still near the door. "You can forget about me, Howard. I'm leaving."

Howard braces to stop him again. "Tell me the things I don't want to know." Beep-beep. The noise is mechanical, not a bug. But Howard is so upset with Josh, and so determined to find out whatever he has to tell, that the oddness of the noise only half sinks in.

Josh is not pushing to get free of Howard this time. He is all of a sudden, calm, the eye of the hurricane. Something deep inside him seems to be adjusting, changing, like water coming to a new level. He stands with his back to Virginia while she goes over to the bed and stands next to the baby, stroking his hair. The baby is still asleep. Maybe it was even noisier with Dick and Thelma and Sharon and Christianson.

"Listen, Howard, I've turned my stock over to Christopher, with Virginia to do any voting about it, voting to sell if she has bat-brains. I don't want anything that belonged to my father. Not anything."

Behind Josh, Howard sees the case of the Old Man's binoculars, the well-worn leather case, on the bureau near the oranges. "So, how come you have Father's binoculars? You can't say everything he had was bad. I wanted those too. But I want you to remember. Remember how the Old Man jumped up from the breakfast table to get us to look at robins pulling worms, or woodpeckers, or the hummingbirds on the butterfly bush that Miss Bounce planted? You used to fight to see whatever it was first."

Josh actually grins, though the water level is still somehow shifting inside him. He grins and his eyes are sad. "I remember the time he caught us looking at the skinny woman down the street who forgot to close the venetian blinds when she took a bath." He leers and winks. For just a split second, Josh is the brother who used to make Howard laugh. The brother Howard told ghost stories with. The one he could tell he was afraid of the dark. And then Josh's mouth goes grim. "We had some good times. But you tell Virginia what our house got to be like, Howard. Tell her about the silences between Father and Miss Bounce when he came home at all. Being married couldn't stop that. A marriage contract is not love. Love is working together to prevent the end of the world."

If Josh gets on that subject he'll never stop. Of course the end of the world is important. But it will still be important after Howard's deadline. Josh, shut up.

"There's one spot downwind from the Andes, Howard, where scientists say human beings might not be fried by radiation if a nuclear war isn't too large. I wanted to take Virginia and Christopher there. We were trying to find a way to move the commune there. But Virginia won't go."

Virginia raises her head sharply. "I don't want to spend my life waiting for the world to be blown up. I want to live. I want Christopher to live." Beep-beep.

"Blown up! My God, that beep is a time bomb!" Howard remembers his car door swinging crazily, smells hot destruction. "Get out of here! Bring the baby, quick. Someone tried to blow my car up. They're trying to blow us up now!"

Now it is Josh who is holding onto Howard, wrestling with him, holding him down to prevent him from running out the door. And all the time laughing that crazy laugh on two notes. Miss Bounce is right. Josh has lost his mind. He's the mad bomber.

But Virginia is not insane. She walks toward Howard holding a small rectangular object like a cigarette pack. A red light blinks and the thing beeps again. "It's the Geiger counter—Josh's Geiger counter." The baby almost drowns her out, awake and yelling.

Josh seems pleased. He has shocked Howard and waked up the baby for a chorus. Josh is always comforted by his ability to shock. "I keep this Geiger counter in case a nuclear power plant blows up or a nuclear waste truck turns over on the highway. Then we'll know which way to go to get away from the radiation. The beeps get faster when you're near high radiation. Except it won't be 'us' now." The pleasure drains. "Only me."

Howard is still shaking. He sits on the edge of the motel bed, stares at the ornate motel plaster lamp and tells them about his car. He sweats.

Virginia cradles the baby against her shoulder. Josh sits down heavily next to Howard, making the bedsprings squeak, and puts his calloused hand over Howard's. "What a mess we're in. What can we do about it but love? And we can't even love."

Josh jumps up, squeaking the springs again, strides over to the bureau, picks up the oranges and begins to juggle. What a time to juggle. On a good day Josh can keep twelve oranges flying. It's his only parlor trick. He says it's great because you can't think at the same time. He juggled twelve oranges just before the Old Man got so angry and threw him out of the house.

"Josh, stop making me wait. I have had a hell of a day. So tell me what you know."

A shudder passes through Josh. He closes his eyes and opens them again, without dropping an orange. The water has reached the final level. "Our father killed a man."

"He what?"

"You think I'm lying, don't you, Howard? You can't believe our father was a killer." The oranges still fly in whirring ellipse. Surrealistic.

"I won't believe without proof!"

"You think I'm lying. I said I'd like to kill the Old Man when he threw me out, didn't I? He called me a druggie." In a rage, Josh actually roars. Framed by oranges. "Are you wondering if I killed him, good old brother?"

Howard feels dizzy.

"Josh wouldn't kill, Howard." Virginia runs over and grabs Howard's arm as if she can drag him to the truth. She is gut-positive, you can hear it in the way her voice comes up from her toes. She still loves Josh.

"So how do you know our father killed a man, Josh? How do you know, you and nobody else?"

"Because there's one way I'm more like the Old Man than you are, Howard." Josh is calmer. Why can't he put down those damned oranges and just tell the story? He has hypnotized himself. The story is a sing-song. "Now and then, I, Joshua, take one whole night and spend it getting drunk, right? Mostly the Old Man held his liquor. But I remember three times he got stinking drunk. In good company, of course."

Josh catches the oranges one by one and slowly puts them down on the bureau. Good riddance. Virginia is still holding on to Howard. She seems to have forgotten to let go. Josh stands as if he is reciting in school, ready to tell the story.

"Once, Howard, when Father was a new reporter he went out and got drunk with Hank in the sports department. And he told Hank he could never go back where he came from because he killed a man. And since Hank died of cancer last year, maybe I am the only one who knows what our father told him when they were both smashed.

"Anyway, years later Hank went out and got smashed with me when I was mad at the Old Man. And he told me maybe the Old Man yelled at me because he killed somebody years ago. That sounds odd, but you get the idea. Hank said he'd never believed the killing bit, just figured it was liquor talk, but maybe it was really true."

Josh is telling the truth. His eyes are black with pain.

"Dear God, why didn't you tell me, Josh?"

Josh considers so long that Howard almost can't bear it. "Because I didn't believe my father could kill a man, Howard. Hank didn't tell me any details, if he had any. Just that one sentence. I was scared to ask more."

"And then?"

"I didn't believe it, Howard, but I also did believe it. It was one of those things I had to not tell in order to make it not true." Now his eyes ask for support. Howard is too shaky to support anyone but himself.

"But when somebody poisoned Father, then I knew it was true."

"That's not proof!"

"Not to you. But I bet you think I should have done something about it then, don't you?"

"My God, Josh, this must have been hell for you. But, yes, I do. You should have told me. You should have told the police after the Old Man was dead."

Josh shrugs in slow motion, looks down at his worn leather sandals, wiggles his left big toe. "It was a damned heavy secret." He is like a record winding down, slower and slower. "I didn't know it was so heavy. Until I let it go just then." All of a sudden he looks up, shy instead of stiff, sad instead of stickly. "I figured if the Old Man died for his secret he had a right to keep it unless the cops were smart enough to dig it out."

Virginia loosens her hand on Howard's arm, lets it drop to her side. Howard hugs Josh and is promptly pushed back.

"Forget the brother-brother stuff. I'm going."

"Josh, we need to talk." He can't go now.

"No talk. I'm through with all that. Through with everything to do with our family." Josh is pleased with himself. Pleased! Mind made up. Smiling. The center of everybody's attention. Virginia picks the baby up and brings him near. Even the baby stares at Josh over the thumb he has popped in his mouth.

"What the hell," says Josh, almost jauntily. He will not go out with a whimper. That's Josh. "I've given my stock to Virginia, in trust for Christopher. She'll send me enough to survive in South America and I'm free! I'm out of the whole mess forever. You stew in it."

"If you run away, the police will think you killed the Old Man. And damn it, we love you."

Josh backs toward the bureau as if he is afraid that love will grab him. "I owe nobody anything." He picks up his old knapsack and sombrero and starts for the door, kissing Virginia and the baby lightly as he passes.

No point in grabbing him again. Josh is going.

Howard is surprised to feel totally deserted. What help has Josh been the last five years? What help is he today, blaming everything on the Old Man and Miss Bounce and then running away?

"Wish me luck." Josh bows goodbye at the door, sweeping off his sombrero. Virginia has tears running down her face. Howard gives Josh a strong goodbye hug whether he likes it or not. Howard would like to run away with Josh. He can't.

The door shuts behind Josh with a loud final click. At least, barring the end of the world, Josh has some assurance he'll still be alive this time tomorrow.

Howard does not even know who is trying to kill him.

TWENTY-TWO

HOWARD GRASPS the handle of the door of the Old Man's BMW and something inside him recoils. Cars blow up. But he can't manage without a car. At least nobody knew he was going to borrow this one, which has been on loan to Josh. The silver-gray BMW is out of place outside a Thrift Motel misted in the smell of a nearby hamburger joint. Before the Old Man died, he was the only one who ever drove this car. The Old Man. Either he was or was not what he seemed to be. Howard must find out. A man is innocent until proved guilty. Remember that.

Virginia has given the keys to Howard. She said "Go find that monster who poisoned your father. Find him because you have to, and find him for me and Christopher."

The car door opens solidly with a balanced silent swing. Everything about this car is built to last and to work and to satisfy the senses in a quiet way. Howard slips onto the leather seat. As the door clicks behind him the cheap hamburger smell is gone. He has entered a time machine. The car still smells faintly of cigarette smoke—not smoke from Josh and Virginia, who believe smoking tobacco is decadent, but from the Old Man. The car is so familiar it hurts: seats with feel of sturdy luxury. Extra dials on the dash that Howard's Volkswagen never knew. The Old Man said this car would go 150 miles an hour and stop on a dime. The BMW has more power than I need, Howard thinks. The Old Man said the greatest luxury in life is more power than you need. And this car is full of the Old Man's magic. He did have magic, no matter what else he did. And damn it, his car won't explode. Please God.

Howard turns the key. The car hums to life. He relaxes.

Something fire red looms against the window on the passenger side. What on earth? A person. The door opens as Howard is ready to zoom off. Suzanne jumps in uninvited, smelling of roses, not fire. How on earth did she find him? Suzanne in her red suit and green jade bracelets. Christmas, when Howard feels like a funeral.

"What do you want, Suzanne?" he says. "I can't take you with me." He presses his foot on the gas and the car purrs forward. "I'll drop you at the first traffic light."

"Virginia told me you were here." She's unruffled. At home. She must have spent a lot of time in that seat with the Old Man driving. Driving as always, about eight miles over the speed limit. He said they never arrested you for less than ten miles over the speed limit, so eight miles was virtually legal. The Old Man, driving and telling his funny stories about the buildings and people they passed, probably grinning at Suzanne so broadly that his dimple showed. Suzanne must have shared all that, just as Howard did, maybe more often.

"Suzanne, what do you want?" Howard asks again.

"I heard on the police radio that your car blew up. I wanted to find out what happened. I thought you might borrow this car." She acts just as calm as if she had said "I heard your car had a flat tire."

But she sits too straight. Under Suzanne's calm is a tension, like a horse just before the race starts. Why?

Has she heard a rumor that the Old Man killed a man? Has everybody but Howard heard that rumor already?

Howard won't bring it up, won't start a rumor if it hasn't started. "I'm on my way to see Doc, Suzanne. Doc says he has something important to tell me. God, I hope it's important.

"Something is wrong with Doc," he says out loud. He doesn't like thinking that. The Old Man was so sure about Doc.

Suzanne is silent, as if she knows Howard is talking to himself. They purr past the back of Eckerd's. Two rather thin women come out carrying large packages. No sign of the fat man, naturally.

"I don't just mean something is wrong with Doc because he has teeth like Bugs Bunny. I've been thinking he's too flashy for a sanitary inspector in a suburb, Suzanne. Did you know he wears a ruby ring and an opal ring and a diamond ring on his left hand? He seems like an actor. His hair is dyed. You can tell by the white roots. He looks in back of himself every three minutes. He grins like he's with you in a conspiracy and he's about to stick you in the ribs with his elbow. He insists on being called from a public phone booth and he goes in for silly codes when he leaves messages. I don't think he has any common sense. That's dangerous.

"And Doc's rhythm is wrong. But I can't really tell about rhythm any more. When I was a kid, nearly everybody here was from here, and they all had a kind of right rhythm unless something was wrong. Now the sunbelt is the place to be and half of the people are from God knows where. And there is no right rhythm. Doc is from Connecticut."

He remembers that Suzanne was born in Connecticut. She still says nothing. Maybe she wants him to forget to put her out of the car. He hasn't put her out yet, has he? Somehow at this moment it helps to have a listener, even Suzanne.

They are floating around Courthouse Square, where even the familiar statues are all of people who were from here. Damn it, why do all the statues look so pleased with themselves when life is such a mess? Suddenly he understands the kid who horrified the city by throwing red paint on the Confederate general.

"So," Suzanne asks, "if you don't trust Doc, what are you going to do about it?"

"I don't know. My father's last words to me were 'Trust Doc.' You don't ignore your father's last words."

Suzanne turns, opens her dark eyes wide and stares at Howard as if he has two heads. "Come off it," she says. "You don't count last words unless someone knows he's going to die. The last words he said to me were 'Why aren't all the pencils around here kept sharpened?' I don't intend to spend the rest of my life sharpening pencils. You have to have a better reason."

She's right, Howard thinks. He has been feeling sorry for himself about Doc, sorry and melodramatic. No steel in that. He needs steel.

"Doc has given me good stuff before. I can't risk not going. And I might catch the person who's been following me. I think he overheard what I said to Doc in a phone booth."

Suzanne goes so white that Howard turns and stares at her. "Someone has been following you, Howard? A fat man?"

"Yes. Why? Do you know who it is?"

"A fat man has been following me. Off and on." Now Suzanne's rhythm is wrong. Literally off beat. Being followed upsets her a lot. Who on earth would follow them both? He would have had to start with Howard, switch to Suzanne, maybe back to Howard. Bounce back and forth. But why?

The BMW purrs past the morgue. At least Howard doesn't know anybody in a refrigerated drawer right now.

He admits to himself they are past the point where he can drop Suzanne at a bus stop. And maybe he shouldn't drop her off by herself anyway. Though there's no tail in sight.

"Maybe you could hide in the bushes on the cliff overlooking the racetrack property and see if there is anything or anybody I miss from the ground below when I meet Doc."

"O.K., sure." She takes on the prospect of scrunching in bushes in high heels with a casual shrug. A surprising girl.

They follow Loudermilk Road out past the new housing developments, through undeveloped patches of woods, February-bare and scruffly. There's a side road here the cops sometimes use as a speed trap. The BMW is so silent and smooth, feels so much like it is really standing still, that Howard has to keep looking at the gauge to be sure he's not going too fast. All he needs now is to get stopped for speeding and miss his meeting with Doc. Just twenty-six hours to deadline.

He turns in the abandoned driveway of the house on the cliff above the track site. The house burned down two years ago. He covered the story. The house belonged to a professor at State who hasn't rebuilt. The stone chimney and foundation stand bleak in the cold. Howard and Suzanne are early. Ten minutes until Howard is supposed to meet Doc.

"Should we try these?" Suzanne asks, and picks up something black from the dark floor of the car: the Old Man's binoculars. The case in the motel was empty, the binoculars left in the car. The only thing of his father's Josh said he wanted, which finally he didn't take.

They park in back of the ruin where the car will not show from the road or from below and crunch through the winter-dry underbrush toward the edge of the cliff to take a look. A clump of scrub evergreens is cover. Suzanne hands the binoculars to Howard. Howard's hands know the rough black leather cylinders well. He raises them to his eyes and feels the cold metal eyepiece against his face. He turns the dials which change the plain below him from fuzzy to clear.

There's Doc, his Chevrolet pickup parked a little back from the tree, walking importantly toward the lone maple in the middle of the site. He is early. He strides along, hands in pockets. An absurd plaid wool hat with a brim covers the place where his rabbity ears ought to be. Nobody else is in sight.

Doc walks eagerly right under the tree. Then the thunder starts. The ground actually spurts up around him as if by a water spout and drops again. The tree itself jolts sideways and when the dirt geyser recedes the tree is lying uprooted. Doc has vanished. The ground did that! Not an object like a car, but the very ground itself exploded. Howard is shaking.

Suzanne says "God help us all" and bursts into tears.

He puts his left arm around her and holds the binoculars with his right hand. He sees small branches blown loose all over the ground almost the way he's seen in pictures of the aftermath of a twister. The earth is plowed into a jagged hole next to the tree. Now a police car speeds across the bumpy ground toward the tree, jiggling and twisting, siren hiccupping. There must have been a speed trap within hearing distance.

He and Suzanne are crunched down behind a bush which he hopes hides them. He adjusts the small dials on each binocular lens to see closer, then farther. Through these binoculars with which he once searched for birds' nests he sees hazy shapes, then bits of shredded branch and loose rock spewed from the hole. And then a hand. A hand all by itself. Bloody. He shudders. That must be Doc's. Howard makes himself keep moving the binoculars around. He sees a policeman, looking nauseated. The man doesn't like severed body parts any more than Howard does. Mixed in a pile of dirt is hair. A policeman takes a stick and gently, like an archeologist, he unearths what's left of a face. Doc's face. Howard is numb.

"Let me see, too," Suzanne demands. He starts to say "No. It's too terrible." But he realizes Suzanne wants to know exactly what it is, terrible or not.

Another siren whizzes by. Reinforcement. Howard can go down and get mixed up in this or go back to the office and call and find out what the police have discovered. What can there be here that the binoculars haven't told him? He's made himself go over each bit of ground carefully, even looking at the leg so obviously torn out of its socket by its roots, but still wearing brown oxford and white sock. Doc couldn't wear colored socks. They irritated his athlete's foot.

Howard has trouble keeping the binoculars steady. He sees the Old Man all of a sudden, eyes narrow, talking about death. "Death," the Old Man had said, "is a lion. You are the lion tamer. You have to persuade the lion you are not afraid. Then he won't eat you."

But Howard is afraid. Somebody has tried to blow him up twice. Doc simply got to the meeting spot before Howard did. That could be Howard's torn hand out there, pointing at his blown-off head, six feet away. The killer's motto: If at first you don't succeed, try, try, again.

"This happened to Doc because he wanted to tell me something!"

"No, don't take that guilt trip." Suzanne is imperious. 'Doc wanted something to be known."

"Poor Doc. Doc was a ham. He enjoyed being alive."

"And you could be just that dead if you'd arrived at the tree before he did."

Howard must decide what to do next. His hunch is strong: stay away from the police. They will ask questions, not answer them. And don't be sentimental over Doc just because he enjoyed being alive. You didn't even like him, Howard Justice. And there is no time.

SUZANNE STARES THROUGH the binoculars at the plowed earth and desolation and blood. The man she half fears as the instrument of this is not fat, has such vanity he would never let himself get fat. And he has no reason to blow up Doc or blow up Howard. Why should he? She had better keep her mouth shut.

TWENTY-THREE

"Boy," says Lance, "you look like you've seen a ghost." He thumps Howard on the back, makes him sit down in the well-worn chair by his desk and hands Howard a mug of whiskey with "Editor" on it in gold letters. "Medicinal," Lance says from under those wild eyebrows. He sits down heavily behind his desk. "Now, spill it all." Howard knows he does not mean the whiskey.

Lance shakes his head, squints his eyebrows together in a super frown. He groans at the worst parts of Howard's story, like the part about Doc's hand pointing to his head across the rubble. But he listens 100 percent. Howard feels better. *The Defender,* headed by Lance, is in back of him.

"And at least we've got a little progress here, Boy. Young Billy Ryan found this out: Four of the wives of men who are on the board of Gemtrex are on the board of the company that plans to build that racetrack. And this took smarts. All the women use their maiden names, not their married names. Organized crime can use anything, Boy, even women's lib.

"That's not enough to prove Gemtrex is responsible for your father's death, Boy, but it's a step. Newspapers may make money, but racetracks and businesses around racetracks make a lot more, especially if there's not a hotshot newspaper breathing down their backs. Right? More motive for blackmail or even murder, Boy. More motive.

"And Leeroy's favorite bum says your wife knows the answers."

Howard winces. He is tired of Leeroy's bum. But he has to admit that the total disappearance of Honey and Maurice Poole is odd.

"Thank God you're here, Lance."

Lance shakes his shaggy head. "But, Boy, we've flopped on one thing. We can't find where the Old Man came from." He sighs like a baby hurricane, gets up and begins to pace. "I've called every courthouse in Mason County trying to find his damn birth certificate. Even his army records aren't right. We've called every police or sheriff's department, every newspaper, looking for an old murder story that might fit. We've looked for a place with the nickname you described: Heaven high, hell deep and river wide. No luck, Boy. No luck."

"How can that be? How can there be no record of a man being born?" Howard asks.

He's interrupted by Bullethead walking in the door, ears still stuck out to hear the worst. It turns out he hasn't even heard yet about Josh leaving town. He doesn't even know yet that the man blown up on the racetrack site was there to meet Howard. Bullethead is here to talk about Howard's car blowing up. That seems so long ago.

"I ought to arrest you for leaving the scene of a crime!" he barks. He gets madder when he learns that Howard left the scene of the explosion that killed Doc, too. He picks Howard's brains for four hours. May what's in my brain do Bullethead more good than it's doing me! Howard thinks. The clock on the wall ticks louder and louder. Finally Bullethead leaves.

Howard is exhausted. I'm not going to make it, he thinks. I'm going to fail at the one thing that matters to me: keeping this paper. Howard can never remember life without *The Defender*, without the excitement of knowing what is happening first, of having a finger on the pulse of life. The paper is like a living thing to him, and yet he is going to lose it to people who will kill what it is and turn it into something else. He does not have the strength he needs.

Midnight comes. For two more hours Lance and Howard brainstorm over coffee that tastes bitterer each hour. No use.

2:00 A.M. HOWARD FALLS asleep in an overstuffed chair in Lance's office. When he wakes up with a start it's 8:10 A.M. And by 5:30 of this day Howard has to have proof that Gemtrex—which at this moment cannot even be reached— was responsible for his father's death.

Lance is on the phone, still dressed in his wrinkled blue shirt and crooked necktie from the night before. A funeral Goldfish, all dressed in black, brings them hot, strong coffee that lightly steams her glasses. Everything seems almost, but not quite, normal.

Leeroy lopes in. He's still trying to track down Maurice Poole who presumably knows where Honey is. The man has no phone, and pays for his flea market booth in cash.

"It's odd," Howard says, "you looking for my wife or the man she's with. But maybe she'll talk to you more easily than she will to me." Still, Howard has a hunch that wandering around looking for Maurice Poole is not what he ought to be doing. He's not sure what he should be doing.

He goes back to his father's office. Whatever is wrong, whatever caused his father's death should have left a clue in the place that was most his. Howard is so used to that office, he hardly sees it. What is out of the ordinary? He knows it's odd to have a full-length mirror on the back side of an office door. But that was just because the Old Man had to make appearances, be a guest on television news shows, talk to the Rotary Club. He liked to check himself out whenever he left the office.

Perhaps it's odd to have a small refrigerator in an office. For ice cubes. And with a still sealed bottle of cold champagne inside, in case, the Old Man said, of a sudden need to celebrate. He said it was bad luck not to celebrate a stroke of good luck. But those things: the mirror, the champagne, are merely unusual, certainly not lethal.

Howard walks over and stands by the globe of the world, looking out at the street. The morning noises of people and cars headed for work seem eerie. Nothing is ordinary. It's 9:05 A.M. and by shortly after dark the Justice family may sell this newspaper. Fast, because they're angry. That's not even smart.

And what does Howard know? That Josh says their father killed a man. Howard did not tell Bullethead that. It may not be true.

Leeroy says the Old Man was being blackmailed. Lumberton knew something about the Old Man's death but God knows what. Lumberton, who came to hate the Old Man and had a heart attack when he saw Howard. He won't ever tell what he knew now.

Freddy on his damn park bench said two things: A one-eyed card shark knows the answers and Honey knows the answers. At least he allows a choice. How generous.

How can any of that fit with poison on the Old Man's bourbon or strange Maurice Poole who reads tarot cards or with a car Leeroy says tried to run down Suzanne or with a bomb in Howard's car or with Doc being blown up? Nothing makes sense.

There's a noise behind him. He whirls around. It's Honey! She has on a drab raincoat, her hair slicked back in a ponytail. She looks ready to turn around and leave, and she's pouting. He wants to grab her and shout with joy and say: "Please know the answers." That won't work.

"I'm mad at you," she says before he can open his mouth. "Sending that man to track me down. I was in the laundromat, and I looked up and there was this man staring at me through the window. I was scared to death."

Who tracked her down? Who is she now in her khaki raincoat? Honey is always playing somebody. If he can figure out who, it may help.

"Then I saw it was that man who sits in front of the paper," she says. "He always said good morning to me so when he came in the laundromat I couldn't scream. And he came right up and said you were looking for me."

Howard doesn't know what to say. He is amazed. It won't sound good if he says he wasn't looking for her. It won't sound good if he says "Thank God you are here so I can ask you questions." He is still her husband. He should hug her and say he's glad she's back.

He hugs her and says "I'm glad you're all right." It is a lukewarm hug. Mutually lukewarm. "I need to talk to you," he says. She looks at him with half-closed eyes, distrustful. "Oh, hell, Honey," he blurts, "we didn't fit, did we? We tried and we didn't fit. I'd like to be your friend. That sounds corny but it is how I feel. Not like a husband."

"And the bum?"

"Tells Leeroy things. Picks up scuttlebutt. He says you can tell me what I need to know about who killed the Old Man."

He expects her to blow up at that.

"My lawyer will talk to you about a divorce," she says, very prim. "I'll talk to your lawyer, not a bum."

He goes over and shuts the door. She stands beside her double in the mirror. "Honey, if you know something about my father that could help me find who killed him . . ." How is he going to appeal to this woman he no longer loves?

"I have to help you," she says. "The tarot cards say I will have bad luck if I don't."

Does she really know anything? Is he going to learn the truth from Honey the actress and Freddy the drunk?

She takes both his hands, and hers are cold like the morning outside. She smells of recently dry-cleaned wet raincoat. Impersonal. But once he loved her, once he even found her acting was fun, and she cared about him. Dear God, let her really have some answers.

"Can you keep this secret, Howard?"

"I can try."

Long dramatic pause. Honey loves pauses. He must be patient. "Maurice is a kind of detective. The flea market is just a hobby. He sells information." Dramatic pause again.

Howard understands why Honey has come—not just because of Freddy, not just to serve notice her lawyer will be coming, not just because of the tarot cards, but at least partly to amaze him, to pull a rabbit out of a hat, to make him gasp. That's more like Honey. And thank God.

"What kind of information does Maurice sell?"

"Maurice was hired to find out where the Old Man came from."

Why does she drawl so slowly? "The people who hired Maurice had only heard some vague story that your father did something terrible back where he came from, and they wanted to go there and find out what." She whirls the globe beneath her tapered fingers. She shifts feet, as if her loafers hurt. "Maurice believed the people who hired him were the people who wanted to buy the paper." She looks at her feet.

"Then, Howard, Maurice found out that some old guy named Lumberton, who wanted revenge, knew that your father really did do something terrible back there, and the old guy had clues about where it was. All sorts of clues which he'd picked up, one here, one there. Maurice really did need the money."

"For God's sake, quick. Tell me where my father came from." And cut the drama, he wants to yell. There isn't time.

"The place was not in Mason County. It's near the line. It's not even in this state. Maybe the house was half in Mason, but the town was over the border. And your father wasn't born Isaiah Justice. He was born Job Justice. He changed his name when he left that place."

"What place?"

"Maurice won't tell me that. He says he can give hints, but he swore he would never tell anybody what he found out. That's part of what they paid him for. Maurice has a strange kind of loyalty even though he was never able to actually find out for sure who he was working for. But if they killed your father, he wants to help you find that out."

Howard runs to the chair next to the globe and grabs the atlas lying nearby. He flips to the right page and runs his finger to the area around Mason County.

Only above five places are conceivably possible. One should be nicknamed heaven-high, hell-deep and river-wide. Lance will figure this out in ten minutes, if Honey is right.

Honey walks over and stands beside him, tentatively puts her hand on his shoulder. "Please don't tell anybody where you found out any of this, Howard. O.K.? Maurice is my friend. Not my lover, just a place to stay, but also my friend."

"When did you learn all this?"

"Yesterday."

Suddenly Howard knows who Honey is in her khaki raincoat. Detective's assistant. He jumps up and gives the detective's assistant a passionate thank-you hug. "I won't tell." He's so glad she's not his any more.

"Honey, didn't you tell me Maurice believes that pimple in his forehead is a special eye for enlightenment." A blackmailer's assistant, with eye for enlightenment. Great.

"Yes, I guess so. He does."

"Good Lord, I'm thickheaded. I heard I should look for a man with one eye. That must have been mixed up from an eye for enlightenment. It may not be a real eye, and the cards he sharks are the tarot cards. But nothing about what is happening to me is real. Not one single thing."

The speed with which Lance finds the spot where the Old Man was born is real. Impressive. It's Moody, on the Rocky River.

"I tried that town before, Boy, on the off chance. But I got the wrong man, young fellow who didn't know what they used to nickname the place. But this is our lucky day. An old fellow who knew came in just as I called. And your father's birth certificate is recorded in that county. So he was born Job. You wouldn't publish a newspaper, Boy, and call yourself Job Justice, now, would you?"

TWENTY-FOUR

SUZANNE WALKS DOWN the hall toward Lance's office, high heels determinedly click-click-clicking. She salutes the more-than-life-sized picture of the Old Man. The photography department has just hung the blowup between the windows in the hallway near the office that was his.

"Today," she promises the paper face, "we're going to find out who poisoned you."

What happens before she gets any further is that Sanders from Sports walks past the door to Lance's office and drops a Styrofoam box which pops open, spilling two sausage-gravy biscuits on the floor. He wipes at the mess, but Sanders is not neat. He picks up the pieces and goes on. Suzanne would hardly notice except for what happens next.

Howard comes out of Lance's office and even as Suzanne calls "watch out," he slips on sausage gravy. His feet slip right out from under him. He half rises, half falls through the air, clutching at space, and lands with a loud thud in a mixed-up heap. He blinks, groans, sits up and gingerly touches his right foot with his fingers.

She runs to him. "Are you hurt?" Why on earth didn't he tell Sanders to wipe up that floor better? Why doesn't Howard look where he's going? The whole thing is silly. And serious.

The oversized face looks down on them. She has the crazy urge to tell the Old Man to mind his own business. The Goldfish and several young reporters come running. Howard is grimacing as he touches his right ankle.

Suzanne is by his side, kneeling. "I studied to be a nurse."
Actually her higher education is one year in nursing school
plus reading everything from *The Defender* to books her
brother Nello leaves in the bathroom. But she's good at
sprained ankles.

"Get me some ice and strips of cloth," she tells the
Goldfish. Leonora can usually come up with what is needed.

Suzanne gently feels the ankle and makes Howard take
off his shoe and wiggle his toes. Then she uses Lance's paper shears, which appear in his hand, to cut strips of the
flannel cloth the Goldfish brings. What cloth! Flannel covered with teddy bears and small blond children. A baby
shower present? It will do.

"Never mind doing too much," groans Howard, winc-
ing. His brown hair dangles in his eyes like a kid's. "Just fix
me so I can drive. I know where the Old Man came from
now. I have to get there."

"You don't have time for a sprained ankle, but you have
one," says Suzanne.

She pulls the bandage tight. "I'll drive. I need to know
what happened, too." That's a trial balloon. Will Howard
say no? She ties the end of the bandage. Howard has square-
cut sturdy feet, even if the one she just bandaged is a little
swollen. Can the rest of him be all bad? The Goldfish hands
her a plastic bag of ice from the small refrigerator in the Old
Man's office "to apply along the way." Lance pulls Howard
up to balance on one leg.

"Bullethead!" yells Leeroy, who is standing near the front
window. What? "Bullethead is coming in the front door of
the building right now. If you're going, hurry!"

LEEROY HATES HIMSELF. Bullethead could have stopped
Suzanne and Howard from going off together. Or Leeroy
could still insist on going in Suzanne's place. But he won't.

He watches how she helps Howard down the hall, one lovely round arm around his shoulders, one of his corduroy arms around her. Leeroy feels as empty as the empty robin's nest in the park. But Suzanne makes her own choices. That is what he loves about her. He stands perfectly still by the window and watches her go.

HOWARD'S WATCH SAYS 10:35 A.M. It will take about five hours to get to Moody. That'll be about 3:35 P.M. Howard's deadline is 5:30 P.M. Tight.

Howard hop-leans down the hall with help from Suzanne and they make good time until they get to Madison's door. Madison must be out or he would have certainly come during the commotion. But his door opens just as they get to it.

Madison staggers out directly in front of Howard and Suzanne. He acts like he's blind and deaf.

Howard catches his balance. There's no time to stop. Bullethead must be coming up in the elevator. Madison grabs hold of Howard as if he's about to drown. In Boy Scout camp Howard learned how to break a stranglehold. He almost does that automatically.

But something is terribly wrong with Madison. He tingles with hurt. Tingles like the electric toaster that Howard and Honey had, when the wires began to short-circuit. His voice is changed too, a screaming whisper. "Howard, Cleo jumped. She jumped from the seventh floor. Someone from the police called. Cleo jumped."

Howard sees Cleo with the blood-red scarf by her side. Pool of blood. Now on cement. Her delicate bones are broken. He feels knocked flat, but he's still standing. More or less.

"I've always been afraid she'd kill herself, Howard. Always been afraid." Madison lets go his stranglehold, and

Howard steadies himself against Suzanne. Madison hardly sees him. "Howard, she's dead."

Howard wants to cry out "It's not my fault." He is not sure that is true.

"Madison, I'll do anything you want me to do to help. What do you want me to do?"

Madison is not focused on what he wants Howard to do. He is struggling with what's happened. Still half blind.

"Madison, I found out where Father came from. It was in Hay County. That's where a blackmailer went to find something from his past. I was going there to find out what, and if, somehow, that led to poison. But if you want me to stay I will. I will do whatever helps you." Howard hears himself with horror. He has to go. But how can he leave his brother now?

Madison focuses sharp and hot. Sun through magnifying glass. Laser beam in a pinstriped suit. "Go find the damn people who started this mess. Find those people Howard, and push them out a window.

"Push them hard."

TWENTY-FIVE

SUZANNE AND HOWARD have left the cities and the Interstates, been through the foothills and are in the backcountry mountains now. This is the most dramatic place Suzanne has ever been. Maybe the most dangerous.

On the left side of the BMW the mountainside sheers off... down, down, down to a point she can't see. A long fall. She imagines getting out of the car, going to the edge and peering over, but she keeps driving. In the near distance a mountainside rises from the abyss, woolly with evergreens. Abrupt rock faces loom grayer and more austere than the front of the tallest building back home. In the far distance the mountains fade into blue. Compared to these mountains, even compared to the nearer rock face, the BMW is tiny. A car far behind, that may or may not be following them, is tinier. Above all soars the blue sky with a few clouds. The day is strangely warm for February. Suzanne has the car window open. She takes great breaths of the crisp air, so pure that each breath she draws is like a sip of wine, almost making her head swim.

Next to her, Howard looks like he has indigestion. Like her Uncle Carlo after three helpings of squid: bad color and cloudy eye. With Howard it's not squid but indigestion of the spirit, she figures—indigestion made worse by the sheer beauty and silence of the mountains, and by the fact that with his right ankle sprained, he can't drive. So he's fermenting. Haunted.

"You think it's your fault, don't you, Howard? Your fault that Cleo killed herself?"

"She might not have jumped if I hadn't been so hot to ask her questions after Madison begged me not to."

"Do you think she'd jump out the window, just for that one reason?"

"What do you care?"

"I liked her. She was human. Sometimes I like you."

He turns abruptly and looks out the car window on his side. Not for the view. On his side of the car there's nothing but a rough rock face with black streaks of water running down it. The back of his neck is stiff. O.K., Howard, be hostile.

"Howard, I never thought Cleo was more than five minutes from jumping off a window ledge. I used to wonder why."

"So I gave her the final push." He spits it out. Good. Angry is better than sunk.

"Do me a favor. Be honest. If you had it to do again would you do anything different? When you didn't know what was going to happen?"

Long pause. Stiff neck. Grudging answer.

"No. Not if I didn't know."

"And you didn't know."

He turns back from the blank rock face and stares at her exactly as if she was a blank rock face. "Why do you care?"

A hawk soars up among the clouds that are thickening and turning gray. It's going to rain. "I don't like riding next to someone who looks like he's going to be sick all over the car."

He sends her a dirty look. Lightning hidden in the haze eyes. And off in the distance the hawk or whatever it is floats downward in a circle. I'd like to be floating in the sky like that, she thinks. Like to be free. I'm haunted, too.

Now he acts like she's stabbed him. "Maybe it's dumb of me to feel awful that Cleo splattered on the sidewalk, but I do." He certainly paints the picture.

"Of course. I do, too. But don't feel like you're God who caused it all, Howard, and don't lose your lunch. We need our strength for whatever we find out in Hay County. Maybe before that." She glances in the rearview mirror at the road snaking around the mountainside. Sections of it vanish and then come back into view. Is that the same blue car back there? Hard to tell at such a distance.

She remembers the car that maybe tried to run her down, grips the wheel tighter and glances down the steep drop of the mountainside. There are not even trees on the down-slope to break a car's sheer tumble.

"Howard, you don't have time to give up now." He needs a shock treatment. Good, because Suzanne needs to shock him. Here goes.

"My mouth is dry, Howard. Could you give me a mint from my pocketbook? And don't be surprised by the gun. It's my father's but I can shoot it. And before we are through, I may need to."

He picks up her green purse as if it might explode and snaps it open. "Loaded?"

So reassure him: "Yes, but the safety is on." His color is improving. Maybe now is the time for full shock.

"The reason I carry that gun is my business, Howard, but it could become your business. I hope not.

"You are the first person I've told this to, and unless there is some good reason to tell it to the police, I hope you'll keep quiet about it." Suzanne begins to feel uncovered. A target. But she owes the truth to Howard now.

He hands her a mint and examines her small revolver.

O.K., Suzanne, get it over with: "Three years ago I was married, Howard. After three weeks Gordon was so jeal-

ous because I spoke to another man that he beat me until I
had to crawl next door and call the police—crawl, dripping
blood all the way, because he split my lip and knocked a
tooth out. I don't have to take that.''

She's surprised how the blood rushes to Howard's face.
How he grips the gun and then quick lets go. Guns go off.
"Beat you up! You couldn't tell he was like that? You're
afraid he'll show up here? You think he had something to do
with my father's death? Is he trying to kill you?'' She's hit
a vein.

"I don't think he had anything to do with the Old Man's
death. I would have told you that." So now explain. "He
was in prison still when your father died. Howard, when
Gordon was arrested for what he did to me, his company
checked some things and discovered he had been milking
money out of their computer. He went to prison because he
stole the money he was using to impress me." She winces to
remember how the gold cufflinks and vest with gold watch
chain turned her on.

"He was a con man. He conned you." Howard's voice
shakes with fury.

"He knew how to make me feel valuable. He bought me
perfume and diamond earrings. He quoted Shakespeare. He
was so impressive. He'd been a Green Beret. He'd been an
airplane pilot. He had two Ph.D.s. Or said he did. Nobody
that impressive had ever treated me as if I was valuable.''

"But he beat you up?'' Howard is still red in the face.
She's touched that he is so upset.

"Yes, but when the police came to get him he was crying
and asking me to forgive him, Howard. He really did think
I was valuable. God, I was sorry for him. But I knew I had
to end it neat and quick. You don't cut somebody's head off
slowly. That doesn't help.

"I divorced him, Howard. He went to prison. I left that place, left a good job with a chain of motels out there. I came home."

"And now you are so afraid that you carry a gun? Why haven't you told us? Why haven't you asked for help?"

Howard is not going to understand. "Because I don't trust you, any of you, not to think I'm a fool. To be taken in by a man like that.

"He may want to hurt me now that he's out of prison. I think maybe he tried to run me down with a car. At the time I hoped some unknown drunk was in that car. But I expected it to be Gordon. Even if it was, unless somebody besides me gets hurt, it's my business, right?"

"But you may be in danger, for God's sake."

"We may both be in danger."

Howard is shocked silent for a full minute. Then he asks "Did my father know about Gordon?" So, O.K., murder kills privacy.

"Your father knew. He helped me. He told me each person has to do what is necessary in order to survive. And that's what I did. And he said I had to keep busy every minute. And he kept me busy. And it did help. And he said you have to find every little crumb of life that needs to be enjoyed and enjoy it. That all helped. And I knew that for some reason your father had to do all those things himself. He understood."

Tears make the curvy road dangerous to drive on. None of that now. She tosses her head, holds on hard to the steering wheel. "I'm telling you all this because there is a blue car which may be following us. I shouldn't have come with you, Howard. But I had to come."

At least the sun is out again. Howard turns and looks behind them as if the rearview mirror might cheat. "There isn't any car I can see. If a car is back there we are well ahead of it. And armed." Suzanne is actually pleased to see that

we-will-conquer, knight-in-armor look on Howard's face,
that look which has sometimes made her want to stick him
with a pin.

And then a crazy wry grin comes over his face. "But
you're telling me Gordon may not be in some blue car following us, aren't you? That the car may be a coincidence.
You're telling me the car trying to run you down just after
Gordon got out of prison may be a coincidence!" He laughs
out loud. "This whole damn thing is so crazy, maybe everything about it is a coincidence.

"Suppose Lumberton collected sexy pictures of Cleo because he was a dirty old man and she turned him on, and not
because he was looking for a way to blackmail my father.

"Suppose Maurice Poole wanted to impress Honey with
being more than a flea market bum. Maybe he told her he
was a detective working for the blackmailers. Then he
started rumors that the Old Man did something terrible back
where he came from. All to back up his story."

Of course, Howard is out of his mind, but suddenly they
are both laughing. Maybe a little hysterical. Why not? The
sky is bright, the sun actually warm. Some nearby pointed
pines are green as spring.

Suzanne's stomach hurts from laughing. "And, Howard,
suppose it was only the Goldfish who wrote those threatening letters to you and Madison for a practical joke?"

Howard likes that one. "Just because she likes to cut
things out and put things together. The Goldfish loves
glue."

"Suppose," says Suzanne, "Roosevelt Lincoln Worthington read in the paper how the Old Man died, and how
Lumberton died, and then he heard and improved that rumor about blackmail in order to get even for not having all
his letters-to-the-editor published."

"Suppose..."

HOWARD AND SUZANNE are laughing hard when they come to the high point in the road. Then the road pitches sharply down. Howard's stomach rises into his mouth and knocks the air out of his laughter. He sucks in a long breath. "Here we go down to find the truth."

"Or part of it," says Suzanne. "There were a lot of parts to the Old Man. All the truth won't be in one place."

The mountainside drops down to a silver chain of river. Heaven-high, hell-deep—but, so far, the river is too far down to look wide. The sky is suddenly darker.

He wonders what there was to laugh about. They are on a fairly straight stretch of road and Suzanne steers with her left hand and laces the fingers of her right hand through his. He is surprised at the comfort and warmth of her strong smooth fingers. "Whatever happens," she says, "you have some good memories. I do. Like the time the Old Man said we needed to be kids for a day and took me to the circus. What is the happiest time you remember with your father, Howard?"

The clouds above are so high, the river in gathering gloom so far below, Howard feels like a tiny speck on the present. He feels back into the past. He remembers how the Old Man walked, arms swinging, fast, jaunty, and yet like he was picking his way. Like a tap dancer in a tuxedo in a mine field. Oh, God, he thinks, forget that.

"Once we fed the pigeons crumbs by the statue of the War Mother on Courthouse Square. My father wasn't in a hurry. He wasn't asking me for anything. We just stood in the sunshine and fed pigeons on a spring day. That was the best time."

Suzanne withdraws her fingers abruptly and Howard misses them. Both her hands are on the wheel because a battered car is overtaking them. Howard opens her purse and takes out the gun. The car passes.

TWENTY-SIX

ALREADY 3:35. Raining. Howard and Suzanne pass a stone church, then a house with a clothesline on the front porch, laundry blowing. Then they are in the town, long and narrow in the gorge cut by the river. Moody: a grim town, although the line of old-fashioned storefronts is brightened by the Hay County Electrical Co-Op, a glistening glass and aluminum building, plainly new.

No blue car has been in sight for some time, but Howard notices that Suzanne is all nerve-endings, not jittery but with eyes in the back of her head and on both sides. She'll be a good ally in a crunch if it comes to it—either from her Gordon or whoever blackmailed the Old Man.

On their left, the river side, is a dime store and a rather prosperous-looking brick bank. Across from these and built into the side of the mountain between two auto dealers is a storefront with venetian blind awry behind gold and black lettering on the window: Hay County Argus.

Howard hobbles over, leaning on Suzanne because they can make better time that way. She smells of roses and rain. Inside, an older man, white haired, maybe seventy, sits at a pine desk at a word processor. He gets up slowly, sticks out his hand: "Howard Justice? And you must be Suzanne Mancini. I don't expect more than one visitor today with his leg bandaged in torn baby pajamas. I'm Army Morgan—Armbruster for long. I know about you because your editor finally got hold of me and filled me in. Phone's been out here. Local company. Sometimes it works. Sometimes it doesn't."

Then Armbruster Morgan laughs: "Ha. Ha. Ha. Ha. Ha." Like machine-gun noise in slow motion. He's boney, stoop-shouldered, faded. But his eyes are electric blue. Bright. This guy misses nothing.

"I enjoyed talking to Lance Jones. We don't talk to the editors of many big city dailies here. Strictly cornball. Ha. Ha. Ha. Ha. Ha."

He hobbles over to the bound volumes of the paper and picks out the cumbersome volume marked 1940-41. He lays it on top of a work table and says "You want to start with the issue of March 12. That's what I understand from your Lance Jones. You want the story about Job Justice.

"Now, excuse me. I'm right on deadline, but I'll be through in a while and we can talk. Mayor convicted of rape here. Big story. Ha. Ha. Ha. Ha. Ha. I'm writing an editorial. I'm against rape. Ha. Ha. Ha. Ha. Ha. I'm always against rape and for civic improvement. Just have to remember which is which. Ha ha ha."

The papers in the bound volumes are tan and brittle. Howard finds the March 12, 1940 issue. The largest headline:

TWO KILLED IN FLOODING

A slightly smaller head, in two layers, is what they're looking for. It reads:

SHOOTING ON RYE ROAD
IS CALLED SELF-DEFENSE

Job Justice, 18, of Rye Road called Sheriff Bill Brank at 10:30 P.M. Wednesday, March 10 to report that Justice had shot an intruder who broke into a second-story window, the sheriff said. John Hutton, found dead by the sheriff in an upstairs bedroom where Justice said the man forced his way, was shot in the right temple and left arm. A wooden ladder was found against the outside of the house.

Hutton was well known to Justice and to his mother, Lou Justice, with whom he lives. Hutton's wife, Mary Jane, sometimes worked for Job Justice's mother. Hutton himself had sometimes done odd jobs around the Justice farm.

Sheriff Brank is looking into the circumstances around the shooting.

Both families have lived in the area for generations. Lou Justice is the widow of William Justice, much-respected Baptist lay preacher who died in 1931.

John Hutton grew up on a farm down the road which has passed out of his family. At the time of his death he and his wife rented a cabin nearby. He is survived by his second wife, Mary Jane. The couple had been married only a year and were childless. Children by his first marriage are demanding a thorough investigation. They are Bill Hutton of Old Sow Road and Ernest Hutton of Dry Creek. A daughter, Martha Hutton, lives in Henderson.

Howard turns to the next issue. A whole week later. Imagine having to wait. The rumors must have been popping like firecrackers. Rumors about the Old Man. Not old then. Ten years younger than Howard is now. Howard is numb. He and Suzanne do not speak. They simply read the largest headline in the March 17 issue:

JUSTICE CHARGED WITH ATTEMPTED MURDER

The sons of John Hutton, who was shot by Job Justice of Rye Road last week in what Justice called self-defense, have charged Justice with attempting to kill them. Justice is alleged to have shot Ernest and Bill Hutton during an altercation at Harlee's on River Road around 7 P.M. on March 14.

The two Hutton men entered the establishment, apparently looking for Justice, onlookers said, and accused him of murdering their father when the elder Hutton tried to stop Justice from having carnal relations with their stepmother, Mary Jane Hutton, 23.

Bill Hutton of Old Sow Road and Ernest Hutton of Dry Creek became enraged when Justice denied the charge, onlookers said, and in the fracas that followed the two brothers were shot. They are at County Hospital, Bill Hutton in stable condition with a gunshot wound in his right shoulder, Ernest Hutton in critical condition with a wound in his neck and another in his right leg.

The brothers have preferred charges against Justice for assault with intent to kill.

There are more stories. All depressing. Week after week. About the Old Man's mother mortgaging her property to raise his bail. The grim woman in the black dress. Who Miss Bounce said looked like a guilty conscience. But she raised his bail. There are stories about the demand for a change of venue because feelings were too high in Hay County.

And finally there's a story about the acquittal. Somehow the Old Man got himself acquitted on the grounds of self-defense in both cases, and left the county. What else could he do? But he must have heard the final story. Someone must have sent it to him. His mother's house burned down the following year and she died in the blaze. "My grandmother," Howard tells himself in amazement. "Even if I never knew her."

The story adds:

Local volunteers fought the blaze by the light of the fire itself and the full moon, with a bucket brigade to the river. But the flames were already too high to save Mrs. Justice.

The sheriff has not been able to find evidence leading to charges against anyone for setting the fire, but many local people believe the fire was meant as revenge against Mrs. Justice's son, Job, who was tried for the murder of John Hutton and the shooting of his sons, Bill and Ernest Hutton. Job Justice was acquitted on the grounds of self-defense in a neighboring county.

"But he never acquitted himself." Howard shuts the volume. "Not during those black moods when he locked himself in his room."

"No." Suzanne nods. "He never acquitted himself. And that is why blackmail could destroy him. Because owning the paper made him feel like a good man. But to shut up about the past, those people demanded that he sell them the paper. How could he decide either way?"

Howard throws himself into the chair in front of the editor's desk. The plain straight chair where people come to tell him stories. Maybe the Old Man's mother sat in that chair and told the editor she knew her son was innocent and she intended to raise bail. Howard buries his face in his hands, feeling on his left hand the silver ring his father gave him when he graduated from high school, and feeling hopeless.

"Bad stuff," says Armbruster Morgan. "Bad stuff to read about your own father. And he wasn't a bad boy. I knew him."

There's a knock on the front door. Not a "May-I-come-in" knock. Somebody on the way in bumps against the door. Suzanne stiffens, clutches her pocketbook, but Howard is so depressed he has to force himself to notice.

Through the door bursts a tow-headed young woman who looks at the editor and says "Ready?" False alarm.

"Ready," says Morgan, and he hands her the editorial he has been typing. "My daughter," he explains. "She's my right hand. She takes the copy to the printer. Paper'll be on the street tomorrow."

"Now," he says, "come to my house and we'll talk. We may get wet. Sure is raining! Three days ago, rain in buckets, day before yesterday, snow and sleet. Today rain. Some weather! Ha. Ha. Ha. Ha. Ha."

TWENTY-SEVEN

4:48 P.M. HALF AN HOUR plus two minutes to Howard's deadline. He and Suzanne have come in out of the rain to the editor's dusky front hall. Howard picks up the phone from a small table near a coat rack to give Lance a progress report. Certainly he knows enough now so that his family will believe his father was being blackmailed. Will that be enough?

He puts phone to his ear: no dial tone, no noise of any sort.

"May work in a while," says Armbruster Morgan. "Fickle as a woman. Ha. Ha. Ha. Ha. Ha."

Morgan gives Howard a glass of whiskey and hands a glass to Suzanne, too. Then the editor sits down in front of his wall of books, old bare books in muted reds and greens and blues and faded black, interspersed with gleaming dust covers of the newer books. So much like the books in the Old Man's study at home.

The editor rocks gently in a dark wood rocking chair, an old man with young eyes. "I liked your father, Howard," he says matter of factly. "Your father was a bright kid. He'd stop by the paper and bring me news from the time he was six or eight. The Jones' mule got in the Haywoods' corn. There's an outbreak of lice in the schools. Little things, but a country paper needs that kind of stuff. I used to lend your father books. I wasn't so old myself. Just about twenty-three. Ha. Ha. Ha."

Howard forces himself to see his father as a kid, maybe sitting in the high-backed chair where Howard sits now. His father would have wanted to know everything in the wall of books. Howard also sees his father holding a gun: grounds for blackmail.

"Job did little jobs for me. He needed to get away from his mother. A good woman. Maybe too good. She never let him be. She was like a hen with one chick."

Why should Howard care about hens? Morgan demands it.

"A hen usually has ten or twelve chicks. When there is only one she clucks all around it. Your father had to do something to prove he was himself and not just his mother's wing. Ha. Ha. Ha. He took up with women. Married women. They're safer unless the husband finds out."

"But the husband found out?"

"That," says the editor, beginning to rock back and forth more briskly, "is how it seemed to me."

"And my father killed him." Howard hears his voice loud and accusing. As if the editor is guilty.

"Rather than be killed."

"I would have done the same thing." Suzanne raises her head, sits straight on the shabby couch. Howard realizes he and the editor had almost stopped noticing her there. "If the gun were aimed at me, I'd shoot first."

"Yes." Morgan nods his white head. "So would I. So would every man in these mountains. That is why your father was acquitted." He is so calm.

"But listen!" Howard cries out. "One man dead, two men shot, the house burned and my grandmother burned with it. All that because my father had to shoot first. And now, more than thirty years later, my father was murdered, my brother's wife killed by jumping out a window, another man blown up. All that began with my father shooting first. Just because another man would have shot first, that doesn't make it all right."

There is an awkward silence. Morgan and Suzanne give him space, but uneasily, as if they feel he has a right to be out of his mind for a little while.

Howard's eyes fall on Morgan's square clock, sitting on the table littered with books: 5:17. He has no right to be out of control. He's here for a reason.

"Who came to look at the records before us?"

"A lawyer fellow." The editor is rocking again, sipping his drink. "Said he was doing some research on a case. Arranged to borrow the bound volume and get the stories copied at the town hall."

Prompt Herbert says the Gemtrex lawyer has a birthmark like a mushroom on one cheek. "Did he have a birthmark in a funny shape?"

"Like a toadstool."

Howard jumps up. "He used those copies to blackmail my father. I have to use the phone. It has to be working now."

But the phone by the door is silent against his ear. No dial tone. Now he's really in shock.

"Crazy local phone company," says the editor. "Comes and goes. Interrupted my talk with your editor this morning or maybe I'd have told him about the lawyer. But look here, I'm sorry about the blackmail. I didn't know at the time. Is there anything I can do to help?"

"I've got to get through or my family is going to sell *The Defender* to the company that had been blackmailing my father. They can sell any time after 5:30."

The clock now says 5:20. Morgan pushes Howard hopping toward the door, and talks like a whirlwind: "Nearest phone that ties with another phone company is half an hour from here, on the Interstate. In the Amoco station. Half an hour by the river road. I'll keep trying to phone Lance, too." He whips open the hall closet door and grabs something out as he talks. "Turn-off to the Interstate isn't too far. One old bridge to cross, weakened in earlier floods. Don't worry. No bad floods in February. Bad ones are in March.

"And, here." Morgan thrusts a wooden cane at Howard. "To help you hurry. Left from the time I broke my leg chasing a pretty girl. Ha, Ha. Ha. Ha. Ha. Ha."

TWENTY-EIGHT

OUTSIDE THE PELTING RAIN forces its way into Howard's ears and mouth, turns his clothing liquid, rushes under his feet. As he hurries to the car, leaning on his new cane, words pour out of him as if his insides are melting, melting and pouring out through his mouth. "I believed in him. I believed in my father. From the time I was little."

The Old Man said "Believe nothing you hear and only half of what you see." He meant without proof. Howard has proof his father killed a man, and hid it from his family.

Suzanne runs ahead through the driving rain and opens the car door for him. The rain turns her hair into glistening black rivulets with clear drops at the end, her lashes into black points.

Howard slides onto the cold leather car seat which squeaks with his wetness. It's almost 5:30. Miss Bounce and Madison and Alice may be getting out their pens to sign, to sell *The Defender*. They are a majority. The BMW still smells faintly of the Old Man's cigarette smoke, now mixed with the aroma of wet clothes. Suzanne starts the motor and against its low hum Howard hears his own voice louder: "All that good stuff—standing up for justice, finding the truth—all that was just to cover what he did."

"Yes," Suzanne says evenly, eyes on the road. "He needed to prove he was a good man, and to keep on proving it again and again and again."

The rain sheets down the windshield, more than the wipers can remove. The water sheets and twists in rivulets at the window edges, and Howard sees Cleo twisting and turning

n the water which is smooth like her thighs, supple like her
rms.

"We felt we had to live up to him. Maybe me the most,
ut all of us in the family felt we had to live up to him. Even
he ones who married in, like Cleo, felt they weren't good
nough."

Suzanne is quiet, concentrating. Water pours off the side
f the mountain in small impromptu brooks, gleaming in
he car lights. The rain is melting the last of the ice and
now. Suzanne holds the steering wheel tight. She puts all
er intensity into keeping the car steady. Howard admires
er concentration. And hates it.

"He used you, Suzanne! Don't you care?" Cleo still
himmies in the rain water. Suzanne would be just as lovely
aked—lovelier. And her smooth body was like one more
rink of whiskey for his father. A way to forget without
bligation. "Don't you care that he treated you like a
hore?"

"He didn't." Suzanne grips the wheel so hard that the
ones stand out on her slender hands. She keeps her eyes on
he road. "He needed me. I knew he couldn't be tied down.
accepted that. That is not being used. Being used is not
nowing."

"Like me. My father tricked me." A sharp slap of water
its the landward side of the car, which swerves. Howard
els slapped. Suzanne wrestles the car back straight.

Howard ought to be quiet. He sees how hard the driving
. God knows he wants to reach the phone that works. But
e words keep pouring out. "My father made me feel I had
mething to live up to, something so great it didn't matter
I forgot about everything else, didn't matter if other peo-
e got mad at me. Because he said I was right."

Gusts of wind seem to be trying to blow the car right off
the road. Then the wind lulls and the road turns up, farther
from the water. A breather.

Suzanne turns and glares at Howard. Does he deserve
that? Her nostrils distend in the faint light from the dashboard. Her mouth puckers in contempt.

"Maybe you helped trick yourself, Howard Justice
Didn't you like being Number One? Didn't you like feeling
so important? I did when I was tricked. Didn't you?"

"I helped him do it? Me?"

Suzanne raises her chin, a proud silhouette in the half
light, daring him to agree. "Swindles work like that, don'
they, Howard? Playing up to fear and hope and greed so the
person helps swindle himself. You did a story about swin
dles. The poor widow. You ought to know."

He remembers the widow who gave her money to a for
tune-teller to get the curse taken off so the money would
multiply. She got back a purse of shredded newspaper, be
cause she wanted to believe in magic.

"You think I'm like that stupid widow?"

Suzanne turns toward him again and this time the fain
light shows a wry smile. "Why shouldn't you be human
Howard? Personally I like you better human than wearing
that damned halo. I like you sweating a little like the rest o
us."

He begins to sweat, all right. The road has wound back
right down to the river and the water is rising fast, coming
close to the edge of the road. The rain is so hard the wind
shield wipers can't keep up. The roar of the river invades th
car, changing constantly. Higher, then lower, with occa
sional snaps and crunches.

There is water on both sides of the road now. On the sid
away from the river, the water from streams on the moun

tain crashes into a natural trough in the land and makes another river.

"We have to turn back." Suzanne raises her voice and still Howard has to strain to hear. She has been driving very slowly, leaning forward and peering through the sheeting rain. "We aren't even to the bridge yet. We won't make it to the road that turns up to the bridge. Help me look for a place wide enough to turn."

Howard opens his window on the river side of the car and leans out into the wet to look for wide spots, and to warn if the car gets too close to the rushing muddy water. The water writhes and falls over itself as it rises.

He turns and sees how strongly Suzanne holds the wheel. She looks as determined as the masthead on a ship.

"Suzanne," he blurts, "I love you." She does not appear to hear. The river is too loud.

In fact, the voice from the back seat only gradually separates itself from the roar. "You are not going to turn around." A man's voice, gravelly and menacing and theatrical as if he's playing himself in a soap opera. Except plainly he's not playing. He must have been crouched down in the dark behind the seat when they got in. Howard even threw his cane in the back without seeing him.

With one fast motion, Howard snaps on the flashlight lying on the seat and turns, sweeping the beam of light past Suzanne until the round spot circles two white pudgy hands, holding a gun.

Round black hole at the end of black blunt barrel: that's where death comes from. And behind that is the larger black cylinder head-on like an old-fashioned telephone dial. But each number on the dial is the rounded end of a bullet, waiting.

The face in back of the gun is sick-pale in the faint light and Howard recognizes its roundness.

"You've been following me. Who are you?"

"Ask your woman." The voice glows with contempt. Howard would like to shake the man like his dog once shook a rat, but the gun aims right at Howard's neck.

"You set two bombs."

"Assuredly I did. You thought you were clever to avoid them. So now I am here in person."

"Gordon, you look terrible." Suzanne must be looking at him in the rearview mirror. She keeps driving slowly.

"I got too flabby when I was in prison, thanks to you."

Suzanne reaches casually into her purse as if she's reaching for a handkerchief.

"We have to turn around or we will all drown." Howard speaks harshly to annoy Gordon, to divert him from Suzanne. But Gordon leans forward as fast as a snake striking and touches his gun to Suzanne's neck. "I don't know what you're reaching for in that bag, but give it to me. I don't trust you, my sweet."

Moonface opens the bag, pulls out the gun and laughs. "Trust makes way for treachery." He sticks Suzanne's pistol in his pocket. What can Howard do? Exactly what the man says while the gun is on Suzanne.

Moonface makes Howard open the glove compartment and also take off his jacket and turn the sleeves inside out. Howard is numb with cold and he hates the way Gordon's mouth puckers like a baby refusing spinach.

"Now, drive on," Gordon orders Suzanne, "straight into the flood. I've dreamed of this, my dear. We'll be together dead." His gun points at the back of Suzanne's beautiful live head. "This whore—I'm glad you agree she is a whore—sucked my money, led me into crime and then left me in prison to rot without one letter while she jumped into bed with a richer man. That is the kind of a woman she is."

Howard would like to defend Suzanne. Whatever she's done, Gordon has no right to be here with his gun. But Howard is sure that Gordon is not here to be reasonable.

"I mean your father, of course." His voice is oily and pleased with rubbing in what Howard does not want to think about.

"What do you know about my father?"

"My dear boy, I have friends who did write. I made it my business to find out where Suzanne was and exactly what she was doing." Still that poetry-reciting voice.

"It was just like my whore of a wife to jump from the dead man to whoever inherited his money. And when I reached the scene, I could see you'd be the one, young man. That's why I have been trying to kill you. You are obviously the type my wife likes. Naive. Pliable."

"I am not your wife, Gordon." Dear God, don't let Suzanne make him so mad he shoots.

A break: the road turns in from the water, but up ahead Howard is sickened to see a swirling stream at right angles to the road. The stream comes sharply down a rocky course and part under, part over an old bridge with cement post rails. That must be the bridge that Morgan says needs replacing! Howard hardly breathes as they float more than drive across the bridge, already swept by water. Thank God the BMW is so heavy, so dependable, not one bit more power than they need. The motor sputters when they are almost across, but momentum carries the car and the motor catches again.

"The next place will catch us in the torrent. 'There is a tide in men's affairs which taken at the flood leads on to fortune.'" Gordon laughs. "I intended to drive us off the mountain, but now I think we will just keep driving between the river and the cliff until the river washes us away. More suspense to that, don't you think, Suzanne?"

Ugly laugh again. "I became wiser in prison, Suzanne. I know exactly what I want, now, and I won't even let you go to hell with another man. We'll all go together."

Josh used to sing a song about the end of the world: "Oh, we'll all go together when we go."

At least the road is going uphill now, even if the gun is still at their backs. Howard would like to choke that pale fungus in the back seat. If he tries anything, a bullet will be in Suzanne's brain. She is driving steadily forward so that lights high above them on the right seem to move. They seem too faint for electricity, must be candles. So the power is out.

The house on the mountain must be on a parallel road at a higher level. Above the flood.

Behind the car comes a greater thunder and Howard shouts "The bridge!" The cement bridge is breaking into pieces in back of them like a cake crumbling.

"So we can't go back," Gordon exults. "Nature is your executioner."

And then Howard sees water swirl ahead. A crashing stream from high above has cut a channel through the road cement, which ends jagged. A chunk breaks off and is washed away. Suzanne whistles. Even the car seems to react. The motor finally dies. But then there is no place to go.

They all get out and Gordon hands Howard his cane with a bow. They walk through the rain to the edge, not the crumbling edge of the road but the dirt by its side. The dirt is at least safer because it washes away in layers, not huge undependable chunks. Gordon stands by the flood, grinning. Suzanne stares at it, frowning.

The channel is too swift to swim, and yet just four car lengths across the foaming water the cement road begins again, jagged at the edge.

Howard can feel Suzanne draw in her breath hard as she grabs his arm. She points. Something long and rounded like a huge fish is bobbing past. The thing is hard to see except by the shine of its wetness in the headlights, dark, with one end showing white as it tosses and spins. And then the light spot comes clear as a face. The river is carrying a dead man hurling past their feet. A man who trusted himself too close to that current.

"We'll be like that." Gordon stands in the headlight glow, nodding his head with satisfaction. Howard would like to see him bobbing dead in the water, paunchy stomach up. Alone.

"And your paper will be sold to the mob. I was hired to help make that happen." He shouts to be heard. "You see how clever I was. I got paid for what I wanted to do. I'll die rich. We will all die together."

A rock that stood back from the water's edge is now surrounded by a swirling eddy. Howard would like to pick up that rock and bash in Gordon's rich skull. Another chunk of the near end of the road, undermined, sags and breaks away with a splash.

"Salvador Smith, revered by the mob, will be publisher of *The Defender*. They call him 'The Hermit.' The only thing that man fears is publicity he can't control. You are going to die. He is going to flourish."

They all step back from the rising water. Howard is desperate to give Gordon a push. He can feel his hands heaving that bulk. But the gun is still pointed at Suzanne. Howard has maneuvered himself next to the left side of the man. Suzanne is on the other side.

The water, so close to their feet, tears at the land hungrily. A surge goes over Howard's foot.

"How long were you in prison?" Howard shouts over the flood. Dumb question. Moonface doesn't answer. Howard wonders desperately how to divert the man.

"There are lights up there moving. Someone is coming to help us." The lights do not move, merely flicker, but they catch Gordon's attention, throw him off balance for a second. Suzanne steps in back of him. Howard spins and grabs Gordon's gun arm with both hands, twisting it to make him drop the gun. Howard won the office arm wrestle year before last and the stakes weren't nearly as high. But Gordon is surprisingly strong, also slippery. He is trying not just to keep hold of the gun but to topple them both into the flood. Howard's feet are slipping in the mud. He is not sure at any moment which way the gun is pointed as they tussle. Suzanne is kicking and pulling Gordon from behind. Howard can feel her impact through the bulk of the man as Howard struggles to pull back toward the land. They teeter and slip on the edge of the water.

Suddenly Howard is rocked by an incredibly loud flat pop. He knows he's been hit. A flash of light between their bodies lights up Gordon's pale grinning face.

Howard keeps hold of the man's gun hand, forcing it away. Howard is not dead yet. He won't let Gordon shoot again. Howard is dizzy. There's a smell like black pepper. Gordon is not struggling. A trick? Suzanne is down beside them crying. Am I wounded that badly? Howard wonders. Nothing hurts. Maybe he is in shock.

Gordon does not move except that one arm in the water wavers in the current. Howard touches Gordon's chest and his hand comes away bloody. Then the rain thins the red to pink drips.

Gordon is dead and Suzanne is weeping for him. "He wasn't like this," she sobs. "He wasn't so ugly when I met him. He wasn't even so stuffy. He even looked good."

"Thank God," cries Howard. "Thank God he's dead—and we're alive."

Suzanne tosses back her wet hair and stops crying. "He was ugly inside, but it didn't show. Until he beat me up, God rest his soul. Thank God he's dead."

Still on her knees beside Howard, she throws her arms around him. She's slippery with rain and tears and she cries out "We won't drown. We won't!"

Howard is damn well going to save Suzanne, whether it is possible or not. He remembers what the Old Man said: "When you see no hope, start fighting." He was right about that.

IN THE MIDDLE OF the rain and flood Suzanne feels the presence of her grandmother Mancini who is at home with death. Who talks quietly to the family dead, as if they had wandered into the room. Suzanne feels her grandmother there in the night, taking hold of her hand, gripping her hand. She hears her grandmother's voice, rising with fear: "Be careful. He is here."

TWENTY-NINE

HOWARD'S HOPE WAVERS. The fever pitch of fighting Gordon was a high. That's over. Gordon's body lies pushed under the BMW, on the highest spot of their tiny island. Now, what on earth can Howard and Suzanne do? The storm slows to scattered raindrops and the wind holds its breath. But the water keeps rising fiercely, fueled by the streams from higher up. Their island is vanishing under the waves. He must not give in to panic. At least Suzanne will have a clear head. She always has in an emergency.

But Suzanne throws her arms around him. She's scared. She is trembling and cold as frozen iron. Her voice shakes. "He is with us, Howard. His ghost. Pulling us down."

"What?" He holds Suzanne so tight that he feels water squeeze out of her clothes. He can't stop her from shaking. He speaks into her wet hair. "Gordon is dead. We have to save ourselves. To be calm. I love you."

"I don't mean Gordon's ghost!" She pulls back and stares at Howard as if he's lost his mind. He half believes he has. "Your father's ghost is with us, Howard."

Her terror is catching. He feels a negative electricity around them as if his hair is standing on end. Damn it, his hair is not standing on end.

"He's here in the storm, Howard. The Old Man. Unable to let go."

What can Howard do to get her out of this state before it's too late? He doesn't know. She is beautiful even in her terror. *The Beautiful and Damned*. A book the Old Man loved. The Old Man is still with Howard—O.K., it's true. But he's inside his head. Howard can't believe in ghosts. Believe nothing you hear and only half of what you see.

The ghost in Suzanne's eyes flows around him. The Old Man is rage. Rage is all around Howard. Screaming inside his head, shrieking in the wind and water. He is losing his mind. They escaped Gordon. They will drown with the ghost, whether it's real or not.

"Listen to me." Suzanne's lips are against Howard's ear. "His anger is the cold. We couldn't look at his anger while he was alive, Howard. Because he was too alive. Because he laughed too much. Because he willed us not to. Now, it's here. Loose against us."

"No." He shuts his eyes. Her lips are soft against his ear. She's alive and close. For how long?

"My God, Suzanne, he's gone and I'm still here. You can see my father's damned ghost and not even see me. And we may be about to die." He wants to make love to her. He wants to shake her until her teeth rattle. He is out of control.

She wants him to feel possessed. The thought makes his stomach churn like the flood waters. Makes him shut his eyes. That doesn't help. He hears the lurches and snaps of objects carried away by the water, the wind risen again, the world around him disintegrating. Chaos.

The sound of chaos is like rage. Like the time Miss Bounce threw a glass vase full of roses and water against the wall. Like the Old Man's door slamming. He lets himself feel his father's door slamming rage at having, by God, to be smarter, funnier, more right then any other man, of having to be perfect or shit. Because he killed a man. Rage growing. Because nobody can be perfect. Nobody can make the people around him, who are somehow a part of him, perfect. Not Josh, not Alice, not Madison, not Howard. And Suzanne wants Howard to feel that rage.

Howard is shaking. The whole world around him is that rage, destroying bridges, trees, sucking him into its force field. He's angry too. At what that rage has done to him. To Suzanne. He feels the ghost, almost sucking his breath away.

"I didn't know my own father." His words surprise him. "First I believed every word he said because I wanted to, and then I hated him for it. Oh God, I'm sorry." The water rolls away a stone not far from Howard's feet. A stone. They have no time.

Suzanne disengages herself from his arms, stands straight and tall, arms outthrown, and calls into the storm: "We see you. Go in peace."

She motions for Howard to say it too. He feels like a fool but he shouts it too, his voice in chorus with the wildness of the storm. Then he feels wildly relieved. If he doesn't believe in his father's ghost, how is he suddenly sure it has gone to rest? The ghost is gone. His mind is clear.

But Suzanne is shouting something very strange. "Howard, my grandmother loves you."

Howard hasn't even met Suzanne's grandmother. Not that he knows of. It's Suzanne he wants to love him. But first they must survive.

THIRTY

THE WIND WHIPS Howard's wet hair. Suzanne's hair whips against their faces as they kiss.

"We have to fight." Now Howard is angry. "Fight with what? A few rocks? The car?" He remembers Gordon had the flashlight. He must have dropped it in the water. Score one for Moonface.

"There must be some way." Suzanne tugs him toward the BMW, still solid on the crown of their tiny island. The BMW: more power than the Old Man needed, now stalled with headlights pale.

"We could take two tires off the car and float on the inner tubes," he scoffs. Radial tires don't have inner tubes. "We could shut the windows tight and float away in the air bubble of the car."

"And when the windows broke or the air gave out, then we'd die." In spite of saying that, Suzanne opens the car door and climbs in.

Inside, at least they don't have to shout. There has to be some escape. "We could send an SOS with the lights," Howard suggests. "Except with the motor dead, the lights are dim, and getting dimmer."

"I'll try to start the motor." Suzanne is already turning the key.

Even if they manage to send Morse code with the lights, who will see them? The lights that flickered above are gone now. The people must be asleep. Or maybe they like sitting and looking out the window in the dark. Maybe they have insomnia. Dear God, let whoever lives on the ridge have the worst case of insomnia in history.

The motor coughs like a death rattle again and again.

There must be water on the wires, but if they raise the hood to wipe them dry, the wires will only get wetter.

"Let me try, Suzanne. Sometimes a change of people will make a thing work." With all the use he's had to give it, Howard's sprained foot is actually feeling better, not worse. That's odd, but thank God. Suzanne gets out, to examine the water level, she says. There's not much else left.

He turns the key. Death rattle again. Outside, a tree floats by, branches ghostly in the dark. The outreaching tip of a branch scrapes against the window of the car. The water is that high. Thank God the branch is on the opposite side of the car from Suzanne. He turns the key again. There's a little catch. Then the rattle. The spark almost catches, but not quite.

Suzanne climbs back in, leaving the door a little ajar to watch the water level.

He turns the key again. A tentative catch, a tentative rattle, and the car starts. They both cry out. There's a chance. He pulls and pushes the knob for the lights. On-off, on-off, on-off. He learned the rhythm for SOS in the Boy Scouts. Still no light on the hill. On-off, on-off, on-off. A large tree on the other side of the flood channel appears and disappears as the lights flash. The tree is on the safe side, not that far away, but impossible to reach. He keeps flashing the lights until his hand is sore. He opens the door and looks out because Suzanne is not telling him how high the water is. He can see why. It's only a couple of feet from the wheels. On-off, on-off, on-off. Howard would like to forget the SOS and spend his last moments making love to Suzanne. This is going to be a useless way to die. He doesn't deserve it.

How long have they been flashing the lights? It seems like hours.

He leans across the passenger seat and gestures to Suzanne to flash the headlights. She moves across and takes his place. So determined. So vulnerable. So wet. He gets out and yells "Help! Help!" He keeps shouting. Nobody will hear, but it's one last thing he can do. Even standing next to the car he has one foot in water. "Help! Help!" He has been yelling forever.

From the far bank he hears an echo. No. Not an echo! A pale light gleams from the bank near a tree. Is he imagining people there? Four men. Appear. Disappear. On-off. On-off.

Suzanne stops flashing the lights, and whispers "Holy Mother of God." The lights make two uneven holes in the dark, clear enough to show four gangly men without a boat. What can the men do? But they are doing something. Howard and Suzanne get out of the car and stand close, shaking with hope. She stands in back of him. There is no longer room for them to stand side by side.

"They have a rope!" Suzanne cries. "A rope!" Howard holds onto the car and Suzanne holds onto Howard because an occasional wave sucks at their feet. He waves one arm, trying to say "Hurry."

But the men do not hurry. Two of them are tying the rope around a tree, slowly and methodically testing the rope. The water is almost to the wheels of the car.

Then a third man, tall and wearing a red plaid shirt, stands up holding a small log in his hand. The rope is tied to the log. He aims with care and throws toward Howard. But the log falls just short and is whipped away by the current.

The men pull the log back in, hand over hand, three of them straddling the rope, one in back of the other, pulling slowly. The tallest man, the one in the plaid shirt, takes aim again. This time the log falls with a thunk on the roof of the car, and Howard manages to reach and grab it before it falls off. He ties the rope as tight as he can to the front bumper of the car. The water is already lapping at the tires.

"You go first, Suzanne."

"We'll go together."

"No. The rope will be safer with the weight of one at a time. Hurry."

She kisses him quickly, grabs the rope and starts across. He watches, breathing hard, afraid the river will pull her loose, and each glimpse may be the last of that determined dark head. She has one elbow over the rope, using both hands to pull herself along. The current pulls her out flat from the straining rope. Howard prays his knot will hold. He tied it in a mad hurry, but double and triple.

A large squarish tin, gleaming and spinning in the headlights, comes hurtling down the side stream, toward Suzanne. Howard calls "Watch out!" But she can't hear him. The tin wobbles in the current, hits the rope and bounces over it, just in the place she was a moment before, then swirls off twinkling in the main stream, out of sight. The current whips off Suzanne's shoe, flipping it up almost playfully, before it sinks and vanishes. Suzanne is three quarters of the way across, rope strained into a wide curve, water sucking hard against her body.

The water is also sucking hard at the right front tire of the car. Dear God, Howard thinks, don't let the car go yet. Let Suzanne get across, and me too.

Three of the four men on the other side form a chain, one holding tight to the tree, and holding onto the arm of the second man who holds the third. He leans out ready to grab Suzanne. In spite of the branch that comes whirling down the stream and tangles in the rope, Suzanne is almost on the

ar side. The men grab her and pull her up on the hillside.
Thank God.

Now Howard lets himself into the cold grabbing water
and starts across, not prepared for the force of the water,
even after watching Suzanne. The suction is so great he can
hardly hold onto the rope, even with his elbow over. Inch by
inch he snakes across. His clothes become water sails trying
to pry him loose. Two wheels of the car are in the water
now. The river will suck it into the flood and break the rope.
His shoes go, ripped violently from his feet, and he expects
to lose his pants. The river is so cold that his sprained ankle
does not even hurt. The branch is still tangled in the rope
and that makes his elbow-hold difficult. The branch vibrates with the water. But he keeps on, hand over hand, even
when the vibrating branch sends out twigs to scratch his face
and rake his body. A log thunks against the branch and
rope, catches, adds to the weight against the rope. Howard
is three-quarters of the way across. He is praying under his
breath. "Please God, let the rope hold. Let the car hold."
On the bank he catches a glimpse of Suzanne, holding tight
to the tree and watching him. She is very still in the midst of
chaos. Worth living for.

A door, complete with white china doorknob, hurtles
down the stream toward Howard, hits the rope hard, and as
he expects the rope to break, the door skips over with a loud
splash and hurtles on. He prays the door won't be followed
by the side of a house or a roof. He is almost across, beyond the clutching fingers of the branch and he even still has
his pants on.

Then Suzanne screams. He feels what her shout means.
The car is about to go. The men form a chain again, even
though Howard still has several feet to go. He slithers along
the rope as fast as he can. Even near the shore the current
grabs. Just as he is almost to the reaching hands, he hears

Suzanne shout again in terror. His hands fly over each other so quickly that he is almost sucked loose between grasps.

And then he feels hands grabbing his arms as the rope snaps under him, whips against one leg, burning his skin. His sleeve tears loose from a grabbing hand with a sickening slide, and he feels himself about to be carried away after all. But strong hands have his other arm and hold firm even though the arm is almost wrenched from its socket.

His feet are on the slippery ground. He struggles up and grabs the tree. Kneeling because his legs shake, and holding onto the roughness of the tree, half expecting the water to chase him up the shore and jerk him loose. Suzanne kneels next to him smiling. "You can let go, Howard. We made it. Thank God. We just barely made it. The car is gone."

The man in the red shirt puts a large hand on his shoulder. "Boy, the good Lord done sent you a miracle! Come on, Boy. You can't hold onto that tree all night."

THIRTY-ONE

"HUTTON'S Mountain View Motel" says an unlit neon sign in front of a large log cabin marked "office." One of the four rescuers, the tall one, Robert, picks out the sign with his flashlight. Six smaller cabins stand along the road, all dark. Others fade into the blackness at a right angle to the office. Hutton's! An alarm sounds inside Howard's head. The Old Man killed the husband of Mary Jane Hutton, and shot his sons.

The place seems deserted. Howard does not see any cars in front except one empty pickup truck. Probably these cabins are used by summer tourists, and deserted now. In a county like Hay, whoever escaped the flood would head for relatives, not a motel.

Amazing that with the flood down below, on the ridge it's raining, no more. The ridge is safe. Safe? Not if these are the Huttons in the newspaper stories. The rescuers seem too young. But who else is in the family?

Inside, there's candlelight and Mrs. Hutton, who cries "Glory be, boys, you saved 'em!" She adds "Welcome." She is about the Old Man's age, a plump dyed-blond re- axed woman in a cotton housedress and a blue sweater, crocheting by candle-flicker. No husband in sight.

"Do you have a phone?" Howard asks. But when he tries the phone on the rustic motel counter on one side of the living room, it's dead. And there's no easy way to get to a phone that works "unless you want to swim," Robert ex- plains. The road out of here dips through the valley again.

So be it. Suzanne and Howard are alive. Otherwise, one thing at a time.

Mrs. Hutton's first thought is to get something to eat. Good. Howard is ravenous. Howard and Suzanne sit on the orange-flowered couch feasting on leftover cornbread, a hot-dog-and-string-bean casserole and spicy homemade apple cake. Meanwhile, Mrs. Hutton wants to hear every word of their adventures.

Howard omits the Old Man and also Gordon from his part of the story. So does Suzanne. It's still a pretty good story. Mrs Hutton loves it, loves her boys being heroes. "The boys can do anything," she boasts. "They're the best rifle shots in the county, best volunteer firemen." The four boys, sitting around the little room in the edge of the candlelight, laugh at her bragging, but they are pretty pleased with themselves, too. They pitch in and tell how their lights went out and after a while they all told ghost stories in the dark with the grandchildren, who have gone off to their house now with their mother. ("My only daughter," says Mrs. Hutton with pride.) Robert tells how Sandra Sue, who is ten, threw one of Mrs. Hutton's crocheted pillows at Mary Ann, who is eight—threw it so hard she broke the windowpane right out. "Because, you see, the pillow missed Mary Ann and the window needed putty." And when the boys boarded up the window they saw the SOS. Howard shivers. Talk about close calls.

Mrs. Hutton has almost adopted Howard and Suzanne into the family. She's so pleased with the family bravery, the family good deed, the family ability to break windows at exactly the right moment.

"And what did you say your last name was, Howard?"

He knows he mustn't hesitate. Justice is a common name Maybe Hutton is a common name around here.

But after he tells Mrs. Hutton there's an odd silence. He hears the rain on the roof. The four boys fidget, frown.

"And you're not from these parts?" Mrs Hutton asks.

"Just visiting Armbruster Morgan."

"Well, I expect you're tired. Robert, show Mr. and Mrs. Justice to the double cabin. I turned on the heater when I was getting the food."

Howard tries the phone once more. Still dead. He prays that Armbruster Morgan has gotten through to Lance.

"We've not got but one cabin with a phone," says Mrs. Hutton. "We'll put you in that one." Good. He can make collect or credit card calls. She hasn't entirely banished him from trust.

She fills out a form, very businesslike, and Howard pays her. No, he's not a member of the family anymore. But there are rewards to truth telling and button-up pants pockets. He can pay her with his credit card. He is also rewarded for not telling more than he was asked. He will share the cabin with Suzanne. And there's an extra bonus for looking wet and tired even after sitting next to the kerosene stove: Robert slips him a bottle of corn whiskey. "Just gimme $12 and don't tell Ma. After a day like today, you sure need a little something."

The cabin is clean and simple, and contains two three-quarter-width beds with green spreads, two green plastic chairs (he sits in one), a table between them, and—thank God—the telephone. Still dead, but the editor says it comes and goes. A candle lights the room pleasantly. A gas heater has already taken the chill off. Suzanne goes in the bathroom and he hears the water running. "Hot water!" she calls happily, then goes over to the bed farthest from the heater and pulls a white sheet off.

"I am going to take a very hot bath, Howard, and then dress myself in a nice dry sheet like a Roman Senator. Then

I'll warm up even more sharing a glass of that whiskey with you."

Howard is warm just thinking about it.

Even in her half-dried, rain-wrinkled suit, and with every bit of make up washed off, Suzanne is beautiful. Even at the end of a day like today, adventure shimmers in her eyes.

Howard tries the phone again. A dial tone! Now he'll find out whether Miss Bounce and Madison and Alice sold *The Defender* instantly or waited just a few hours to find out what they discovered in Hay County. He says a prayer and dials. Miss Bounce can be pretty damned determined. The deadline is past. He calls Lance first. He holds the phone right against the side of his face and listens to the ring.

He'd rather hear the worst from Lance.

But Lance's hello is cheerful. Relieved. "There you are, Boy. We were worried."

"And the paper?"

"Is still O.K." Thank God. Lance sounds downright casual about that. "Boy, things are pretty upheaved around here with Josh vanished and Cleo dead, and Madison drunk for the first time I ever saw, and you off drowning in a flood for all we knew. Everything about the paper is on hold. What did you find out up there?"

Telling Lance about the Old Man hurts. But then Lance is wildly excited about the definite mob connection with the purchase offer. He's all set to look into Salvador (the Hermit) Smith who is supposed to be in back of it. "You say he hates publicity? Boy, we'll show him the meaning of the word."

Lance sounds ready to shoot a cannon and pour champagne. "Boy, you've done it! Proved those bastards who want to buy the paper are crooks. Boy, I love you." At the same time Howard can hear the splash of Suzanne's bath-water.

So now Howard feels strong enough to call Miss Bounce. To tell the story again. She listens. Says almost nothing. Is she angry? Pleased? Is she quiet because she's trying not to cry? "Thank God you're safe, Howard." Subdued. That's how she sounds. Amazing. Howard is touched.

He calls Madison last, because that's hardest. As he waits for his brother to answer, Suzanne slips out of the bathroom. No Roman senator ever filled out a sheet the way she does. She gets two glasses and pours the whiskey.

Madison is even quieter than Miss Bounce was. Monotone. "Madison, I love you. I know what a hard time this is for you." What else can he say to poor Madison, who hates scandal, whose much loved wife will never comfort him again because she killed herself.

Howard hangs up and sighs. Suzanne sits down in his lap and says "I'm sorry." And he soars. Soars with the joy of being alive instead of drowned, being alive and close to Suzanne. The pain in his heart and in his rope-burned leg and sprained foot, all that pain is part of being alive.

Suzanne hands him a glass of whiskey. So. She studied to be a nurse. He takes a few sips of her medicine. "Wait until I put on my toga," he says.

The motel may be simple, but the shower is piping hot. The storm seems far away. So does his father's ghost. Was there a ghost?

He puts on his sheet and laughs. Julius Caesar, move over. He perches on the chair across the table from Suzanne. He feels the warmth of the heater, the warmth of the whiskey and most of all the warmth of Suzanne sink into his bones, like rain after a long drought. Forget rain. He also forgets about the four Hutton boys who are crack shots, forgets that he killed a man, forgets about Josh waiting for the end of the world, about Cleo, about the Old Man. He gets up and the pain in his legs is part of the fierceness of being alive. Suzanne gets up, too, and stretches out her arms to him. The sheet, which was anchored under her arms, drops away and she stands with her dark hair curling around her, skin glowing in the yellow candle glow which lights her round breasts and proud chin from below.

Howard remembers a picture that hangs in Leeroy's apartment. The nearest Leeroy has to a pin-up, Venus stepping from the waves. Suzanne is a dark Venus stepping from the waves of the sheet. He forgets Leeroy, who would like to be here in his place.

As Howard and Suzanne step together they both trip over the sheets around their feet. They get into the motel bed laughing.

THIRTY-TWO

9:00 A.M. WHILE SHE SOAKS in the bathtub, Suzanne does not know that Howard is peering out through a chink in the motel curtain at a red Datsun pickup truck with guns in the gunrack and the four Hutton boys lounging around it.

The bathtub, surrounded by pink plastic, is a place for taking stock. She stares at her toes, long slender toes sticking up out of the water, attached to long slender feet with high arches. The Old Man said she had aristocratic toes. She smiles. Her legs, glistening, half submerged, are long and round enough so the bones don't show. Suzanne has always been glad that she has a pleasing body. A pleasing body makes the world exciting. Or so she thought.

But her body is part of a trap. Not the whole trap, because she can't keep her feelings sorted out that coldly. Oh, sometimes she feels guilty for not following the teachings of the church she learned as a child. But the trap is more than that. The small black triangle of curly hair is just the tip of the iceberg. Wrong word. Marking danger. The spot where she can feel such ecstasy that she's not herself. So she can't go back to being the person she was yesterday.

She sighs and an electric shudder through her whole body makes the water ripple in the pink plastic bathtub.

With Gordon she was dazzled, shocked, and then guilty. Now she's glad that he is dead. She is dreadfully sorry to be glad.

With the Old Man she kidded herself that she was almost free. And he helped with that raw-wound hurt after Gordon. She knew he couldn't belong to anyone, but losing him hurt bad.

What has happened with Howard is something else, something deeper and more dangerous. She shivers again. Even so, her whole body from head to toes feels light as if she might float, but at the same time more alive and defined. Her nipples point at the watermarked ceiling. She has goose bumps. And at some place inside herself, something has let go, let down its guard, ceased to be Suzanne alone and become Suzanne and Howard. She thinks of those corny hearts entwined on cheap valentines. Now, what is she going to do?

For the first time in her life, Suzanne is really afraid. Oh, she was afraid in the storm, but something could be done about that. Now she crosses her arms across those silly pointing breasts and hugs a shoulder with each wet hand. Because now she has something to lose. Something so valuable that she can't just raise her chin and make up her mind to look after herself.

Suppose something happens to Howard? Suppose she never looks into his wise hazel eyes again? Suppose she never sees him square his shoulders for action in that idealistic vulnerable way, like a slightly comic knight without a white horse. His Volkswagen has been blown up. His borrowed BMW washed away. She knows he needs somebody practical like her around for moral support.

She's cold. Her goose bumps have turned blue. She gets out of the bathtub and dries on the skimpy motel towel, staring in the mirror at the tight mask of her face. I have to be careful, she thinks—caring is so damned dangerous. But what else do I want? To help run a motel in Alaska? To work for a newspaper in Hong Kong or Australia? Yes, part of her would like to run away. But she's going to stay and face being afraid. God help me, I have to do it, she thinks—

I won't run. She raises her chin defiantly, tosses her dark hair and puts on her clothes. Except shoes, lost in the storm. She wears a worn-out pair of Mrs. Hutton's old pink slippers.

A door slams outside with a metallic click, and she looks through the bathroom curtain crack to see a large man in a dark suit just putting a suitcase in the trunk of a shiny new black Ford. Another guest, on the side away from the office.

Out in the motel room, Howard is peeking through the curtains toward the road at the front. He stands so lightly on his toes that she knows he is hiding from someone on the other side. She wants to hug him, but this is not the time.

"The Hutton boys are in front with guns, Suzanne. They may just be going hunting, or they may intend to hunt me because my father killed their kin. Am I being paranoid?"

"Who cares. If there's a chance, don't be heroic. Out the bathroom window I saw a man packing a car in front of one of those cabins at the side. Come on, let's climb out the bathroom window." From now on Suzanne won't take chances. Not without a good reason. Better to look dumb than dead.

She does feel a little silly climbing out the window, but the man packing the car is so intent on getting his stuff in just right that he doesn't even notice. What on earth has he got in all those boxes and suitcases?

He's impressive in his dark suit. "Good morning," he says, so heartily that Suzanne prays the boys on the other side of the motel can't hear him. He smiles like a pumpkin. He has small feet in double-shined black shoes and white even teeth.

"Beautiful day," he beams. "I didn't care for yesterday, but every day has its purpose."

Howard explains that the BMW washed away in the flood yesterday. That he and Suzanne need a ride to the nearest rent-a-car place.

Shiny-teeth says he's going right next to an Avis place. They'll be there in three quarters of an hour. This seems too good to be true. In Suzanne's experience, things which seem too good to be true are. But Howard has already arranged a ride, already asked if the man will mind if they both sit in the back seat since they are so exhausted that they'll go right to sleep. Of course, Howard has arranged the back seat bit so that their new friend won't see them duck down out of sight when they pass the "boys" in front.

That works. White-teeth does not seem to notice when they grovel on the car floor as he drives out of the place.

Out on the road to the city, they hug in relief. It's a beautiful, sunshiny rain-washed day. Up on the ridge, downed branches are the only signs that last night there was a flood in the valley.

"I waited for you," says their friend.

"You what?"

"I get my orders from the man upstairs. And he wants you."

So, out of the frying pan into the fire. The Hutton boys seem friendly compared to a member of the mob, if that's who this is. Why, maybe the Hutton boys really were going hunting!

"The man upstairs has been waiting for you all along and this is my chance to bring you to him." Shiny-teeth drives fast around the curvy roads, while Suzanne's mind races, thinking how to escape. He swerves once to miss some men removing a downed tree from the road, bumps through a low section of the road where small rocks have been washed onto the asphalt, but never slows down. There's no chance to jump out of the car.

"That's why I overslept," their captor says. "He was directing me that even if the revival had to be canceled last night, I could bring his good news to you this morning. You've come close to death in the flood, my friends. Now is the time for you to be born again in the blood of our savior Jesus Christ.

"And in the time it takes to get to the city, I can explain the heresies of the Methodists and the Presbyterians and the Baptists and all the others. My church is the true church, the Church of the Revelation of the Word. In those boxes, I have for you a free Bible. I also hope you will make a small contribution. Who knows what lies ahead for you, my friends? Is your soul prepared?"

THIRTY-THREE

LEEROY BOWS TO Freddy on his park bench. Leeroy brings a message from Howard, via Lance, also a cold bottle of champagne from the Old Man's office refrigerator.

"Howard suggested we share this. And when he gets back from out of town he'll be by personally to thank you for finding his wife." Leeroy doesn't say that he'd just as soon be outdoors on the park bench because he's too blue over Suzanne to work. He doesn't say he's here to find out what more Freddy has learned. He takes two plastic champagne glasses out of a paper bag and begins to fill one.

Freddy darts his eyes right, then left. "Listen," he hisses, "we're being watched." Leeroy sees nothing but the ordinary morning traffic, a tan Chevrolet and a red Ford, two young women entering the Defender Building.

"Listen, Leeroy Hicks, people will think you've lost your mind, drinking in public with me at eleven in the morning." Freddy pulls up straight. "You ought to be more dignified. You represent the press. Your last story was magnificent."

Maybe Freddy with his cauliflower ear really was a high school English teacher once, just like he says.

Leeroy fills the second champagne glass. Hands one to Freddy, raises his. "To news, whether we like it or not."

Freddy does not raise his glass. Even the eye with the scar opens wider than usual. "Why?"

"Because of your help in finding Howard's wife, we're nearer truth. But how come that Maurice Poole got in his van with all his stuff and left town so damn fast?"

Freddy takes a sip of his champagne, ignores the question and smiles. "I hear old Justice killed a man. Stop gaping. Of course I know. The rumor only had to cross the street. You look like a damn fool."

"O.K. Freddy, you know everything and guess the rest. So why do you play games? Why do you waste my time?" All of a sudden Leeroy has let Freddy get to him. "Why on earth did you tell me to look for a one-eyed card shark?"

Freddy pouts, innocence put upon. "Howard Justice knew Poole said he was growing a special mystic eye for enlightenment. At least, Howard's wife did. That was a good hint."

That's what I need, Leeroy thinks bitterly, a mystic eye for enlightenment.

"And Poole asked me questions about Isaiah Justice. He asked me who would know exactly where he came from." Freddy grins at his own importance.

Leeroy chokes on a sip of champagne. "You! Why didn't you tell me?"

"I protect my sources, and my ass. I gave Poole names. Isaiah Justice was murdered. I steer clear of murder."

"So why do you tell me now?"

"Poole got his story to Howard, then left town. I'm in the clear."

"He got his story to Howard!" Leeroy spills champagne in his lap, almost drops his glass.

"Sure," says Freddy, grandly. "He was sworn not to tell. But he sent you hints. You ought to be grateful. He was such an honest man his conscience hurt. Just like me."

"You knew Maurice Poole?"

"He was my valued friend. I give you information, but he paid for it. With other information, or wine."

Leeroy is so furious he feels himself turn red. Freddy is a stool pigeon. Leeroy has helped him be one. Damn.

"You sell information!"

"Sure," says Freddy, "so do you."

"You mean to say this Poole knew all along that the racetrack people were the ones who wanted to buy the paper? He knew they killed the Old Man? He knew the details of that and God knows what else, and you kept your mouth shut and let him get away?"

"Calm down," says Freddy in the gentle tone which Leeroy knows he should be using. "Poole figured the people who wanted to buy the paper must have killed Isaiah Justice. Makes sense."

"And he just 'figured' they were the same as the race-track people? Out of the blue, for no reason? Come on!"

"Oh, no," says Freddy, "that was my idea. It made a better story. You needed a good story to save the paper."

"You lied. And we don't know who killed Isaiah Justice."

Freddy is shaking his shaggy head as if in disbelief. "I saved the paper from being sold. I saved your job. And you aren't even grateful." Then he laughs. "And you haven't even proved that what I said isn't true! It could be. Or not."

Freddy raises his glass in the hand with the scar. "To the murderer, still hidden." He winks.

"And yet he's a well-known man. Whoever killed your boss, Leeroy, became instantly famous. *The Defender*'s circulation has jumped because of him, right? National TV follows that man. Everybody is guessing who. That's true fame." Freddy's gravelly voice is full of admiration.

"You sound as if you knew him personally."

Freddy pours the last champagne from the bottle and tosses the bottle into the public trash can near his bench. "Leeroy, I need power because I'm a bum." He nods slowly like a sage. "I'll always be a bum. It suits me. But this killer could be someone who felt like a bum and couldn't bear it.

So he made himself famous. Clever fellow. I like that idea. Better than the mob.''

Freddy is totally outrageous, totally unreliable, and yet, damn it, Leeroy thinks, he often has the nerve to be right.

"Leeroy, stop shaking. You mustn't get carried away. I never saw you get carried away before except when you looked at that woman.''

"What woman?'' The nerve of the bum!

Freddy winks again. "That Suzanne Mancini.''

Leeroy could hit the man except he has such a gentle smile. "Anyway,'' Freddy says, "Suzanne Mancini isn't the right girl for you. I've watched her going in and out of that building. She's a handful. You need someone like my wife, motherly and not too demanding. You'll get over Suzanne.''

Leeroy jumps up and turns to leave without even saying goodbye.

"Remember one thing when it comes to murder,'' Freddy calls, "look for someone who wants power. That's not a tip. That's my whole philosophy.''

THIRTY-FOUR

HOWARD'S WATERPROOF WATCH says 3:45 P.M. It's proved itself. Now he has to prove himself by dealing effectively with his mother. He wants to comfort her and persuade her to vote to keep *The Defender*.

Miss Bounce stands in her front doorway puffy-faced. She's been crying. And she's out of uniform, in a plain cotton I'm-not-going-anywhere dress and soft slippers. She sometimes wears those slippers in the evenings of bad days to comfort herself.

Maybe she's changed, softened. Maybe. He's not so sure that he's ready to tell her how he feels about Suzanne yet. One thing at a time. Suzanne has gone home to change her clothes before she meets Howard at *The Defender*.

Howard gives his mother a big hug and she hugs back hard. Why on earth does she smell like curdled milk?

Miss Bounce out of character makes Howard nervous. He remembers the frontier adventure book he loved as a kid where the hero knows his house has been ambushed by Indians because it's "too quiet."

Miss Bounce settles too quietly on the couch under the portrait of the Madonna painted by the ex-convict, and by habit Howard moves as far as he can to the other end and twists to face her. He tells her briefly about the flood and how the "boys" saved him.

"Thank God," she whispers.

The hard part is to tell her about the newspaper stories in the bound volumes: about his father's arrest and trial, and about how his grandmother burned in her house. As he tries to make that story as bearable as possible, his right hand nervously fingers something fuzzy. He tells Miss Bounce what the editor said about the Old Man as a boy, a good boy.

Tears shine his mother's cheeks. She asks for every detail. What did the town of Moody look like? The editor's house? The valley?

And then she cries out "Why, Howard? Why couldn't your father share at all?" She is not expecting an answer. A piece of cherry pie sits forgotten on the coffee table, one bite gone from the point.

He moves over and puts his arms around her, still holding onto the fuzzy thing. Wanting to be comforted, himself.

"Why couldn't he tell me what happened? Why? Didn't he trust me?" She's getting angry, sitting straighter, angular. That's more like Miss Bounce. "I could have helped. I could have listened." She clenches her fists, clenches her whole body. "I hated him for shutting me out. I hated him!"

Then she leans limp, head curved down against Howard's shoulder, shaking. "And I loved him. Even at the end, I loved him."

Howard raises the hand with the fuzzy thing into his lap. He is holding a child's toy like no toy he ever had. A fuzzy white unicorn, well-battered.

He holds it up in surprise.

"It's the baby's." A smile twists Miss Bounce's puffy red face. "Virginia and the baby just moved in with me, Howard." Now she's radiant. "Christopher is asleep in your old bedroom right now. Our darling child."

This rocks Howard. Last he heard, Christopher was a bastard, child of a loose woman. Virginia must be persuasive to have converted Miss Bounce so fast.

"Virginia and the baby are going to live here with me till she finds an apartment. She's going to work in the photo department. Did you know that Virginia is an accomplished photographer? That girl is amazing. At least Josh..."

Without warning, Miss Bounce is crying again. Howard changes the subject so he won't cry too.

"What are you going to do now, Mother?"

"I may go back to work myself." Sunshine again. "Back to the Life-Styles Department. Yesterday, after I talked to you, I began to wonder if I might like that. Obviously we can't sell the paper to crooks, and I was happy working, Howard. Mary McFee is leaving Life-Styles because she has an offer from the *Los Angeles Times* that we can't top. I'll try her job."

Howard would like to jump up and down, shout, do a cartwheel. Miss Bounce in Life-Styles could be 400 shares not to sell *The Defender* at all. But good grief, Miss Bounce will be just down the hall ready to give him advice at a moment's notice. How much can his mother change in two days? Forget cartwheel. Never mind, he says to himself. First keep the paper. One thing at a time.

He still doesn't know who killed his father.

THIRTY-FIVE

SUZANNE IS HAPPY one minute, apprehensive the next. She sees herself reflected in the Defender Building's glass front door, beaming like her Aunt Louisa who married, had twins and gained 100 pounds. She makes a note not to gain 100 pounds.

Next to her, Howard beams, even with his nose red from blowing. A cold is a small consequence of nearly drowning. He's full of bounce like a puppy on a spring day as they push through the glass double doors. And yet he walks straighter in his blue nylon jacket than he did two days ago. He's lighter on his feet in his running shoes. His clothes look too young for him. He has more presence than he did a week ago and she's proud.

Arthur Mason, the red-headed book-page editor, is stepping out of the elevator. He pumps both their hands, grinning wide. The Lassiter sisters come out of Circulation, excited. Arnold Smith, who moves heavy objects and sweeps, runs over. Suzanne and Howard are surrounded. Mouths say "Glad you're back safe." Eyes say "Sorry about the Old Man. And damned curious."

Suzanne and Howard manage to get through to the elevator and close the doors behind them. Howard kisses her as the elevator clanks. Upstairs, Lance and Leeroy have already heard from the grapevine and are waiting.

Lance rushes over and gives Howard one of his bear hugs. "Thank God, Boy. Thank God you're O.K." He hesitates, then throws his arms around Suzanne. So he accepts them as a couple, a relationship. Maybe Lance isn't so bad.

Leeroy has never been a hugger. He shakes Suzanne's hand. He must see the relationship, too. That's why he's so formal. She'd like to squeeze Leeroy and say "It's going to be all right." She'd like to say "Leeroy, you know perfectly well you don't want to marry again, even shack up again. You just want to daydream about it." But his loneliness is real. She can see it in the curve of his neck. She can feel it hurting.

So why is she, all of a sudden, heart-pounding scared? Is she scared of Leeroy? Nonsense. Scared of Lance?

Is she scared because she has something big to lose now? That again? Happiness can end. Yes, but why scared right this minute? Since I love Howard, she thinks, my head isn't screwed on right any more! Why, she realizes her cheeks are wet.

"We have to be careful," she gulps, "because whoever killed the Old Man is in this building."

Howard and Leeroy turn and listen. "How can you know, Girl?" Lance demands.

"I know because . . . because I just know." She runs into the ladies' room to the left of the elevator to repair her face. At least the outside of her can look normal. Maybe that will help.

THIRTY-SIX

HOWARD DOESN'T LIKE the idea of Suzanne's going off into the ladies' room alone when she thinks the killer is in the building. But if she had the intuition to know if the killer is in the building, she'd have the intuition to know if he was in the ladies' room, right? She is overwrought by the three deaths and the flood. That must be it. She wants to be alone a minute. He respects that.

He stands in the hallway under the twice lifesized picture of the Old Man. Howard feels pretty bad himself. The Old Man smiles, absolutely self-assured—that's how he looked so often, as if nothing could ever go wrong.

Howard stares up into his father's huge determined eyes and speaks to the picture. "Listen, life is not all a glorious crusade, not like you said it was." But he might as well laugh as cry. "Life," he says, "is like juggling a dozen oranges."

He thinks what the expression will be like on Miss Bounce's face when he tells her he's going to marry Suzanne. He smiles. "Twelve greased oranges."

"Amen." Lance chimes in. Leeroy has left.

"My brother Josh could juggle oranges but he couldn't juggle his own life. I wonder where he is now? Somewhere off waiting for the end of the world alone."

Lance puts a great steadying paw on Howard's shoulder. "He's as far as Mexico by now, Boy. At least his shirt will feel at home."

Behind Howard the elevator doors swish open. He and Lance both instinctively whirl fast.

Out hurtles a black man in a wheelchair. He propels the wheelchair with his powerful right arm as if he's going to ram Howard against the wall. As Howard jumps back he notices that the man's left arm and legs are missing, but that doesn't tame the man. He stops short and hovers, facing Howard who braces for him to pull a gun or a knife. At the same time, Howard has to stop himself from laughing. Because this wild man is dressed almost as much like an ambassador as Madison in a brown pin-striped suit, off-white shirt and wine and yellow striped tie with tie pin. The legs of his trousers are tucked so neatly under him they almost have hospital corners.

"I want a job!" So that goes with the clothes. But the body English says "Your money or your life!" The man is a force like gravity or lightning.

"My name is Roosevelt Lincoln Worthington. I told Leeroy Hicks what to look for—which was blackmail—and you went to look for it, Howard Justice. You did, didn't you? You look like you found something out. Now you owe me a job. I can write editorials. I can write anything."

Howard points. "Go in the newsroom and find an empty desk. Write an editorial about how to prevent the end of the world. Let's see what you can do." Does Lance resent Howard's blurting that out? Lance is editor. Thirteen greased oranges.

Worthington is caught with more anger about to pour out. He snaps his mouth shut, slams the wheelchair around and rolls off.

Madison is watching from down the hall near the door of his office. Madison with circles under his eyes. What is he doing at the office so soon after Cleo died? The funeral is tomorrow. Howard runs over and hugs him. Madison feels droopy and prickly, resigned but mad at the world. He smells of whiskey.

Lance pulls them both into Madison's office. Shuts the door. What's up? Howard doesn't want the door shut long. He wants to keep an eye out for Suzanne.

Lance pulls his bushy eyebrows into a worried V. "Look, I've held up an important story for the first time in my life: the story about Howard tracing the Old Man's past. O.K., maybe to hold it up temporarily in order to get it exactly right from you, Howard. But Madison here is saying not to run the story at all. We can't do that."

Howard wants to yell "No! Don't run the story. I can't stand it." He remembers the cousins who acted as if the Old Man's murder was just what they had expected. Also, the man who leered over his prayerbook at the Old Man's funeral. That man will give a party to celebrate when he hears the truth. The world acquitted the Old Man of murder whether he acquitted himself or not. The world will convict him of being a hypocrite for hiding his past. Satan on the poster grins.

Madison sits down on the edge of his desk under the picture of the devil. There's an open bottle of whiskey on his right and a glass half full, next to Cleo's photograph. Whiskey is what is getting Madison through the day. Well, one problem at a time.

Howard squares his shoulders. "Madison, we've got to print the story. It's our job." Lance nods.

"No! I'm a stockholder in the paper, and now that this paper is all I've got, I say no!"

"Madison, somehow everybody in this building has found out what I discovered about the Old Man. You can see it in their eyes. There is no way we can keep what I found out a secret."

"Then let somebody else print it, not us!"

The door whisks open. It's only Alice. No. Alice and Suzanne. Arm in arm, sparkling. What on earth?

"I told Suzanne," Alice sings, as she runs over to Howard and holds out her arm full of bracelets, jingle-jingle. She ignores Madison's glower.

"Told Suzanne what?"

"I'm so glad you didn't get killed in the flood, and I have this new charm that Arthur gave me." Her little-girl voice loves everybody as she holds up a silver baby carriage. "I am going to have a baby, in fact Dr. Adams says the last woman who took the same fertility drug had quintuplets!"

"We have to settle something serious." Madison glares at Alice. He doesn't think quintuplets are serious.

Madison's jaw muscles bulge. His vulnerable mouth is pursed in an angry O. "How can we print what the Old Man died to keep quiet? We owe it to the Old Man to shut up!"

Suzanne puts her hand lightly, tentatively on Madison's arm, her lovely hand pale against the gray flannel. "Madison, I think your father would be glad you were able to be braver than he was. Enough of him was brave so he would want that."

Lance nods. "Exactly. And, Boy, do you want the people who blackmailed him to blackmail us? They tried to blow Howard up and shoot him. They'll try anything."

Madison explodes. "Do what you please," and stomps out, taking the whiskey bottle with him. Poor Madison.

"I look at it this way," says Alice, and Howard realizes nobody thought to ask her. "The Old Man always said we all had to give up things we wanted for the paper. Why shouldn't he give up his halo? That's fair. And we don't have to sit around and think about the past. We can think about the future. Our father's grandchildren."

And some of those grandchildren may be quintuplets all just like Arthur. Well, one problem at a time.

At least Alice and Madison don't talk about selling the paper to Gemtrex any more. But where will they stand i another offer comes? Madison against selling because the paper is "all he has left," or for selling because the paper exposed his father? Alice satisfied that her income will raise quintuplets? Or wants to be a millionaire? Virginia liking her job? Or wanting cash?

And Howard still doesn't know who put the poison in his father's whiskey. He needs a handkerchief. He sneezes.

THIRTY-SEVEN

SUZANNE IS GIDDY, heart and mind on overload. All the phone lines into her psyche ring joy.

Maybe that's why she feels such sympathy for the Goldfish, even while Leonora sends out stay away signals: a kind of electric fence with eye-power. Why, she's jealous! Suzanne is sorry. Leonora stands so alone behind her desk, and the gold-framed portrait of Baby the cross-eyed cat.

But wait. The cat is gone. The frame sits at exactly the same angle, but Suzanne does a double take. She sees Howard do a double take and try to hide it. The frame contains the Old Man, smiling his Franklin D. Roosevelt smile, eyes to the right, just like the cat's.

Suzanne is not tempted to laugh. The Goldfish has bizarre ways of showing her feelings. But today she has reason to grieve, and maybe for denying grief. The Old Man was her hero, wasn't he? She gave him most of her talent and energy, and hero-worship was her only real reward. Now she's had to learn that the Old Man once killed a man and then, even though the court acquitted him, twisted his life to hide his human failure while publishing how others failed. That he's been blackmailed. Fallen heroes hurt.

Whatever she feels, the Goldfish covers with crisp efficiency. "Rupert Murdoch called at 10:45," she says to Howard, consulting a note on her desk. "He wanted you or Madison to call back."

Rupert Murdoch buys newspapers. What will Howard make of that?

Howard sneezes. "Not now, Leonora. One thing at a time." He's on overload too.

Then he grins that wry grin and he says "Suzanne, life really is juggling thirteen greased oranges nonstop. But, you know, I'm getting used to it."

Suzanne sneezes in chorus with him, and they both laugh. Life works better that way.

So they both have bad colds. Better than drowning.

"What we need is a drink," Howard says. "We'll feel better. Let's drink a toast to being alive." His voice and his eyebrows say he's surprised to be alive. That's what's fun about Howard. He is surprised so often.

The Goldfish walks sedately over and opens the pine cabinet under the map of the state, the cabinet with the small built-in icemaker and the compartment where the Old Man kept glasses and whiskey. Also champagne, but that's been presented to Freddy.

"There's a full bottle here. Your father always said whiskey was the best cold remedy, Howard." Leonora holds up the whiskey bottle in the small hand with the bitten nails, almost enthusiastic. "This is Wild Turkey. Your father was saving it for a special occasion. He said it was the smoothest whiskey in the world."

Leonora holds out the whiskey to Howard. Suzanne notices that she presses the fingers of her other hand hard against her lips.

As LEONORA DESCRIBES IT, Howard can almost feel the warmth of the whiskey in his gut. He inspects the seal on the bottle which certainly appears unbroken.

Suzanne stands close and says she'd love a drink too. The Goldfish never drinks, but Howard offers her a glass out of politeness. For a moment she seems about to surprise him by saying yes. She eyes the bottle of whiskey as if she can imagine the taste, as if she could love it. But she shakes her head "no" as always, holding one hand over her mouth as if to stifle the urge to drink. Leonora should let herself have more fun.

Howard pours the whiskey into two hand-blown glass tumblers that Miss Bounce gave the Old Man one year for Christmas. He hands one to Suzanne. He can hardly think of anything but the smooth touch of her fingers, the way her eyes hold his.

She tinkles the ice and laughs, then raises the glass. "Let's drink to life as a gamble."

Howard glances at his father's empty chair, where the red cushion even now holds the longtime imprint of his sitting. He remembers the Old Man, pink-cheeked, eyes full of fun, raising a glass of whiskey and toasting: "It matters not if you win or lose, it's how you play the game."

Suzanne holds her highball glass high and her shining eyes still hold Howard's. "Let's win more often than we lose, and laugh when we lose and roll again." Another toast of the Old Man's. She's remembering him, too, and it's all right.

The Goldfish is not all right. She watches as raptly as if her eyes were whirlpools and she'd like to suck in Howard and Suzanne. Because she has no life of her own? She stands by the globe of the world, her whole body poised as if she's waiting for something, as if maybe it's her sixth birthday party with the cake and candles about to arrive. And yet the small oblong fingers of her left hand press her mouth hard as if she wants to keep herself from crying out. The fingers don't prevent sound. She speaks through the gaps, down-beat. "I lose, when I win."

A part of Howard cries out to find out what's wrong. Another part just wants Leonora to go away, to stop ruining this moment.

The office glows with the warmth of Suzanne. It's not quite dark outside but the office lights burn and burnish her curly hair. She has on Howard's favorite blouse with the four-leaf clovers. Her eyes sparkle. Her cheeks are flushed. She stands so lightly between the small bar cabinet and the Old Man's desk, head thrown back, about to drink.

The Goldfish is breathing hard and trying to hide breathing hard. Why? Howard remembers something ridiculous: the Old Man's picture in the cat's frame. Leonora wants to remember the Old Man, not the cat. Something is about to happen that concerns the Old Man.

Suzanne swirls whiskey and ice. Howard is caught in a wave of fear. Because Leonora covers her mouth with her hand. The day the Old Man died she covered her mouth.

The picture flashes back. She sits at her desk with index and longest fingers over one corner of her mouth, ring and little finger over the other. Words come out between: "Your father is dead."

Howard is lightning-struck. He sees. She's holding in her nervous telltale tongue. Her tongue licks at the corner of her mouth whenever she breaks a rule. Poisoning breaks rules.

Suzanne has begun to tip her glass of whiskey, ready to take a fatal sip. Howard jumps. He knocks the glass out of her hand, so hard it knocks against the leg of the Old Man's desk, splashes and breaks. The rug is poisoned.

Suzanne cries out in surprise. Leonora does not. She stands frozen by the globe of the world. Her glasses are ice, her white blouse snow, her face blank.

Howard finds himself next to Leonora, holding his whiskey glass close to her face and shouting. "You drink this. If it's not poisoned, drink it!"

Leonora shrinks and through clenched teeth she says "No."

The door of the office opens, the mirror on the back reflects Howard and Leonora, seeming to slide and then vanish as the door moves. Leeroy hesitates in the doorway, tall and sad, then closes the door behind him with a click, hiding the mirror with his lanky frame, the Old Man's mirror which seems so strange in an office.

Leeroy strides toward Leonora, puts his long arm around her, and rests his hand on top of the globe, on the North Pole. He looks down on Howard. "Leonora doesn't have to drink anything."

Who the hell does Leeroy think he is? The Civil Liberties Union? Does he understand that Leonora has tried to kill Suzanne, not to mention Howard? That she obviously killed the Old Man? And what damn possible reason did she have to do that?'

But Leeroy hugs Leonora as if she's a lost child instead of a scorpion. And in that ridiculous mother-father voice, he says, "This has been terrible for you, Leonora, hasn't it? You are the only one of us who's been entirely alone."

"She poisoned my father," Howard yells. He hears his voice crack like a teenager's.

"I had that poison on my closet shelf behind a shoe box a long time." Leonora is almost matter of fact. "I could have killed you all seven years ago." She lifts what there is of her chin as if she's proud of herself. "That's one reason the police can't trace the poison. I kept that poison on the back of the closet shelf so long. Not to use it. But to know I could use it."

She stands forward from Leeroy. Damned if she isn't pleased with herself. She preens. Howard remembers Madison once told him how he saw the wind blow the Goldfish's skirt up and under a sober gray dress she had on a magenta petticoat with blue lace.

All of a sudden, her expression goes with magenta petticoats. "Oh, I felt good. When Al Arthur was manager at the community theater and he made me paint scenery instead of being on stage, I knew I could kill him if I so desired. That felt good. When they finally let me be a maid in *Charley's Aunt* and I walked on stage with sandwiches and they laughed even when I never said a word and wasn't supposed to be funny, I new I could have killed any one of them. That felt so good."

Howard has never heard Leonora say anything felt good, or talk so nonstop, or seem so pleased with herself. Leeroy is patting her damned shoulder.

"All my life they made me be in the back row corner in class pictures, and didn't ask me to be the bridesmaid in weddings, and even made me sit on the back row in the church choir. And nobody knew how clever I was. I got hold of that bottle of poison in a way that even the police haven't traced. And never will. They'll never find where I took it from because I made an exact duplicate of the bottle and left it there. Who tests their cyanide?" She laughs.

"But you never intended to use the poison." Leeroy sounds like he's singing a lullabye. He looks like a mother horse, damn him.

"I never intended to use the poison until somebody started blackmailing your father." She grins like a shark.

"Gemtrex was blackmailing your father and then he was so low that he could care about me. Me! He said 'Leonora, you are the one who has always backed me up. I have to love what you are. You care what becomes of me. You are wonderful.'" She sings that out, a hymn of triumph from her shark's mouth. Howard is amazed.

"I remember exactly his words. He had been drinking. His voice was not slurred, but he smelt of strong drink. And we were in bed together. The sheet was twisted around one of my feet. We were really in bed together. It wasn't one of my daydreams.

"And then before long he drank enough to tell the truth, and I knew it was the truth, even though his voice was slurred." She starts to shake, and of course Leeroy steadies her.

"Isaiah Justice said this to me: He said 'Leonora, I could really love you if you weren't so damned ugly. Do you know what they call you behind your back? They call you the Goldfish. Because you look like a goldfish. Howard noticed that when he was five years old. Why the hell can't you look like Suzanne?'"

Howard shudders. Why couldn't his father shut up? Suzanne is almost as pale as Leonora, as if she can't bear what she is hearing.

"I guess I knew I was sometimes called the Goldfish, but I never really felt it until he said it. I never really understood that around this newspaper I was a joke. Useful, but a joke." Howard hates to hear the rest. He can't escape.

"So I went straight home and got the poison and put it in the whiskey at the office and at his hideaway. Nobody but Isaiah knew I had a key to that, and a key to the back basement door. I got him with the workhole poison. But I missed Suzanne."

Leonora runs over to the small bar. She picks up the Wild Turkey bottle and holds it up in those small ugly hands. She hugs the bottle. "I wanted Gemtrex to buy the paper and kill that part of that bastard Isaiah Justice, too. To kill everything he cared about." She shakes the whiskey as if she likes to hear poison slosh in the bottle. "I wrote those cut-out letters. I called about Lumberton. I wanted you to know what a bastard your father was." Now she's practically crowing. Doesn't she know she can be executed for murder?

What is she going to do with the poison? Is the stuff lethal if you throw it at someone? Is it absorbed through the skin? Howard backs away from her. Suzanne has edged toward the door, perhaps getting ready to call for help.

If Leonora starts to throw the stuff at Suzanne, Howard has to be ready to jump and throw off the woman's aim. That is better than trying to grab the thing if she doesn't throw it. Who knows which way it would spill.

Leonora laughs at Howard, a shallow laugh from her chest where she clasps the poison. "You'd like me to kill myself. That's why you are not taking this bottle away from me." Her magnified eyes glint with hostility.

"I won't kill myself. And you'll have to publish every detail of my trial, which will make you look bad, not me." Leonora is shaking with laughter. The electric lights jiggle in her glasses.

Leeroy crosses over to stand beside her again. His eyes say "I'm listening."

So who the hell is Leeroy? A Boy Scout gone insane? The master interviewer, even at the gates of hell? Or what is it between Leeroy and the Goldfish?

LEEROY'S PAIN at his own aloneness goes into his arm around Leonora. Leonora, the eager pre-med student, who learned about Professor Koch's poison, and later stole it. He'll check that out, but in his heart he's sure.

Leonora is laughing hysterically. She catches her breath, looks up at Leeroy. He feels as if she is studying his face for a clue, all eyes. He knows there is nothing on his face but sorrow and listening. No hope. Only God can help her.

She cries out "Oh, my God, it's true. I'm all alone," a long wail, echoing against itself.

With one swift motion she raises the whiskey bottle and drinks from the neck. Almost comic, she is so small, the bottle is so large, except she's drinking death. Why didn't Leeroy stop her? Because she caught him by surprise? Because she had a right to decide to die? Leeroy is not sure. The bottle drops to the floor with a crash.

He catches her in both arms, holds her tight against him and feels the jolt of death hit her vitals, the quivering jolt that he will describe in such exact horrifying detail in his story that will win a Pulitzer prize.

"I killed her with kindness." He is not sure whether this is a terrible joke or just the truth. He will spend the rest of his life wondering if he did the right thing.

HOWARD IS HORRIFIED, relieved, ready to cry, ready to pray, angry, triumphant and floored. Suzanne bursts into tears and runs over and puts her arms around him. He's also comforted, happy and miserable.

He must digest all that. Must pull himself together before the police come. It's expected of Howard Justice, son of Isaiah Justice.

He raises his head, determined, and finds himself looking at himself in the mirror on the door. Looking beyond Leeroy, who has eased Leonora to the rug and kneels over her like a lost scarecrow priest.

Howard is surprised by the angle of his own raised head in the mirror, the determined flare of his nostrils, the fire in his eyes. Surprised to realize he looks exactly like the Confederate general's horse. And because he's not a horse, he looks inhuman.

Without wanting to, he suddenly remembers the summer afternoon when he and Josh invented Leonora's nickname: the Goldfish. Invented it, yelled it over and over and laughed themselves sick. Goldfish: the name which the newspaper staff called her for twenty-two years. Which will not appear in her obituary.

He remembers how once he and Josh put a small gray garter snake in her top drawer with the stamps and paper clips to see if they could crack her iron efficiency. They wanted to see if she was human. They brought the snake to the office in a Duke's mayonnaise jar with nail holes punched in the lid, all concealed in a brown paper bag that crinkled. When Leonora's back was turned they tipped the snake into the drawer. They could not make her scream.

She never screamed then or later, never complained, and then committed murder.

With Howard's encouragement Suzanne goes to comfort Leeroy.

Howard goes and sits on the red cushion in the chair behind his father's desk where he has never sat since his father died. He weeps and is not ashamed. He weeps and then begins to compose in his mind his contribution to Leeroy's story about who killed Isaiah Justice.

A weird story about snakes and jars and strong whiskey and adultery and loneliness and what it feels like to kill a man rather than be killed. Human interest. The Old Man would like that.

COFFIN AND THE PAPER MAN

Gwendoline Butler

First Time in Paperback

A
JOHN
COFFIN
MYSTERY

A PROMISE OF DELIVERY

Sixteen-year-old Anna Mary Kinver is raped and stabbed in the dank Rope Alley section of Leathergate. A former psychiatric patient, covered with blood, is picked up for questioning and subsequently let go.

Soon thereafter, John Coffin, chief commander of the Docklands district, receives the first in a series of notes from an anonymous letter writer calling himself "the Paper Man," who promises more bodies if Anna Mary's killer is not caught.

As the case goes unsolved, more bodies turn up. Who is the Paper Man?

"Coffin...solves a complex puzzle in this richly textured police procedural."
—*Kirkus Reviews*

Available in December at your favorite retail stores.

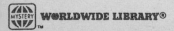

WORLDWIDE LIBRARY®

COFFINP